Mark Hurst

Her Last Days

Accepting what she has done will set her free... or will it?

Wooded Hill Books Limited

www.woodedhillbooks.com

This is a work of fiction. Names, characters, businesses, places, events, locales, and incidents are either the products of the author's imagination or used in a fictitious manner. Any resemblance to actual persons' living or dead, or actual events is entirely coincidental.

Dear reader,

A guiding note from the author:

To maximise your reading enjoyment of what has become an unexpected trilogy, the author's suggested reading order is:

1. My Partner's Friend
2. Your Secret
3. Her Last Days

My earlier books, "**My Partner's Friend**" and "**Your Secret**", are written as two separate standalone stories. However, the closing chapters of both books have the two respective lead characters heading towards a shared destiny in "**Her Last Days**", and their story continues to develop when the two of them decide to work together on a mutually beneficial project in the United States of America.

As a result, informative background to the two lead characters is contained in the earlier books, and although "**Her Last Days**" can be read as a standalone book, reading this book first may impinge on your further reading if you choose to read my earlier books later. Then again, if you do decide to read "**Her Last Days**" first, the earlier books will certainly add the background context to this story… the choice is yours.

Mark

"... there are known knowns; there are things we know we know. We also know there are known unknowns; that is to say we know there are some things we do not know. But there are also unknown unknowns - the ones we don't know we don't know."

Donald Rumsfeld, 2002

Prologue

'No, he's not breathing. I'm sure he's dead. There is blood everywhere. He pushed me too far, and I've killed him.'

Dropping the phone handset to the floor, I leave the line open and stagger back across the room as the distant voice tries to entice me back to the phone. I think I've said enough.

The police will be here any minute, and I guess I'd better prepare myself. Taking a deep breath and exhaling, I stand upright and walk to the front door, opening it in anticipation of the officers' arrival in a few minutes. I return to the living room, and as I cross the open doorway to the kitchen, I look down on his lifeless body lying in a large pool of blood on the floor, surrounded by blood splatter and arterial spray over kitchen cupboards and worktops, the result of multiple wounds I inflicted. The only thought going through my head is that it's going to take a lot of effort to get all that cleaned up, and thankfully, it's one mess I know I won't be tackling.

Continuing across the room, I drop down on the dry, cracked leather of his favourite armchair, exhausted by it all, feeling cold and empty inside. He shouldn't have said what he did after everything I've been through and endured, but he got what was coming to him after all those years of goading and blaming me.

Now I have to face the music; there's no denying I did it, I'm covered in his blood, and I've just made my confession. He will have been missed at work tomorrow, and someone will want to know where he is, so it's best that I take the lead as quickly as possible, confront my actions, and try to get in front of this as best I can.

Distant police sirens pierce the night's quietness. They're coming, getting louder, ever closer. I need to be careful now, or I could be shot by accident. You hear of these coppers getting pumped up when they suspect they are walking into an armed scene, all trigger twitchy and nervous, and I don't fancy dying in a hail of bullets, deciding to get down on the floor, lie on my stomach with arms and legs outstretched, in anticipation that's how they want me to be when they enter the room.

Turning my head and placing my right cheek on the rug, I notice my left hand and arm; my blood-soaked sleeve dripping everywhere, my hand thick with it, strangely coating my engagement and wedding rings; it's as though I've dipped my hand in a bucket of thick molasses. All these years of keeping a clean house and a tidy home, of being the best wife I can, all of it forgotten when he said those words that finally pushed me over the edge. He went too far. He caused this. Weirdly, after all these years, the release is liberating, and it feels like I'm breathing fresh, clean air for the first time in over twenty years.

Cars are screeching to a stop outside, with shouts and general commotion getting louder. Undulating first responder lights seep into the room through the partially closed shutters, transforming what was our home into some macabre party room.

They're at the open front door now, and I take in a deep breath, hold, and then exhale.

'Crockett Police Department! We're coming in!'

Here we go.

Someone enters the living room, their boots firmly pounding on the wooden floor as they enter with purpose.

'Police! Do Not Move!'

I don't intend to; I know it's best to lie still.

'Slowly put your hands behind your head. Interlock your fingers. Do it now!'

As I move my arms, I wonder what kind of risk I must present to them. Obviously, they're trained to be like this, but really? Short of cuffing myself, I don't think I could have been any more accommodating.

'Is there anyone else in the property?'

'No,' my simple reply.

'Do you have any weapons on you?'

'No.'

Multiple feet enter the room, and a voice calls out. 'In here, there's one down. Cover me.'

'Go.'

A large, powerful hand shrouds my interlocked fingers, closing tightly over mine, forcing my entwined digits firmly together, and I feel handcuffs being placed around my wrists.

'Clear,' from the other room, followed by similar calls around my house.

From nearby the kitchen doorway, a female voice adds to the scene, 'Christ, look at the blood in here.'

'Any pulse?'

'You're kidding, right? No, nothing. From the looks of it, there'll be nothing left for his heart to pump.'

As hands grab me under my armpits and start to lift me from the floor, another deeper, familiar voice of authority takes control, 'Get him out of here! If he pukes all over my crime scene, there'll be hell to pay. For fuck's sake, Jesse, get that rookie outside!'

Forceful hands spin me around, and I look up, steadying myself, straight into the startled face of a Rotary Club colleague.

1

Emily

George Bush International Airport, Houston, Texas

As the plane touches down, the peace and relaxation I enjoyed during the flight suddenly changes to anxious expectation, tinged with trepidation, as to what I am about to experience over the next few days and weeks, but it had to be done; I had to get on this plane and come out here to meet my biological mother, especially in her current situation and condition, and to find out the whole truth of everything that had happened to me, and to my mother, Angela Collins.

We haven't spoken person to person yet, with our intermediary, Mary, serving as the conduit for our reconnecting. I've spoken with Mary quite a few times now, using video calls, and she comes across as kind, caring, thoughtful, and, above all, supportive; she understands and appreciates the sensitive predicament my mother and I are in. And I just love her soft Texan accent and the way she speaks.

My mother's health is very poor, and it's clear she doesn't have long to live, not because she is on death row, and that has a finality about it, but because of the damage she inflicted upon herself following her attempted suicide. The drug cocktail she consumed during her trial crippled some of her vital organs, and she has been on the decline ever since. She is now an inmate in the Patrick O'Daniel Unit in Gatesville, although it is not likely she will survive long enough to have the sentence carried out, thereby avoiding that lethal injection, an ironic and cruelly sad situation.

Several campaign groups are fighting against her conviction for capital murder, given the extenuating circumstances she experienced, as well as groups demonstrating and fighting legal campaigns against the general principle of capital punishment in the US. I'd never looked into any of this before until I found out she was my mother and on death row, and I was surprised by the polar opposite viewpoints of the sides and interested parties in the debate. However, at the time she killed her husband, this was a capital offence, exacerbated by him being an employee in the local courthouse.

Apparently, after hearing I had been found and was still alive, these various action groups were reinvigorated in their campaigns, bolstered by the belief that given Angela's limited time and the Christian principles of forgiveness, they have been calling on the State Governor to intervene to show compassion with either a full pardon or at least commuting her sentence to life imprisonment. However, again, this latter option is meaningless as she doesn't have long left to live.

Mary will already be waiting in the International Arrivals Hall in Terminal E, waiting to greet me and accompany me to my hotel. She should be accompanied by Martin Nicholson, the author who is thinking of writing my life story. I'm looking forward to meeting him, but I'm still not convinced that it should result in a book about what happened to me, let alone that a movie should be made of it. I know there has been a lot of public interest in me and my story since the truth was uncovered and my real identity revealed, but this whole public arena thing is just not me; I'm not that keen on it. What I am interested in, though, is how the process of writing it all down helped him come to terms with his experiences and how a similar approach has helped others recognise and control their issues and troubles. I've decided to keep an open mind about the book and any film or TV adaptation until it's all fully explained, and I can buy into the potential of beneficial outcomes for me.

As the airbridge is coupling with the aircraft, I turn on my mobile phone, and it searches for a cell network. My phone pings, and I presume that through some prior business arrangement, it connects with one of the local providers, giving me a full-strength signal. I receive a text message from my UK network provider informing me of the limits on calls and data downloads, as well as the charges that apply thereafter. I remember my former husband Paul saying to me once, "*Everywhere you go, a person or a business is trying to make a buck,*" how true that seems now. Paul, he's never really that far from my thoughts; it's weird how I don't miss him, but at odd moments like now, I think of him, of some little habit or idiom that seems to have stuck with me.

How everything in my life has changed over the last few months; I was a wife and now a widow, I'm wealthier now than I ever thought I could be, I'm of some fame or interest to others, people I've never met, and now, I'm on a different continent looking to redefine my future.

I receive a further text message and see that it's from Mary, indicating they are indeed in the Arrivals Hall waiting for me.

I pass through US Customs and Border Protection without much delay and recover my luggage from the carousel, then head out into the Arrivals Hall, not really knowing what to expect. There are the usual families re-uniting, business types just motoring through heading directly for the exit, tourists looking for their collection drivers, and then there's me, slowly scanning the crowds looking for Mary and Martin, holding up a small sign with my name on it.

'Emily! Hi! Over here!'

I hear the call out for Emily but carry on walking, looking into the crowd of people at the gate for a familiar face.

'Emily! Here Sugar!' is called out again, and I hear it, noting the unmistakable Texas accent, but it's a little fainter this time.

As I move slowly along with the other new arrivals, I turn my head to my left just as a male voice with an English accent calls out, 'Kate Hunter!'

I stop dead in my tracks, and the person behind bumps into me. That formal use of my former self startles me, and I look back over my shoulder, spotting Mary a couple of people back from the barrier. I apologise to the man for my abrupt stop as he navigates his suitcase around me, and I raise my right hand in recognition, replying, 'Hello.' Mary starts to move along the bank of people, parallelling my direction, and that's when I notice the likely owner of the male voice, Martin, following closely behind her. He looks taller than I had imagined and more athletic than the online photos I've found of him, but still, his features and hairstyle remain familiar to his online presence.

Mary reaches the end of the barrier and the thinning crowd and comes around in front of me, instantly holding out her arms for an embrace.

'I'm so pleased to actually meet you, Emily.'

'Likewise. I'm sorry, Mary, I heard you calling out Emily, but I'm still not used to being addressed as Emily.' We hug each other.

'I understand, Sugar, I do. Do you prefer Emily or Kate?' she asks as she releases me from our embrace.

'Well, I prefer Emily now; there are some things I want to forget about if possible.'

'I understand, sure thing, Sugar. Now, where are my manners, little lady? This fine young gentleman beside me is Martin Nicholson.'

We look at each other, and he extends his right hand to welcome me, 'My apologies, I thought the use of Kate Hunter would catch your attention; I'll use Emily Collins from now on. I'm pleased to meet you; I trust the flight over was comfortable?'

As I take his hand, I reply, 'Yes, I am pleased to meet you also; the flight was fine. No problem; as I said, it's going to take some time to become Emily.' His grip is firm but not overly so, and his smile pleasant. Wearing a white cotton shirt, light blue jeans with a tanned leather belt, and a pair of leather cowboy boots, he looks to be adopting some of the Texan ways I've imagined over the last few weeks, but there is no mistaking his Englishness when he speaks.

'Here, let me take that,' he says as he reaches forward for the handle of my suitcase. 'We have a car waiting outside to take us downtown'.

Mary holds out her right hand, gesturing to take my shoulder bag, and I graciously decline her offer. 'Thanks, Mary, I'm OK with this.'

'You'll be tired from that flight.'

'Yes, I am a little, but I did manage some sleep.'

Martin leads the way to the exit and our waiting car, with Mary and I falling in behind him. She links my arm and pats my hand, 'I kinda got some exciting news to share, can't wait to tell you, but not until we get in the car; we can talk further at the hotel if you're OK with that, Sugar?'

'Er, yes, OK, good, I could do with some exciting news, I don't seem to get much these days.' She pats the back of my hand again. We exit the Hall into a large, multi-car lane pickup area, and as Martin comes to a stop at the kerb edge, a large dark minivan with tinted windows pulls up in front of him, and the doors open automatically. The driver steps out and speaks with Martin, the discussion being inaudible to me, given the vehicle noises around us.

Martin hands him my suitcase, and as he moves to the rear of the vehicle, Martin gestures for us to enter the rear seating space. Letting Mary step inside first, I notice a small group of people with cameras, and a reporter with a large microphone sees us and, at pace, heads in our direction.

Martin steps forward to intercept them and outstretches his arms in a blocking motion.

'Jump in Sugar, or those coyotes are sure enough liable to go have you for lunch.'

I look back at Martin and see the film crews aiming their cameras around him in my direction as he speaks with the reporter.

I don't wait for a second invite; I've seen all this before. Entering the car and taking a forward-looking seat, the driver quickly closing the sliding side door behind me, then the rear tailgate, before reoccupying his driving seat.

'Looks like word's gotten out about you coming out here.'

I sigh and turn to Mary. 'I was hoping we could avoid all this media attention.'

'Well, that's it, Sugar, you are the news today; that's what's exciting.'

'How do you mean?

'Well, your mom's been pardoned.'

The front passenger door opens, and I quickly turn my head towards the distraction as Martin climbs in and firmly closes the door behind him. He looks at the driver, 'Let's go, Ernesto, straight to the hotel, please.'

'Yes, Sir.'

I turn back to Mary, unsure if I heard her correctly, 'Sorry, did you say she's been pardoned? Really? When? Today?'

'Yes, Sugar, a full pardon; just announced this morning, and with immediate effect.'

As Ernesto pulls away from the kerb, leaving the coyotes, as Mary refers to them, behind by the roadside, Martin, fastening his seatbelt, twists slightly to look back at me and then glances a look to Mary. 'She knows then, Mary?'

'Yes, Sir, she sure does.'

2

Emily

Journey to Downtown Houston

I can't believe what Mary just said, and Martin knew, too.

'I was aware appeals and action groups were trying to assist my mother, but when I boarded the plane in London, they were just that, actions in hand. What happened?'

Martin remained quiet, leaving the dialogue to Mary. As we pull away from the airport, Mary speaks up. 'Yes, Sugar, as you know, there have been plenty of people continuing the fight for justice for your mom, fighting for clemency; there were even some optimistically trying to obtain a full pardon for her. Then, out of the blue, we hear about you, that you are alive, and you were looking for your birth mother. That was the added spark needed. A couple of the more influential groups joined forces and began lobbying hard on your mom's behalf. They managed to lodge filings with the Texas House Committee on Criminal Jurisprudence and put pressure on members of the Texas Board of Pardons and Parole. They pulled on the emotional heartstrings of the State Governor and followed up any of his TV appearances or speeches or public appearance, with statements and reporter updates to get Angela's, and your, case out there in the public arena. Then, the religious community got behind it all. You are probably aware of this, but what clinched the President getting involved was your coming out here. It was the President who actually pardoned your mother.'

'Really? The President of America?'

'Yes. Apparently, a week or so ago, your British Ambassador in DC discussed your situation with him, and the President was horrified at how your parents had been treated in the UK when you were taken, how they were treated as the prime suspects in your disappearance, and of how they decided to come out here for a new start, but the stress and pressures never left them, and then your mother finally cracked that one day after so much abuse. Her sentencing was harsh and put her on Death Row. Now, the President himself is a proponent of banning capital punishment, and it seems you being alive and here today, clinched her the pardon. He also worked some federal technicalities or grey areas due to your mom's husband working in the justice system. When he was told of Angela's condition and that you were coming out to meet her for the first time since you were taken as a baby, he acted quickly, speaking with the State Governor. They worked together to get this done before you arrived. The full Presidential Pardon was issued just this morning, a couple of hours before you landed.'

'Oh my god. That is just... it's just fantastic news. So, is she out of prison now? Can I see her today?

'No and no, Sugar, but we are driving up to Gatesville tomorrow to collect her; you will be the one that walks her out of prison as a free woman with a full pardon,' Mary replies with a beaming smile.

Martin looks over his shoulder at me, gently nodding and smiling. The instantaneous release in me surprises even me as I burst into tears. Tears of joy and of guilt. Mary leans into me, raising her arm over my head and wrapping it around my shoulder, pulling me into her, 'Awh, now there, Sugar, now there, this is a wonderful day.'

'I know, it's just…' and I continue to let it all come out. Maybe it's because I'm tired, the travelling, the heat, the media circus that is sure to follow, the fact that I will be in my mother's arms once more, or all of it, I don't know, but the emotions just flow out me. Martin reaches around, and Mary takes a white cotton handkerchief from him and passes it to me.

'Thank you,' is all I can say as I put the handkerchief to my eyes whilst sniffing away, trying to control my emotions.

We turn onto a large freeway, and I collect myself. 'Is it far to the hotel?'

The driver replies in deep drawl, 'We'll be on the sixty-nine for the next twenty minutes or so, if the traffic is good, then a few minutes into Downtown.'

I look up at his internal rearview mirror and note he is looking back at me. 'Thank you,' I reply.

'You're welcome, Ma'am.'

Martin glances at the driver beside him, 'Ernesto, are we being followed?'

'No, Sir, it looks like we avoided them with our quick exit.'

I collect myself and ask Martin between sniffles, 'Will there be reporters at the hotel when we arrive?'

He looks over his shoulder to me, 'No, there shouldn't be any there. I reserved the room in my company name, but no doubt, they will find out soon enough and start to hound us. However, they're bound to be at the prison tomorrow when Angela is released.'

Mary chips in, 'Well, in that case, should we control the narrative and hold a conference late this afternoon? If we give them what they want, they may be a little easier to work with.'

'If it was only that simple,' Martin replies. 'This is big news for a few reasons, and until there is something bigger or uglier to report, Emily and Angela are going to be in every North American living room by six p.m. today, and I'm quite sure international media will have just as much interest. It's not often a Presidential Pardon is granted, especially to a non-American citizen who actually committed what is a capital offence and has been residing on Death Row.'

'Oh, yes, I see,' is all I can say.

'Don't worry, Sugar, we've got your back,' Mary adds.

'So, does this wipe away her criminal record? Is she free of the conviction?'

Martin replies, 'No, your mother's felony remains on record; it's not expunged or erased. It's a bit like picking up a "*get out jail free*" chance card, out of jail but not free of the conviction, or to put it another way, it's akin to time served and walking out.'

'Oh, so she is not cleared of murder; she's just released from prison?' I ask him.

Mary looks at me and answers, 'Correct, but now you will get to spend her last days together.'

3

Martin

The Southern Star Hotel, Houston

It's just the two of us for an early dinner this evening; Mary making her apologies as she's attending a family event. The news crews soon found us when the word was out that Emily was in town, and all credit goes to the hotel security team, who have been perfect in preventing any paparazzi or reporters from getting anywhere near us. When the hotel's senior management team found out who my mystery guest was, they immediately upgraded Emily to the Presidential Suite, which was kind of fitting, given the pardon her mother had received. I had plans to take Emily out for dinner this evening, but with all the attention outside the hotel, the hotel team offered to look after us and made one of their private dining rooms available to us, which was immensely gracious of them.

I decided to keep the conversation relatively neutral over dinner, as there is a lot for Emily to take in now. We chatted about general things, but on balance, probably more about me than Emily. Emily naturally wants to be comfortable with me and know how I might approach her story, so she has quizzed me a little deeper on who I am and my background. For this, though, I can only tell her the official version and nothing of what really happened;

she gets the version I've shared with the world as there are only two still breathing that know the truth of what occurred, me and my brother, and I'm keeping him secret. Curiously, she doesn't touch on the subject of her story being a potential book and the possibility of wider media productions. As I speak, Emily listens attentively and asks good questions at the right time. I probably slightly underestimated her from the background information I had collected on her; she is clearly intelligent, sharp, well informed, and does not dance around a subject, opting more for the direct approach, which I like, I think; there's no point on beating about the bush I suppose.

Emily is young and attractive, and it's easy to appreciate what her deceased husband saw in her; her vibrancy, confidence, and natural beauty would be appealing to most men, especially to any man that Emily showed an interest in.

As we finish our main course, I quietly observe Emily place her knife and fork down on her plate, then, using her napkin, dab the corners of her mouth. 'I don't think I can eat another morsel; the food was delicious, thank you, Martin.'

'It's not me you need to thank; it's the hotel team here we need to thank for looking after us. You're a very special guest, and it seems they wish to pamper to whatever your needs may be.'

'To be honest, I was anticipating room service this evening, followed by an early night,' she replies.

As I look into her eyes, I can see she is beginning to look a little tired, which is all to be expected. She has travelled from London to Houston, landing straight into the breaking news of her mother, with its heightened media frenzy. I have seen plenty of video snippets of her used on news reports and photos in newspapers and magazines at the time she was informed of her real identity and of her biological mother's position and condition, and to be fair, the images of her then portrayed a startled and bemused young woman. In my opinion, I think she has taken all this quite well, probably a result of her strong personality and her ability to appear calm on the exterior while screaming inside, a bit like the proverbial swan, serenely gliding upstream whilst beneath the water, unseen, her legs are kicking away like mad.

'Yes, we probably should retire early; it's something like a three-and-a-half to four-hour drive up to Gatesville in the morning. Are you OK to travel early tomorrow?'

Looking slightly deflated, Emily replies, 'Oh, I didn't appreciate the distance from Houston to the prison. What time are we thinking of leaving in the morning?'

'Mary will be here at seven-thirty with the same driver; we aim to leave about eight; is that OK?'

'Erm, yes, although I'm not sure how I'll sleep tonight with the news of my mother's release coupled with being in a hotel room in a different country and the jet lag, but I need to be there to meet my mother as she comes out, so yes, I'll be ready for seven thirty.' She pauses for a few seconds, then asks, 'Have you been there, to Gatesville prison?'

'No, this will be my first time also, I think it's the same for Mary, so we're all in the same boat on this.'

She nods to herself softly while smiling slightly, I feel, to mask her apprehension. 'Unfortunately, it will probably be a media circus tomorrow, especially as the various campaigners will be attending. A person on death row having a sentence commuted is one thing, but one receiving a Presidential Pardon is something else, especially a person of dual citizenship.'

'Oh, so my mother is also an American?'

'Yes, sorry, I thought you knew. It's what made the death penalty sentence interesting, her being a citizen of dual nationality as opposed to, say, a full American or a resident alien.'

'A resident alien?'

'Sorry, it just means one who is not American but living and working here legally; it's how the authorities refer to us; I'm a resident alien, whereas you are a visitor with a visa, well, currently anyway. We will need to think about how much "*work*" you do on the book while you're here.'

'Ah,' she says. Looking down at her plate and twisting her knife between thumb and forefinger, she asks, 'I suppose there will be no way of avoiding the media circus tomorrow?'

'No, unfortunately not; this is solid gold prime-time news, and the Governor, for one, will want his fifteen minutes in front of the cameras. I'm sure the President will be saying something as well from the Whitehouse, looking to show compassion whilst retaining a strong leadership style.'

'Really?'

'Yes. Anyway, we'll look to keep you away from the media if you prefer; we can look to use your mother's health condition as a reason for privacy.'

She doesn't seem that enthralled or sure, but interacting with the media now, at such a key event, will be of great promotional benefit for any potential book or movie, and I would kick myself if I didn't ask her. 'Will you consider going in front of the media tomorrow to say a few words? I only ask, as it goes to the reason we are here together, writing a book of your experiences and possibly wider publications, and following such a dramatic Presidential Pardon, there will be no better, cost-free public relations potential than tomorrow; you will have the world's media at your fingertips.'

She looks at me as if she is assessing what I've just said. This is a big ask, I know, especially of a person that doesn't want any media exposure. Then, I notice a little smile appear, and her eyes lock on mine. 'The thought had occurred to me earlier when I was grabbing a quick shower. Great minds think alike,' and her smile broadens.

'Yes? You are willing to go in front of the cameras; are you sure?'

'Yes, I think so; yes, I am. You're right; what better way to crystalise our working relationship and project to such a wide audience.'

'Whoa, so you do want to work with me on your story?'

'I'm leaning that way, yes. Maybe tomorrow we don't mention the book, but we can sure raise awareness as to what has happened to both Mum and me and gauge the reaction, the public opinion.'

That's the first time I've heard her call her mother Angela, Mum, and as I'm thinking about it, it must have dawned on her also. She continues, 'Do you think I should refer to her as "*Mum*", "*Mom*", "*Mama*" or "*Mother*"?'

'I would stick with what comes naturally to you, then you won't need to think about it when you are answering questions or being interviewed. You seem at ease with Mum, so I'd go with that, and it highlights your Englishness.' Her smile broadens further, and she nods slightly, indicating agreement.

I can't believe how quickly this has turned around. This was still an exploratory conversation about a book, with Emily preferring to keep a low profile away from the media, but now it seems she wants to actively engage with it. I wonder what changed her mind.

Keeping the momentum of the topic going, I seize the advantage, 'I could plant a question with one of the reporters I trust, something along the lines of "*Given the experiences, both you and your mom have been through, are you going to write it all down? The public wants to know what you both thought when these events took place. This could be showcased in a book or a movie. What do you say, Emily? Will you tell us everything that happened?*" or something along those lines.'

'Well, to that, I would respond, "The thought had crossed my mind, but now that you mention it, that's something I will seriously consider, thank you," and hopefully they'll notice you behind me.'

As she says the words, I feel the excitement in her delivery. She has thought about this quite seriously, it seems. I need to get her signed up before one of the big publishing houses swoops in and showers her with blank cheques and promises of global celebrity status. 'Well then, if you're sure about this, I'll have the contracts prepared, and we can sign them as soon as they're ready.'

'Yes, please do. Best to have it all on a proper business footing.' Stifling a yawn behind her hand, she continues, 'Now, if you'll excuse me, I had best try to get some sleep. We can prepare a statement in the car travelling tomorrow.'

'Yes, of course, no problem. Shall I call your room at, say, seven a.m. to make sure you're awake?'

'No, I'll be fine, thank you.' She stands, pushing her chair back slightly, and I stand a split second after her.

'Have a peaceful sleep, Emily, and I'll see you at breakfast in the morning.'

'Yes, thank you; you too. Good night.'

She turns and steps away from the table, heading for the door. 'Good night, Emily,' I reply after her.

I watch her quietly leave the room before sitting back down and reaching for the nearly empty bottle of wine. Pouring the last of the Cabernet Sauvignon, my mind is racing as I wasn't expecting her to make her decision so quickly; I was anticipating a much harder sales pitch. Maybe it's the Presidential Pardon, the fight being over, the battle won. I'll need to ask at some point, as it could play a part in the book, maybe as a good prologue piece.

The door opens, and a waiter enters, 'Oh, I am sorry, Sir, I thought y'all had finished, and the room was empty, I'll come back.'

'No, no, it's all good, thank you. Please,' as I lay my hand out, indicating to continue. 'Thank you for looking after us this evening; the meal was delicious.'

'You're welcome, Sir. It's not often we have such a famous person staying with us. Oh, sorry, Sir, I didn't mean famous; that's probably the wrong word.'

'No, famous is OK, I know what you mean. Can I take the bill, please?'

'It's already been charged to your room, Mr Nicholson.'

'Ah, OK. Thank you,' and I finish the wine in my glass before standing. 'Please pass on my gratitude to your colleagues; this evening has been perfect.'

'You're welcome, Sir, thank you, I will.'

I turn and head for the door, then stop, turn around, and see him start to clear the table, deciding to pose a question to him.

'Sorry, could I ask you something?'

'Yes, Sir, of course.'

'What do you think of the Presidential Pardon of Angela Collins?'

'Sir, it's not for me to comment.'

'No, please, I would like to hear your personal opinion; it'll stay between the two of us. I would like to know the general feeling of this decision.'

'Well, Sir, I don't quite get it.' He stops and stands upright, looking at me. 'She definitely murdered her husband at home, there's no question of that, so I ain't sure a full pardon is right.'

'It's true she killed her husband, but that followed years of abuse and cruelty.'

'Then, Sir, why didn't she just up and leave him? Ya know, get out of there as opposed to killing him.'

'I don't know, but it's never that simple; maybe we'll find out soon enough. There is a bigger story to tell on this, a history that needs to be told; maybe that will provide the clarity to help you appreciate the President stepping in and issuing a full pardon.'

'I'm not sure, Sir, maybe. But she still killed him, and that can't be taken away from her, can it? That shouldn't be forgiven.'

'No, I suppose not. You think she should have ended her days in prison?'

'Yes, Sir, I reckon I do.'

'Umm. Well, thank you for your honesty.'

I turn to leave, and as I place my hand on the door handle to open the door, he comments further. 'Exodus, chapter twenty. The sixth commandment is clear, thou shall not murder.'

'Yes, that is so, but who is to say it was murder?' Before he replies, leaving my query hanging, I open the door and exit the room.

Walking the corridor to the elevator, my mobile phone vibrates gently in my trouser pocket. Pulling it out, the screen shows the solitary letter "*N*". I look around me at the empty corridor, then back to my phone. This is unusual; Nico rarely contacts me. It's usually me who calls him when I need something. I press accept.

'Hi, Nico, is everything OK?'

'Hello, little brother, yes, all is good. I just thought, as we hadn't spoken in some time, it would be good to catch up. How is America? Is everything good with you there?'

'Actually, yes, everything is good, in fact, it's better than good, it couldn't be any better. I've just managed to pick up a new commission with someone who has been in the news a lot lately. I'm to write her life story, which I believe will be a best seller and will highly likely become a movie.'

'Ah, interesting. Who is this person? Do I know her name?'

'If you watch the news or listen to the news on the radio, you've likely heard her name; it's Emily Collins. Does this ring any bells?'

'In fact, it does. Wasn't she the woman who recently found out she was abducted as a baby, and her true identity has become known through DNA testing?'

'Yes, that's her. There is more to her story, and I'm really looking forward to getting into it with her and her mother. Oh, yes, I should have mentioned that her mother is on death row here in Texas for murder, and she has just received a Presidential Pardon from the big man himself.'

'Oh my, there is much to this story then; I will pay more attention to the news and read up some more on this Emily Collins. So, you are in Texas at the moment?'

'Yes, we are driving up to the prison tomorrow morning to collect her mother; watch the news late tomorrow evening; you may see me, your little brother, on BBC in the background,' and I chuckle softly.

'Fame and fortune; is that what it is that you desire, Martin? I thought it was to write books?'

'It is, I am a writer, and I love the art passionately, but it would be nice to earn something serious for my hard work and skill.'

'Now, if it is money you desire, you only need to ask Martin; you know this, I will happily transfer whatever you need or want without hesitation.'

I sigh quietly to myself; he knows I don't want handouts, that I'm not a leach; we've had this conversation before. 'Thank you, Nico, I know you have offered before, and it's immensely generous of you, but I want to make my own way in life, earn my just rewards from my labours. I am grateful, I am, but I want to do things my way, on my own.'

'Yes, yes, I know, a proud man my little brother is, but always remember, if you need anything, anything at all, I am here for you, anytime.'

'Thank you, Nico, I know.' We pause for a few seconds, and then Nico speaks.

'Now, then, you must tell me more about this book and Emily.'

4

Emily

The Presidential Suite

I still can't get over how large this suite is; it's such a waste for one person, although having two master bedrooms with ensuite facilities will work out great for bringing Mum back here. I kick off my shoes and plant my feet on the sumptuous carpet, scrunching up my toes, almost clawing at the carpet pile. I saw it in a movie once, but I can't recall what it was called; however, it's supposed to help me unwind after a stressful day.

Martin is a nice man, pleasant, courteous, and attentive. I know I should have done some more due diligence on him and his plans for the book, but he feels right, and our shared experience of life-changing events is somehow comforting; actually, he's quite attractive. Whoa, where did that come from? There's no way I'm looking for a relationship at this time; I need to stay focused on Mum and then my story. I should have asked him if he needed Mum's input into the book. We initially started this journey focusing solely on my life events, but her story is inextricably tied to mine. Now that she is to be released from prison, she may want to participate.

I wonder what she is like. Mary has described her to me, both her physical and her mental state, so that I won't be startled by her appearance when we first meet.

However, it's her mental condition that I'm most afraid of. Not the killer bit, no, but the hatred she must have for the legal system and how she was treated here and back in the UK. Her life must have been hell, especially when the one person left that she could turn to was, in fact, her daily abuser, both mentally and physically. Poor Mum, she has had a rotten life since I was taken from her.

Heading to the master bedroom to the left, just off the lounge area, I recall Mary's comments in the car on the way here to the hotel. Mary advised that Mum's medical prognosis is not good, but at least now she can spend her last days free and in relative comfort. Her last days. I never thought to consider where she might want to spend them; she may want to remain here, in the US, or fly back home to the UK. It will be a difficult decision for her, as neither country has provided her with the protections she ought to have had, at least not in her opinion, I suppose. If she elects to stay here, I may need to extend my visa; however, with the Presidential Pardon now being issued, I expect any extension to be a mere formality.

Removing my blouse, I place it on the back of the dressing table chair, then unclip my skirt, letting it fall to the carpet, and step out of it. Standing there in my underwear is when I feel the chill in the room. The air conditioning is on and set a little too low for my liking. I quickly enter the ensuite bathroom, pull on one of the white towel robes, tie it at the front, and place my feet in the white slippers provided.

At the wash basin, I start to remove my makeup, well, what little I had applied, then prime my electric toothbrush and begin cleaning my teeth. As the vibrations gently play in my mouth, the toothpaste and bristles doing their thing, I think of Martin again. He's a very handsome man, and as far as I know, he's available. I'll have to ask Mary about his personal life. Stop it! You've only just got here and met him. Is it the wine and the jet lag, or am I becoming attracted to him, or is it that I just crave some intimate company? No, enough, stop it. I rinse, then stand the toothbrush up beside the sink.

As I pad out of the bathroom, crossing the expanse to the ridiculously oversized bed, I hear a tiny ping from my mobile phone, which reminds me I need to charge the battery while I sleep. Here we go, normal everyday life resumes, well as normal as you can get when in Texas, about to collect your mother who was, until a few hours ago, on death row, a mother I cannot recall ever meeting.

The message is a brief note from Mary, containing nothing of any consequence, just confirming the timings for tomorrow. I put the phone in airplane mode to minimise distractions and connect the charger cable to replenish the battery.

Leaving the air con setting as it is, I slip out of the robe and my underwear and quickly jump into my cotton pyjamas, then burrow my way through pillows and slide beneath the bed covers. My head sinks into one of the enormous pillows, and the cotton bed sheets start to warm from my body. The wine has gone straight to my head, and I realise I'm probably a little dehydrated; I should have had more water, but now I'm in bed, I don't want to move again. Lying on my back, looking up at the ceiling with the lights still on, my thoughts slip backwards to the last conversation I had with Paul, my husband, and how easy it was to talk him into taking his own life. He must have been weaker than I ever imagined, all the time before thinking he was a resolute and strong-minded person. I tut and berate myself; I must stop thinking of him before I go to sleep at night, as it makes it difficult to slip into a pleasant sleep, but it's the empty bed that reminds me of what is absent. I do miss him, his touch, his warmth, his company and his affection, but this is now how it was meant to be. His end, he brought on himself, his own selfishness being his downfall. It's ironic to think if he hadn't shot himself in the head, then the DNA tests probably wouldn't have been needed, and I may never have found out who I really am. These thoughts keep whirring around in my head, the 'but for' event that brought clarity to everything and all the truth out into the open.

Stop it now, I need to stop doing this. It is taking real willpower to resist the sleeping pills prescribed by my doctor; I don't want to take them tonight as I want to be awake early, and I need to be on my best game tomorrow. I reach over to the nightstand and pick up my eye mask. Since all this happened, I have been unable to sleep without the room lights on; I don't know why. Pulling down the eye mask provides the shroud of darkness I need to fall asleep, and I begin my breathing exercises, which the psychiatrist advised, while counting slowly backwards from one hundred.

I can't recall ever counting below eighty.

5

Mary

The Southern Star Hotel, Houston

'Good morning, Sugar. You're looking mighty fine this morning. Did you sleep well?'

'Good morning, Mary, yes, thank you, I slept as well as can be expected.' Emily looks around, and continues, 'Is Martin down yet?'

'Ah, yes, he was down early. He's outside making some calls. He said to go through for breakfast; we've got a big ol' long day ahead of us. He'll come join us when he can.'

'Of course, although after last night's dinner, I'm not sure I can eat much this morning.'

'Sure, you can, Sugar. Come now, let's head to the restaurant. I have some further details about your mom's release and how the day should run out.'

This is going to be a long, tough day, and she needs to have her energy levels at full. Emily walks in front of me, following the maître d' as he glides effortlessly around occupied and vacant tables, and I notice how calm and composed she is. We are shown to a quiet corner table, away from windows, and they exchange a few words as the maître d' withdraws a chair for Emily and then for me. 'Thank you, Sugar.'

A waitress appears and presents us with a quite substantial, leather-bound menu.

Emily takes the menu, lets it rest on the table, and looks at me. 'Forgive the cheeky question, do you refer to everyone as "*Sugar*"?'

'Ha, no, not everyone, Sugar, just the ones I like,' followed by a smile and wink. She smiles back at me and lifts the menu again, opens the cover and starts to read.

I open the menu, then quickly close it.

'Are you not eating, Mary?'

'Sure, just it's all a bit highbrow for me. I know what I like. I'm sure they'll make whatever we ask for.'

'Well, if that's the case,' she replies, closing the menu, 'I know what I want.'

'Good for you, Sugar.'

The waitress notices us close our menus and returns to the table, extracting a PDA to take our order.

Looking at me first, 'Ma'am?'

'Yes, I'll take Texas-style French toast with bacon and eggs and coffee. Thank you.'

Turning to Emily, 'And for you, Ma'am?'

'A single poached egg with avocado on brown toast, please. Oh, and English breakfast tea if you have it, please.'

'Of course. Ma'am. Thank you.'

As the waitress walks away, crossing the restaurant, I see Martin enter and have a quick word with her, gesturing in our direction before he walks over to us.

'Good morning, ladies. May I join you?'

'Sure thing, Sugar,' at the same time, Emily replies, 'Yes, of course.'

As Martin sits, Emily asks me about the day ahead.

'Well, there is a whole posse of reporters and news stations already camping outside Gatesville; they started turning up yesterday and have grown through the night. Local law enforcement is in control up there, and the State Governor is already flying back from Washington to be present at your mom's release. The authorities are aiming to release your mom at two o'clock this afternoon, but apparently, they're never on time; there's always something delaying 'em, which helps build up the anticipation and viewing figures. Going to be one busy day.'

Martin asks me, 'How is Angela? Is she fit to travel?'

'I asked that very question yesterday, and the medical team in Gatesville have forwarded an email of her medications and current condition. It doesn't read that well, Sugar. I'm sorry.'

Emily looks at me before calmly asking, 'Can she travel back in our car or…?'

'No, Sugar. A private ambulance has been arranged, and we have her registered in a local private hospital not far from Gatesville. The medical team suggest she is probably too weak to travel far.'

'Oh,' is all she replies.

I look at Martin and then back to Emily. 'Y'all got little time left, unfortunately, but she is a fighter. The hope is when she sees you again, it will revitalise her; not sure what that means, but everyone thinks it'll pick her up.'

'Where is this private hospital? What's it called?' Martin asks, pulling out his cell phone and opening the Maps app.

'It's a facility south of Waco, less than an hour by ambulance from the prison; it's called The Pontin Institute. The trouble is we'll be hounded all the way. Police have indicated they'll provide an appropriate escort to keep the coyotes back, but they can't guarantee they won't turn up at the hospital.'

'Can we arrange an air ambulance to move her?' Emily asks.

'We could, Sugar, but that is going to be awful expensive.'

'I don't care about the cost, could we do it, arrange one for today?'

'I don't know, Sugar, I've never done anything like that before.'

Emily looks across the table to Martin, and I follow her lead. Martin is already looking down at his cell phone, tapping the screen. The waitress returns with a large pot of coffee and two mugs, along with a teapot, cup and saucer, and places them on the table.

'Thank you, darling,' I say to her as she turns to leave.

Martin speaks while still scrolling his cell phone, 'Well, we can certainly arrange a medical flight, assuming she is well enough to fly, but I don't think it can be done today. Reservations, crew, nursing team, flight planning, and so on will all take some time. And, of course, it further depends on whether we remain stateside or go international with repatriation to the UK.'

'Or elsewhere,' Emily adds. 'So, we need to know where Mum wants to spend her last days.'

'It seems so, Sugar. We'll need to still collect her today and take her to the Pontin this afternoon; then, if she wants, we can move her from there.'

The waitress reappears with a colleague, and they commence serving our breakfast.

As I cut into my French toast, I start to reflect on the situation. This is the first time I've been involved with a pardon, and this is the big one, a Presidential Pardon.

It's also the first time I've been in a discussion regarding a medical flight. I may have to lean a little more on Martin here, as he seems confident about these things. They both seem to get on with each other, which is good, but I am a little wary of his true intentions. I believe Martin is only doing this for the opportunity and money. He says he has altruistic intent to help others who have suffered trauma come to terms with their experiences, helping release their inner anxiety and frustration and even confront their fears, which is massively commendable. Still, I don't know yet; I can't decide if the money and potential fame from a book and possible film are more attractive to him than the support Emily will need and receive. I suppose only time will tell; I'll give him the benefit of the doubt for the time being.

He looks at his wristwatch and then towards the restaurant entrance, almost as if he is waiting for someone to arrive.

Emily speaks up. 'If we are going all the way up to Gatesville today and then onto this private hospital near Waco, will we be coming back here this evening?'

'Good point, Sugar, no, I suppose not.' I look at Martin, 'Do you want to check out or keep a base here and pack an overnight bag?'

He looks at his watch again before replying. 'Well, it seems sensible to check out as we could end up anywhere subject to where Angela decides she wants to be.' He looks across the breakfast table to Emily, 'I think we should pack up and check out to be on the safe side; what do you think?'

'Yes, as you say, we could end up anywhere now. Do we have time to pack?'

I reply before Martin gets the opportunity, 'Of course, Sugar. Ain't much going to happen at Gatesville until the main player shows up.'

'I thought the player was already there?' she replies.

'From what I hear, it's the mom-daughter reunion that most people are interested in, not that mom has been pardoned. There's definitely mixed opinion on your mom receiving a full pardon.'

As I say it, I notice Martin raise his eyebrows slightly as he cuts into his second egg. He's probably been watching the news reports as well.

'Really? Well, if my mum is as poorly as she seems to be, then there's not going to be much of a reunion to observe.'

'We'll see,' is all that Martin adds.

6

Emily

Hearne, US-190, North towards Gatesville

We've been travelling now for nearly two hours, and I feel like we could do with a break to stretch our legs. On the approach to a town called Hearne, we're paralleling a railway track to our right, the tracks directing some of the longest trains I've ever seen. Everyone in the car has fallen quiet; Mary is reclined with her eyes closed, although I don't think she is fully asleep, and Martin is on his phone again, furiously typing messages. Ernesto, eyes protected with wrap-around sunshades, is maintaining a constant sixty, matching the speed of other vehicles on the road.

'I never thought I get to see places like this; it's not the usual tourist attraction when you think of visiting America.'

Ernesto is the first to respond. 'No, Ma'am, I guess not. What do you make of it?'

'I can't get over how wide the horizon is, how flat the roads are, and how bright the sky is. I'm used to hills with woodland, fields with crops, rain clouds and valleys with towns clinging to hillsides. I am surprised, though, by the green trees and fields beside the road; I was kind of expecting desert or scrubland.'

'Well, Ma'am, you're probably thinking of West Texas. It can get awfully hot out here in summer and very cold, wet and windy in winter; y'all get the same weather in the UK, I think.'

'I don't know about the awfully hot bit, but yes, we get cold, wet and windy winters.'

'I was raised not too far from here, Ma'am; this is my country.'

'How did you end up in Houston as a driver, if you don't mind me asking.'

'Not at all, Ma'am. I joined the Army young and then the Rangers, then spent quite a bit of time away. Then, after picking up an injury and meeting the love of my life, I decided to settle down after some twelve years' service and took to truck driving, but soon realised I was away from home too often; I wanted to be around to see our two boys grow up, y'know, be around them, play ball, teach them fishing and hunting. My wife, Carmen, she's a special woman, she knows me. Her folks live just outside Houston, so that's where we settled. We still come up this way, visit my folks, pay our respects and all. My father still does the finest barbeque in Texas.'

'That's good. You're happy then, Ernesto?'

'Yes, Ma'am, I'm very happy; thank you for asking.'

'Well, I'm sorry to drag you away from home on this journey.'

'No, not all, Ma'am, this is a real pleasure. See, I don't fully agree with capital punishment, the old killing right back argument; no, anyone can make a mistake, especially those in difficult, pressurised situations. However, there are some evil people in this world, and that punishment should be reserved for them, those hell-bent on going out to inflict harm and kill strangers. Now that I know the full story, I think your mom was unjustly treated, and I am happy to see her released. And I'm happy for y'all, too; being reunited with your long-lost mom has got to be the will and blessing of a higher power.'

I'm not sure how to reply to his comments and play safe, 'Thank you, Ernesto. Hopefully, we'll have you home soon, back with your family.'

'As I say, this is a real honour, Ma'am, and Carmen is with me on this. You can take as long as it takes.'

There is real comfort in knowing about Ernesto's past, including his military training and service, his family life, and morals. He appears to be a good, honest man.

Keeping her eyes closed, Mary chips in, 'Y'all better not try Ernesto's barbequing skills though, no sir, his daddy sure got him beat on that front.'

Ernesto laughs, 'Yes, Ma'am and I'm proud to admit that he has, that you can hang your hat on.'

Martin, sitting in the front passenger seat, looks up from his phone and turns to Ernesto, 'Could we pull up in the next town for a washroom break, please?'

'Yes, Sir, no problem, we have time in hand, and I wouldn't say no to a cup of Joe, I know just the place.'

We pass by oil storage tanks and industrial units as we approach the city limits of Hearne, and within a few minutes, Ernesto reduces speed, pulling off the main dual highway into the car park of a roadside diner, 'Best cup of Joe around these parts,' he adds.

Coming to a complete stop, Ernesto opens the side door remotely, and the heat of the morning enters the car. 'Phew, it's hot out there,' is the first thing that comes to my mind.

Mary replies, 'Ah no, Sugar, still a little chilly just yet, wait until this afternoon.'

I fish out my sunshades from my travel bag and exit the car, stretching a little as I move a few paces away.

As we all leave the vehicle, Ernesto locks the doors behind us, and we all head towards the diner. He pulls the door open and steps back, holding it for Mary and me, followed by Martin. As Ernesto brings up the rear, there is a loud call out from behind the service counter, 'Well my lord, looky here, an old cowboy come back to the ranch. Where you bin stranger? Come over here and give this ol' gal a bear hug.'

'G'morning, Sally-May, it's good to see you too'.

Sally-May walks from around the counter, and the pair of them embrace. 'Now, you gone and messed up my apron,' she says as she pulls back from him, brushing herself down while smiling.

'Sally-May, I'd like to introduce you to my friends. This here is Mary, Emily and Martin. These two here are from England, so don't you go getting flustered now.'

She holds out her hand, and we all shake in welcome. 'Any friend of this cowboy is a welcome friend in my diner. Come in, sit, let's get y'all something to eat and drink.'

We occupy a booth by the front window, and Sally-May stands at the head and is already calling the shots, 'I know it's a cup ol'Joe for the cowboy; ladies, what'll it be?'

Mary replies, 'What coke have you got?'

'Lemonade, Coca-Cola, Pepsi, Dr Pepper, Sunkist, all in diet too if that's ya poison.'

'I'll take a Sunkist, thank you,' Mary replies.

Sally-May looks at me, and sheepishly I ask, 'I don't suppose you serve tea, do you?'

'Now, well, we sure do, Miss; is that with milk or lemon?' and I see her wink to Ernesto.

'Erm, I'll take it with lemon, please.'

'Sure thing, and for you, darlin?' looking at Martin.

'Oh, a cup of Joe will be fine, thank you.'

'Coming right up,' and she turns, heading back behind the counter.

I look around the diner, observing a mix of patronage, some single, some in groups, some in work clothes and others in casual attire. Martin looks a little out of place here, having exchanged his casual attire from yesterday for a two-piece, light grey suit with an open-neck white cotton shirt; he is dressed for the events of today in case we are running late. He has his head down again, locked onto his phone's screen, tapping quickly using both thumbs.

I look diagonally across the table to Mary, and she is already looking at me. 'He's in there somewhere, Sugar.'

'Pardon?'

'Martin. He's here with us, I think,' and she winks at me.

Martin looks up from his phone, 'Yes, I'm here, I'm listening, just trying to get a few things organised before this afternoon's distractions,' as he turns his head to me.

'Distractions?' I repeat back to him.

'Oh, no, sorry, I didn't mean it like that. It's just… well, we'll all be on other important matters this afternoon, much more important matters.'

'That we will,' Mary adds. 'Martin tells me you are thinking of going in front of the cameras this afternoon; that right, Sugar?'

'Yes. I think so. Although, I'm not yet sure what I'll say,' I add.

Martin places his phone screen down on the table and looks at Mary, then at me. 'Well, I think it needs to come from the heart, be sensitive, compassionate, and above all grateful to the campaigners for their continued support and belief, to the Governor and, of course, the President. Ask for some quiet time to reconnect with your mother, especially in light of her health condition and frailty; the pair of you have so much to catch up on, reconnect, etcetera. Hopefully, then they'll cut you some slack. However, I don't expect all of them to leave you alone, especially some of the freelancers.'

'Yes, of course, I can do the more formal pleasantries, although I'm aware that some people are not happy with Mum receiving a full pardon; should I say anything about them to appease them? Do you expect some of the more outspoken will be attending the press conference today?'

'Probably, it is a free country of free speech,' Martin replies. 'To be safe, I wouldn't say anything to appease them or recognise them, as you may say the wrong thing. Don't worry about them; there will be plenty of police and close-quarter security present today, and we have our erstwhile Ernesto with us as a guardian angel, eh, Ernesto?'

I look across to Ernesto as he replies, 'Yes, Sir. I won't let any harm come the way of my charges today, not on my watch.'

'Thank you, Ernesto,' Martin replies to him.

The words protection, police, close quarter, and my watch all make me think there is something more to worry about. Still looking at Ernesto, I ask him a question I never thought I would ever ask, 'Are you carrying a gun, Ernesto?'

‘Sure am, Ma’am. I have a permit to carry a handgun, although I generally keep my weapon out of sight.’

‘Oh,’ is all I can say.

Picking up on my hesitation, Mary chips in, ‘S’alright there, Sugar, this is normal for Texas.’

‘Ma’am, I’ll be declaring my weapon when we approach Gatesville, and I’ll follow the direction of the local police and federal officers,’ he adds, smiling back at me.

Concealed handguns: this is a world away from what I am used to; I’m not sure if I like the idea of being in a car with a gun in it or not. Although I trust Ernesto, it’s just the thought of being around a gun that’s making me feel uneasy, especially one I’m not in control of. I wish I’d never asked him now.

Mary speaks up, ‘When we arrive at Gatesville, we’ll announce ourselves at the gate and be taken inside. From there, we will likely undergo some security checks before being fully allowed inside the facility. I’ve been informed your mom has been moved to the hospital wing and is no longer being considered as an inmate. She is receiving some treatment in expectation of being moved by ambulance to another facility. The nurse I spoke with said your mom seems a little puzzled by all the commotion and very surprised at receiving the pardon.’

‘Has she asked about me?’

‘Not that I am aware of, Sugar, but that doesn’t mean she hasn’t,’ followed by that comforting smile again.

Sally-May returns to our booth with the soft drinks and then comes back with two coffee cups and a large coffee pot, proceeding to fill them. ‘So, what brings y’all out this way?’ she asks.

‘Now, there’s a story, Sally-May,’ Martin replies. ‘How long have you got’.

7

Angela

Hospital Wing, Gatesville

I may be old, in a damaged, frail body, progressively weakening by the day, but my mind is still sharp and hardened by years of living in a penitentiary and on death row, rubbing shoulders with some of the worst and vile there is, while at the same time, and I believe, some reformed, and on occasion, an innocent inmate. But it's always been an uphill battle, and I've become too frail to fight it anymore, to fight inmates, and fight the system against my sentence, and to be honest, I'm not sure why I bothered as I had nothing to live for anyway. I'm the first to admit I did the crime, I killed Barry, my husband, and in my opinion, he had it coming to him, but to receive a death sentence was extreme. Anyway, I imposed an early death sentence on myself when I tried to end it all a while back, looking to avoid my extinction at the hands of others, trying to go out on my terms. I couldn't even get that right, but then, I suppose I did; it's just taking longer to reach that end.

Then Emily was found.

I never thought or dreamt that this day could happen, where my life is completely transformed for the better by events outside of my control. I still can't fully appreciate the enormity of it. First, I'm told that my little

Emily has been found, alive and well, after all these years of being missing, and then that she wants to meet me, even in the knowledge I'm in here. We were assigned an intermediary, Mary, who has been linking between us, Emily and I, to support us in our reconnection and, of course, work through all the access hurdles here on Death Row. We managed to arrange a visitor permit, and the Prison Warden had been quite reasonable in supporting this, and it was all scheduled to happen today. Then, completely out of the blue, without any notice, yesterday morning, the Warden had me wheeled up to his office and proceeded to tell me I had received a full pardon, signed by the President himself no less. A full pardon allowing me to leave prison.

So now, when I meet little Emily, I'll do so as a free woman.

Although I guess she is no longer so little, she'll be her own woman. Mary provided me with some photographs and articles to read on how Emily came to be found; it sounds like she's had a terrible time of it too lately, and no doubt she's scarred by events she couldn't control either, travelling a similar twisted path to me. I always knew Emily was taken, that we weren't involved in disposing of her body, although I had to accept the allegations of being negligent in leaving her alone in her pram at the rear of the house, allowing her to be taken, and that, I've had to live with from that day to this; and it's been hard.

I don't know what Emily wants to say to me or what she expects from me, but I know deep down I want to be forgiven; if that is at all possible for her to do, I need to reach a place of atonement before I go. When we meet, I want to be standing; I want to get up out of this bloody wheelchair and show her my defiance and determination, and I'll hold my daughter for all to see. When I said this to Monica, the nurse assigned to me, her first reaction was I shouldn't, that I'm too frail, that I could fall, but now she understands why I must do it, do this for Emily and me, and she said she will support me.

The prison has provided me with some new plain civilian clothes to wear for my release, clothes which I wouldn't have picked if I'd had a choice. Still, at least they have taken away my prison two-piece that replaced that awful white gown I first had to wear when I arrived here; I suppose I'm being humanised again, being prepared for real life outside these walls.

After hearing of my pardon, I was escorted back to my cell, and one of the correctional officers helped me pack up my meagre possessions. As I was wheeled out of the unit to cheers and jeers from some of the other inmates, I handed my small wooden crucifix that used to hang on my wall to Coral as I passed her, another on death row, and I promised to write to her. The tear in her eye was genuine and moved me to hold my head up high as I was wheeled out of the unit for the last time.

I look over to Monica as she prepares my next injection. 'What time is it, Monica?'

She looks at a small watch on her wrist, 'It's just turned eleven. Not long, darlin, you'll soon be free of this place.'

'Yes, I will, thank you.'

8

Emily

Gatesville – Warden's Office

It really does feel like running the gauntlet again, with hundreds of press present, their camera crews, and campaigners waving banners, although local law enforcement has managed to keep a way clear for us to navigate our car through and pull up inside the outer security gate of the facility. It's bringing flashbacks of the noise and commotion back home in England when news broke about my being 'found'.

Clearing security checks and paperwork is taking some time, all of which is overseen by the Warden himself. The Warden apologises for all the formalities, and then escorts us through the building, accompanied by a couple of other prison officials. He is cordial, polite, and well-spoken and is offering us any assistance he can to make today run as smoothly as possible.

As we enter his office, the Warden instructs the other officials to remain outside. Mary and Martin are with me, while Ernesto is waiting outside with the car. He offers us some lemonade as refreshment, and we all take a seat around the rather large, polished mahogany meeting table.

'Well, this is a special, rather unique day,' he starts. 'It's not often such a Presidential Pardon is granted. And may I add, I believe, to a deserving and model person your mom is.'

Martin is scribbling quietly on his pad, and Mary places her glass down and is about to speak as I reply.

'Thank you, Warden, for your welcome and kind words. However, if such sentiments had been aired years ago when my mother was first arrested, charged, and then sentenced, then maybe, just maybe, she would not have attempted to take her own life and, in doing so, resulted in her last days with us being of ill health and suffering.'

I have no idea where that came from; I had no intention of saying anything like that. It shocks me, and from his expression, it shocks the Warden, also.

Mary places her hand over mine and gently squeezes to show she is there, supporting me, and speaks directly to the Warden. 'Emily has had a long journey out here following the revelations of her and her mother's past, and naturally, Warden, Emily here is upset at eventually finding her mother in such, well, shall we say, environment and poor health.'

'Er. Yes, well, I suppose I can appreciate Miss Collins' position and her opinion on this awful situation. Still, we must look forward together to a reunion of mother and daughter and the good fortune that they have the ability to meet and bond once again.'

I look at him and see that I've made him feel uncomfortable, which is not what I intended at all. 'I am sorry, Warden, I do apologise. Mary is correct; I am tired, a little overwrought, and naturally anxious to meet my mother again.' As I say this, I feel Mary gently squeeze my hand again, softly holding her grip for longer. 'Yes, we must look forward to better times,' I add.

'Thank you, Ma'am. My colleagues are escorting your mom here as we speak. When she arrives, I will leave the room to you.' He glances at Mary, 'Please knock on the door when you are ready for my return. The State Governor has just arrived and is making a public address currently at the facility gates. When he's finished, he wishes to meet with Miss Collins here and Angela to convey his thoughts and blessings.'

'Of course,' Mary replies.

There is a knock at the door, and the Warden stands. 'Shall we,' gesturing to the middle of the room, 'I believe your mom is here.'

As he heads towards the closed door, we all stand, and I move to the centre of the room with Mary to my right. Martin, standing, remains off to my left, a couple of yards away from us. The Warden, his hand resting on the doorknob, turns to look back at me, then Mary, and nods slowly, his eyebrows raised, looking for acceptance to proceed. Mary takes my hand, quietly asking, 'You ready, Sugar?'

I take a deep breath, hold it, then exhale slowly, and reply quietly, 'Yes, as I'll ever be.'

On hearing this, the Warden opens the door.

9

Martin

The Warden's Office

I hadn't really thought about my role in this family reunion fully, and now I suddenly feel like an outsider, an observer. I'm not a family member; I didn't know mother or daughter until twenty-four hours ago, and here I am, witnessing one of the most extraordinary newsworthy events of this year. As the door opens and I see her being wheeled into the room, I instantly feel both ashamed and excited in equal measure. We had agreed not to film or take photographs at this first meeting in order to maintain the integrity and privacy of this reunion, but even being here now unsettles me somewhat.

As Angela's wheelchair is pushed into the room, the silence is only broken by the gentle clicking of something catching against the spokes of one of her wheels. No one speaks as the attending nurse keeps the chair moving forward slowly towards Emily. Angela lifts her right hand free of the armrest and holds it out to one side, palm down, seemingly as a prearranged signal for the nurse to stop, which she duly obeys and applies the locking brake.

The nurse comes around to Angela's side and lifts the light cotton sheet from Angela's legs, placing it over the rear of the chair. Bringing both arms back to the armrests of the chair, Angela takes a firm grip on the chair and proceeds to slowly rise, eventually to stand upright. Nobody else moves.

Watching her closely, I see Angela's life-hardened face slowly break into a wide, beaming smile as she holds out her arms, fully outstretched, inviting Emily to enter her embrace.

Emily takes a small step forward, followed by another, slowly closing the distance between them. She lifts her arms to her mother, and just as they are within reach of each other, Angela's strength seems to waiver, leaning to her right as though she is about to collapse. Emily sees this and instantly rushes forward to close the gap between them, throwing her arms around her mother to stabilise her before she has time to fall. Mary also steps forward, as does the nurse, but it is Emily who catches Angela and provides the support that she needs.

The smile on Angela's face is even bigger now.

'I knew in my heart you were still alive and that one day we would meet again. No one would believe me. Oh, my darling Emily. What did they do to you?'

I cannot see Emily's face from where I'm standing, but I can tell from the sobbing sounds coming from them that they are both in a place of hope and love. Reunited at last.

The nurse begins to wipe tears from her face with her index fingers, and I catch Mary also extracting a tissue to wipe her face. The Warden looks at his two colleagues still in the doorway and quietly flicks his head to one side, indicating for them both to leave, closing the door behind them.

'Mum,' Emily says into the top of Angela's shoulder as she holds her mother upright in her arms.

'My little Emily. My little Emily.' Angela whispers quietly, just audible to us nearby.

Then, without warning, Emily bursts into floods of tears, sobbing uncontrollably. Mary steps forward to support both her and Angela, and the nurse clears her throat as though she is about to speak but then decides to remain silent, leaving them to their embrace.

They remain standing in this embrace for a few minutes, which, in Angela's condition, probably seems like an hour. No one moves or speaks. We all appreciate the emotion in the room, the years of lost love and affection that feel as though they are being sucked back into the room through the very fabric of the building. Even the Warden, standing by the door, has his head dipped almost in reverence.

As Emily's crying subsides, Angela, also with tears running down her gaunt, thin and lined cheeks, raises her head and looks directly at me, her painfully thin arms still entwined around Emily. She looks at me as though she is looking right through me as if I'm not standing maybe three or four yards from them but off on some distant horizon. Our eyes are locked, though, and we see each other, and for a fleeting moment, it feels like there is some kind of connection between us, some association or bond. It feels a little eerie looking into the eyes of another killer; can she sense some kindred spectre in me?

It's Mary that breaks the silence. She coughs slightly to break as a gentle interruption and says in a calm voice, 'Shall we all take a seat? There are some details we need to discuss before we leave this room.'

At this, Emily moves slowly, standing upright from her lowered posture with her mother. Sniffing softly and wiping the back of her hands across her cheeks, Emily replies, 'Yes, of course.'

The Warden steps forward with a pair of clean, pressed white handkerchiefs and offers one to Emily and the other to Angela; both are taken with thanks and used. He had thought about what this meeting would mean to the women and had prepared accordingly.

Angela takes a small step backwards and gingerly indicates her intent to sit down again in the wheelchair. The nurse helps lower her back down, bending at Angela's feet and gently lifting them, in turn, to rest on the aluminium foot plates.

Mary takes Emily by the arm, and they return to the table, taking their original seats. The nurse releases the brake on the wheelchair, and it snaps me into action. Moving forward, I withdraw and remove the large wood and leather chair beside Emily to make room for the wheelchair to sit beside her. The nurse smiles at me as she pushes the wheelchair into the vacant slot at the table.

Emily looks at her mother, and they smile, each offering a hand to hold.

The Warden takes a seat opposite Angela. He looks at her, then at Emily and then to Mary. He clears his throat and speaks up. 'Ladies, Mr Nicholson,' looking to me. 'In a few minutes, I'll be joined by some officials to discuss Angela's departure from this facility. An ambulance with an EMT on board, made available by the state, is ready to transfer you to your preferred location. Monica here,' indicating the nurse behind Angela, 'is available to accompany you also if that is acceptable?'

As Mary goes to reply, Angela cuts in. 'Yes, that is acceptable; thank you, Warden.'

He nods back at Angela and then refers to a thin pad of notes he has in front of him. 'The local police will accompany your ambulance and look to keep the media pack at bay. They have also offered to post presence at the hospital you have elected to go to for the next few days to ensure you are not unduly disturbed or disrupted.'

'Thank you, Warden, but I don't envisage it will be for long, no more than a few days, I expect,' Angela replies again.

Whilst frail, her mind seems duly switched on, and she certainly isn't afraid to speak up in front of the Warden. Well, I suppose when you have been living under the shadow of a death sentence, you develop a more robust confidence than you would ordinarily have. Angela clearly has some plans already, although I don't know if she is ignoring her health condition or thinking of a darker outcome arriving sooner. Emily turns her head to look at her mother.

'It's OK darling, it's OK,' Angela says to her as she moves her left hand and places it over their already locked hands.

'Mum?'

'It's fine, darling, it truly is. I have you back now, and the natural order of things is coming about. It's all good.'

Mary addresses the Warden, 'Is the Governor coming here, or are we to meet him outside?'

'Ah, er, he wants to meet outside in front of the facility. Would that be acceptable?'

'In front of the cameras, you mean?' Mary asks.

'Er, yes, that is his preference.'

It's interesting, as an observer, to watch how mother and daughter are emotionally connecting with each other while, at the same time, details of press conferences and political point-scoring are unfolding within a few feet. These people should be left to quietly reconnect and tell the world to go screw itself, but no, there is always a price to pay; someone else is owed a tax.

Then it dawns on me: I'm one of those people looking to collect a share from this story; I'm also taking a tax. But if it's not me, it'll be someone else, some other person who hasn't got my history or experience. At least I can relate to the loss each has experienced from forced separation and the killing of a person with a knife, although the depth and detail of my latter experience no one here knows about.

Angela and Emily are quietly discussing something that I can't hear the words of, although their body language indicates they're becoming aligned on it. Mary knows of Emily's wish to speak up today and of her want to shield Angela from anything in the public eye, and she is simultaneously conveying this to the Warden.

I sit quietly, observing all. The nurse is also quiet, standing professionally behind Angela, where I've noticed her looking at her watch every minute or so as though there is some deadline she is counting down to. Maybe it's for Angela's next medication, or is it something else?

One of those natural silences falls on the room just as the Warden comments to Mary, 'Yes, that is so, but inside this facility, I have the final word on everything, but outside the gates, I can't do anything to assist or support your wishes. You must appreciate that?'

Looking at Emily, I notice a change in her expression, from the joy of meeting her Mum to the realisation of what is outside awaiting her. This feels like an opportune time to ask her if she still wants to go through with meeting the media.

'Yes. Yes, I need to say something, or they'll just keep hounding us.'

'Well, only if you're sure, Sugar,' adds Mary.

10

Emily

Outside Gatesville

Bright sunshine, the heat, and the accents apart, this scene mimics what I experienced back in the UK. The shouting press, the cameras, the microphones, the voice recorders held high, the constantly clicking, although here, it's multiplied tenfold. Looking over the heads of the baying mass, dozens of large vans bristling with satellite dishes and antennas are parked with doors open. To either side and immediately behind the cameras are the crowds, the general public, some here to support and some seemingly not, with flags and banners being held aloft. Regardless of Mum's specific situation, the two sides, pro and against capital punishment, are using this as a reason to congregate here and have their say. There is a smaller group, clearly here to support Mum's release, and to them, I am grateful for the steadfast support for humanity and justice.

The Governor, standing before me on this temporary podium, has been speaking for at least ten minutes; Mary and Martin were right; it's an opportunity for him to showcase his role and policies and bolster his upcoming re-election campaign. I find it a little unnerving that he has several close protection security personnel with him, easily identifiable people with their earpieces, dark shades, dark suits, and stances with their ever-roaming meerkat awareness.

While he's here speaking and I'm in full view, both acting as a distraction, Mum is being transferred to the ambulance for her journey to the Pontin Institute. The ambulance will leave as I stand to address everybody. Mary is accompanying Mum and the nurse, and we're hoping that the majority here miss them departing and remain focused on me.

Martin is standing down below, in front of me, alongside one of the national news crews. Our eyes briefly meet, and he nods once to me, providing just that little bit of extra encouragement. He looks at ease, his strong character seemingly making him stand out from the others in front of me. He doesn't look as though he's in a feeding frenzy like some of those around him; it's almost as if they are not there and he is the sole person interested in me.

'…and with that, The President and I could not do anything other than pardon Angela Collins and return her to the arms of her long-lost daughter, Emily, who is here today and wishes to address us all. I have the great honor of introducing you to… Miss Emily Collins.'

His words ring loud in my ears, and I look up at him as he turns to me, taking a step backwards before commencing to applaud me. This is my cue to stand and approach the lectern. He offers me his right hand, and I shake it, noticing that he has already turned with a beaming smile to the throng of cameras and reporters. He then leans into me and whispers, 'I believe you wish to say a few words, Ma'am. Please…' indicating he is stepping back and offering me the hot spot on the podium.

Shouts of questions and statements hit me like a crashing wave, and the Governor steps forward again with his arms slightly raised in front of him, saying, 'Please… please, can we show some respect. I'm sure y'all would like to hear what Miss Collins here has to say. Please,' moving his palms up and down slightly in a gesture to calm down.

They fall quiet, although from across the way, some chanting from one or two of the campaigners remains, as they are intent on being heard. I see a couple of police officers move towards them, but as free speech goes, I don't think they'll have much luck in quietening them for more than a few minutes.

As I stand behind the lectern, it's then that I notice the dozen or so microphones fixed to it, each sporting a media brand. This unnerves me a little, and I look at Martin again; he is nodding slowly, his right thumb upright in front of his chest, providing me with the encouragement to keep going.

I swallow hard, my throat already dry, and cough slightly. The Governor is quick to offer me a small bottle of water, and I smile at him as I take it, unscrew the lid, and take a couple of small sips. Holding onto the bottle with both hands as though it were some kind of a life belt, I speak.

'Good afternoon. I am Emily Collins, and I was taken. I was abducted from my parents as a baby in the United Kingdom, and only recently I became aware of this. The people I thought were my parents for the last twenty-three years turned out not to be, and my real identity is now known. Naturally, I wanted to meet my real parents again, and this has led me here today to be reunited with my biological mother, Angela Collins.' My nervousness is now subsiding a little now that I've actually stood up and started to speak.

‘My mum, Angela, has lived a very difficult and fraught life ever since my abduction all those years ago. In England, she was accused of being in some way complicit in my disappearance, even being publicly slandered for my murder and the disposal of my body. It is now plainly clear to all that she was totally innocent of any wrongdoing, innocent of all the allegations, accusations, and lies spread about her. Under this constant pressure, Angela could no longer live in England, and with her husband, Barry, they decided to relocate to the United States for a new start, a new beginning.’

I pause and take another sip of water, letting my words sink in with the media.

‘They settled down in Crockett and tried their best to assimilate into community life, but her husband, behind the scenes, would not let her start again, constantly reminding her of the day that I was taken, blaming her, torturing her almost daily with mental and physical abuse. There was no one around to help my mother; she was alone in a foreign country.’

The campaigners had stopped their chanting and were listening, some of them slowly lowering their placards.

‘Then, one day, he did something or said something to her that went too far, and she just snapped. Her defence in court was walked all over and ignored, resulting in her being wrongfully sentenced to murder and receiving the death penalty sentence. Her frail health now is a result of her own hand. Abused, battered, lonely, and forgotten, she tried to take her own life while in custody, and now she is dying slowly. I want that guilt to rest on the shoulders of all those who persecuted her, hounded her, chastised her, and wrongly punished her, culminating in her attempt to take her own life.’

The only sound audible was some distant traffic; everyone was listening, some looking straight at me, others with their heads bowed.

'And then I was found, and not long afterwards, I was informed my mother was located here, in this place. She is a shell of the person she used to be, of a mother, but seeing her for the first time this afternoon since I was a baby, the love and affection between mother and daughter remains, and I saw the light re-enter my mother's eyes today in the Warden's office. Her health is failing, and we don't have much time left together, and this is why I am standing here today. I am going to make a personal plea to you all. I ask that you let us be, that you leave us alone, showing respect and sympathy, so that we can spend my mother's last days in peace; peace she has never been granted or found since my abduction nearly twenty-four years ago. And in return for this peace, I promise the full story of everything will be provided to you in due course.'

The quiet remains. I turn to the Governor, nod my head at him, and then turn back to the microphones.

'I wish to take this opportunity to personally thank the Governor, and of course your President, for allowing us this morsel of time together before it's too late, time to re-connect before my mother passes, and all I ask is that you respect our peace and privacy over the coming days and hopefully weeks. Thank you.'

No sooner had I finished speaking than the first question was shouted out, then another and another. I raise both my hands in a stop signal. 'Please, I don't wish to say anything further. I will, in due course, issue a statement, but strongly ask that until that time, you respect our family privacy.'

As I speak, the security barrier opens at the main gate, and the liveried ambulance slowly departs the prison confines. Someone shouts out, and smaller groups and individuals in the crowd move towards it; I quickly take charge of the situation.

'Wait, please. All, please listen. My mother is not in that ambulance, so it's pointless chasing after it. She left the facility about thirty minutes ago in an unmarked vehicle and is already on her way to a private and secure hospital facility.'

I look down at Martin, standing stock still, unphased in the melee all around him. He raises his eyebrows slowly, almost imperceptibly, nodding his head to me. Hopefully, the ruse worked, and by now, my mother will be almost at the Ponton Institute and checked in before anyone realises where she is.

11

Mary

The Pontin Institute

The hospital was ready and waiting to receive us, and Angela was efficiently conveyed to this secure wing and private room. A police officer is sitting outside her room, as promised, to hopefully fend off any unwanted visitors; another is sitting in the reception area.

'It feels like I'm back in Gatesville,' Angela says as she is being helped into bed by two nurses and has medical monitors applied to her.

'Nonsense, Angela, this is nothing like Gatesville. For one, you're not locked in here and are free to leave at any time,' and looking at the nurses, I add, 'and for sure, this is a much nicer environment.'

The nurses do not respond or acknowledge my words; instead, they remain focused on settling Angela in.

'Well then, why is there a guard outside?' she asks.

'He's not a guard; he's here to stop unauthorised persons disturbing you.'

Monica, the nurse from Gatesville, has travelled with us, and she takes the hospital nurse to one side, conversing quietly in the room corner, no doubt discussing medication and timings.

'I'm tired.' Angela says out loud.

Monica picks up on this and crosses to the bed, 'How are you feeling now, Angela? Do you need some pain relief?'

'Yes, of course I do!' She snaps back at Monica, which surprises me a little. Monica is not fazed by this and is clearly used to Angela's changeable manner.

'Now, Angela, that's enough of that; you know I won't tolerate that kind of attitude. Grace here,' indicating the hospital nurse beside her, 'will be looking after you; I have to return to Gatesville.' She turns to Grace, 'Don't let her talk badly to you, she knows to be good to get her meds; isn't that so, Angela?'

'Umm, if you say so, Boss.'

I flash a quick glance at Grace and notice the surprise on her face. I suppose she's not used to dealing with death rowers or the manner of prison inmates. Monica then turns back to Angela and holds out her right hand to her, 'I wish you all the best, Angela, and godspeed.'

Angela looks at her outstretched hand and pauses, unsure what to do, it seems, but Monica holds her hand steady, waiting for Angela to accept it. Angela looks at me, and I simply nod twice in return, to which she takes Monica's hand and shakes it, no words spoken.

Monica says farewell to both Grace and me, then leaves without any further words with Angela, her charge now passing to Grace. As the door closes behind Monica, Grace asks how Angela is feeling and if she needs anything at this time.

She replies, 'I could do with some pain relief, and then I want to go to sleep, I'm exhausted.'

Grace leaves the room to collect further medication, and I move closer to Angela, sitting on a visitor chair beside her. 'Emily will be along shortly; it seems the ruse worked, and she managed to distract the media at the Gatesville's gates; they don't know you're here, well not yet that is.'

'I'm not sure if I have the energy for more today, Mary; will you tell her that we can meet up again tomorrow? I want to get some rest. Today has taken quite a bit out of me; I'm sure she will understand.'

'Oh, er, yes, I will do,' I reply, a little surprised.

I wasn't expecting that; I thought she would want the two of them to be together as much as possible. I can accept it must be difficult, as truly they don't know each other, and so much has happened to each of them in the intervening years that is different yet equally shocking. Still, given the limited time available, I really thought Angela would want to spend every available hour with her long-lost daughter. It just goes to show how wrong I can be.

'Shall I leave you now to rest?' I ask her.

'Yes, please,' she replies, as she drops her head back on the pillow and closes her eyes.

As I leave the room, Grace returns, and we cross in the doorway. 'Angela is tired and doesn't want any visitors today. I'm just going to call her daughter to let her know.'

'OK, I'll give Angela this pain relief, and then we can leave her to rest.'

'Thank you,' I reply.

Looking at my cell phone, I'm trying to work out how to let Emily know her mother doesn't want to see her today and decide on playing it straight with her; after all, it's not my decision. I scroll to Emily's cell phone number and press the call button.

12

Emily

Car to Pontin Institute

We've been driving for a little over ten minutes, heading towards the hospital, when my mobile rings and I answer it to speak with Mary. The call is short, and as it ends, I continue to look down at my mobile phone in my hand, astounded by what Mary has just said, but naturally, if that is Mum's wish, I'll have to accept it. Martin, sitting beside me, hearing only one half of the conversation, asks, 'Is everything alright? Is it your mother?'

Without looking at him, I reply a little sullenly, 'She doesn't want to see me today; she's tired and wants to rest. We are to meet up again tomorrow morning.'

He reaches across and places his hand beside me, twisting slightly in his seat to look at me. 'Well, I suppose she will be tired; she is very poorly, and this is all happening so fast; just over twenty-four hours ago, she was still facing the death penalty.'

'I know, yes, but we don't have a lot of time left to be together, in fact, we don't know how much or how little time this will be, so we should make every minute count, shouldn't we?' I look at him as I ask the question.

He smiles sympathetically, no doubt appreciating the situation and realising there is nothing to be done if one of the parties doesn't want to meet up.

'Well, on the upside, this gives us the opportunity to head straight to the hotel and use what is left of today to discuss your story and your thoughts,' he replies, 'in fact, it could work out better for us as it may provide us with some deeper background to talk through further with Angela tomorrow.'

'Yes, I suppose so,' I reply, and as soon as I do, Martin instructs Ernesto to head directly to the hotel instead.

I am disappointed by Mum's decision, but Martin helps me accept it. Using our newfound time together today to speak with each other, just the two of us, without other distractions, will be fruitful. It hadn't really dawned on me until now that we've spent very little time alone together to discuss me and my feelings, to explore any assistance and support that Martin can provide, and, of course, the development of the book, my life story.

Looking out of the window, we've left the open expanses behind us, and we're driving through a dispersed town called McGregor. The wide road is lined on both sides with large hardware stores, drive-in eateries, and other depots, all set back away from the highway with vehicle parking out front and what seems like a proliferation of gas stations advertising different petroleum companies. Ernesto slows the car as we approach traffic signals and then enters into a stretch of temporary roadworks. To my right, I see a sign indicating a right turn to a place called Moody, and I laugh a little to myself, thinking the sign is fitting for Mum's temperament. Within minutes, we're through McGregor and back out into the flat expanse of field and blue sky.

As we travel at a constant speed, occasionally overtaking slower vehicles, the monotony of the drive and the brightness have me closing my eyes, placing my head back on the chair's headrest, my thoughts drifting off to events in England leading up to this day. It's hard to believe just months ago, I was in a completely different life, married to Paul, thinking of starting a family with the man I loved. Paul, the man who turned out to be the most devious, conniving, selfish and self-centred person I've ever come across, that was until I discovered what my parents had done, them arguably being worse than Paul. I now find that I am unable to trust anyone close to me; I just can't be deceived again like that. I was too trusting, trusting at the outset, but isn't that what you should be like with your parents and your new husband, to trust them unconditionally until they show that they can no longer be trusted?

My world has turned upside down, and it seems inside out. I wasn't the person I thought I was, my parents weren't my parents, and my husband wasn't the man I thought he was, either. I was hoping for the big reunion with Mum, yet even though I expected it to be within the confines of a prison visitation room, I wanted us to be close again. I wasn't expecting the pardon and the extent of her poor health, both somehow are impacting how I thought we would reconnect and rediscover each other.

Ernesto speaks up, 'We should be at the hotel in about twenty minutes.'

'Thank you,' Martin replies. I remain quiet, lost in my thoughts. Can I trust this man, Martin? How much can I tell him about what really happened? The process of describing my life to Martin has me nervous, as I may say something that leads him to ask more questions, eventually finding out my part in Paul's death. If I stick to what I said to the police and what they think they know, then I should be safe. After all, those interviews carried much more consequence than the ones I'll be doing with Martin.

13

Martin

The Merlin West Hotel, Waco

Re-arranging the desk in my hotel room to place a chair on either side seems to be the best professional working environment I can muster with such limited resources at short notice. My laptop is ready, and my trusty digital recorder is at hand, accompanied by a selection of coloured pens and my leather-bound notebook. Two large bottles of mineral water, along with two glasses, are on the side cupboard. The notes and paraphernalia I have collected on Emily Collins, or I should say, Kate Hunter, about her life and events, are stacked into three neat piles on the bed. They comprise her abduction and investigation with publications of that time, then background on her life after abduction before becoming aware of her real identity, and finally, events that followed after she found out who she really is.

It feels incredibly insensitive and cold to compartmentalise a person's life like this, but this is research, and these piles represent the significant milestones in Emily's life. To some extent, her life is not that different from mine, but only Nico and I know the full extent of all the events that happened to me and around me, and it needs to stay that way.

Normally, I would spend some time getting to know the subject, Emily, in this case, before embarking on any guidance or support, as each case is so uniquely different, with the individuals involved affected in different ways. One person can handle, say, the violent death of a loved one seemingly quite well, while for others, it affects them dramatically, causing all kinds of breakdown and trauma. But what I've learned over the last few years is that those who, on the face of it, handle it well often bury it deep down and try to keep it away from daylight, keeping it bottled up. These are the ones who need real help, but they just don't know it. It can eat at them, or it can be the start of a gnawing hunger, them wanting to avenge the death of their loved one or to inflict injury on others; it's something I've experienced myself, personally, and I can see it in others when they let their guard down. This is why I need to get to know each subject first, but with Emily, we're on borrowed time, at least with regard to her mother. There will be time enough to spend with Emily to help her, but we need to work with Angela now, given the sand in her timer is slipping away quicker than I expected. So, Emily and I need to start now, just in case there is something we want to ask Angela before she passes.

Looking at my watch, Emily will be here anytime. I know she was close to her husband, Paul. Still, she is one of those who seems to be handling his death well, surprising given the dramatic and shocking method of his exit. It was this method of killing himself that led to exposing Emily's parentage deception and abduction and bringing us here today.

The gentle knock at the door announces Emily's arrival. I cast a quick glance around the room to check if everything is OK, and to be honest, I don't know why it wouldn't be. Shaking my head, I step across the room to open the door.

'Hi, Emily. Please, do come in.' As I'm saying this, I think it's all a bit formal, considering we've just spent the best part of five hours over the last twenty-four hours together, sat next to each other in a vehicle, and having dinner together last night.

I step back, allowing Emily to enter; she is wearing tight blue jeans, a white and blue horizontal-striped t-shirt, and her hair pulled back into a ponytail. Her plimsoll shoes don't make a sound as she seemingly glides by me, leaving a soft light scent in her wake, teasing my senses.

'Please, take a seat,' I say while closing the door.

On turning back to her, I see her standing, looking at the three bundles of documents on the bed.

'Research?' she asks.

'Er, yes. Background I have been collecting to help build the story.'

'Umm,' she replies, as she turns to the desk and selects a chair. 'Well, Martin, where would you like to start?'

I wasn't expecting her to be so forthright again, and whilst I admire her for it, it may take a little getting used to. 'Well, given time is against us on certain parts of your story, I think the best place to start is when you found out you were an abductee. We can then explore your initial reaction and feelings upon hearing this and how you felt when informed about your mother, your biological mother, Angela. Is that OK with you?'

'Yes, why not? We need a place to start, and that sounds as good a place as any.'

14

Emily

Martin's Room, The Merlin West Hotel, Waco

He asks me again, 'So, how did you feel, Emily?'

'Well, naturally, I was shocked. At first, I thought they had it all wrong, the police, that there had been some kind of mix-up at the testing lab, but then they said they had double-checked, and confirmation was beyond doubt; I struggled to comprehend the enormity of it. I had no idea I was somebody else. I had always thought Julia and Duncan were my parents. Then, when confronted, Duncan initially said he was not my biological father, and it was shocking enough to hear just this, but then, they already had their perfect story planned in case I challenged them; how was I to know it was anything more than this and that the reality was something more grotesque?'

'After finding out Duncan was not your biological father and that they said they had used a clinic to become pregnant, how did that make you feel?'

'Then… well, stupidly, I ended up feeling even closer to my mum, I mean Julia, but knowing what I know now, I have to accept I never knew them at all, it was all a lie, they stole me from my real mother and her life spiralled thereafter, her life totally ruined. I am so angry now that I felt closer to Julia, that she… she…'. I pause; deep down, I know I'm not ready for this just yet. 'Can I have some water, please?'

'Yes, sure.'

He collects the water from the side table and returns, pouring me a glass.

He sits again, and as I sip the water, he continues, 'What were your thoughts when you realised that Paul's death was the reason you found out the truth about your so-called parents, that Julia was not your biological mother and that her and her husband, Duncan, had abducted you?'

Is he trying to catch me out on something here? Why has he asked me that? No, he doesn't know about my involvement in Paul's death; he can't. I need to stop being paranoid. The only people who know are locked up in prison in England, and they said they would keep my secret. Or, no, have they said something to… no, stop it, he doesn't know anything about it.

'Emily?'

'Oh, er, sorry, I was miles away then. What was the question again?'

'Paul's death being the reason you found out about your abduction, how did you feel?'

'Oh yes, well, ironically, him shooting himself in the head was the reason DNA tests were carried out for him, but really, it was my stepsister's actions that caused us all to have our DNA tested and well, the rest is history as they say. I was found.'

'But how did you feel?'

'Well, how would you feel if you found out you'd been lied to for the whole of your life?' I snipe back at him quickly, unexpected for the both of us.

He raises his hands, palms showing towards me, 'I'm sorry, I know this is hard, but this is what readers will want to know, how it affected you personally. From the outside, your parents weren't your parents; they abducted you as a baby. Your husband committed suicide because he cheated his lifelong best friend into taking DNA tests, which culminated in your half-sister murdering him, your real father. Then, your real mother turns out to be a convicted murderer on death row here in Texas. That's quite a collection of events and facts. The readers will want to know your inner thoughts on all this.'

In my head, I'm screaming; they can never find out about the truth behind Paul's death, that I talked him into it. Ever since being asked to do this book, I've worried that I might say something that trips me up. I feel guilty enough now that I know all the facts, but at the time, Paul convinced me he was my biological father, and the ramifications of that were huge. His suicide, I thought, was the best outcome then, so we could keep it all buried, a secret to have been taken to the grave.

He's looking at me still, waiting for more from me. I decide to deflect slightly and move the topic a little. 'Yes, I see that, but I'm still processing most of it. Anyway, what about you, what brought you out to the US?' and, as I ask it, I realise how lame a question it is as he addressed it in his autobiography.

15

Martin

My Hotel Room, The Merlin West Hotel, Waco

Classic deflection technique. I need to tread carefully with Emily, as she is still quite raw from everything that has happened. She's dodging sharing her thoughts and feelings with me, but this sharing is essential for the book, and more importantly, it allows her to come to terms with the events that have affected her, enabling her to move on with her life.

I don't know if this is the so-called sixth sense, but I get a feeling she is not being entirely honest about something. She seems cautious, for what I don't know, but she is holding something back, something that stops me from getting her to talk about her feelings. It's maybe the deflection or the way she replies, but I feel there is something there. Whatever it is, it can't be any worse than what I've done. I thought my past was deeply buried, locked away, never to see the light of day again, and that I could control my emotions, but clearly, that was not the case. The double killing I did I thought would end up in my arrest and being imprisoned for life, but as events unfolded, I managed to dodge that bullet. I'm even more determined now to never stray again into the dark side of my mind, to let it take over my actions and direct me.

'I came out here for a new start,' I reply, 'and I'm glad I did. There is nothing left for me back in the UK anymore, and with investors interested in my story, I thought I'd try life in the US; and, so far, it's been very good, enjoyable.' There is Nico back at home, but our relationship is something no one needs to know about. I continue, turning her query into something for me to gain, 'What do you have left to return to? Do you have any family over there?'

Her expression changes to one of emptiness. 'Actually, I've never really thought about that until now. There… there is no one back there for me, nothing that I must return for. I have my house, of course, and business interests, but even they can be remotely controlled, and if I decide to leave the UK, selling the house wouldn't be a problem; the business interests will either look after themselves or I'll appoint a manager.'

The business interests were Paul's that she has inherited, but I note how she refers to a house and not a home, a word choice that may indicate she has a more materialistic mindset. It was the home she made with Paul, her husband, that they bought together to start their new life, but she clearly doesn't think of it that way anymore. Exploring this with her and wanting to keep the dialogue going, I ask her, 'You refer to your home as my house but not my home; is there a reason for that?'

She looks away from me for a few seconds, then back at me, 'I thought that would be obvious; with everything that happened to me, it's just bricks and mortar now. The dreams we had for that place have long since evaporated. And with Paul's suicide there, I can easily leave it behind me, so yes, my house is no longer my home.'

'Ah, I see, yes.' I had read it somewhere but forgotten that was where he had taken his own life. I continue to push at the edges of this topic, 'I presume Paul's family, his son and daughter that is, are distant from you now?'

'Yes, why would you think that would be any different? In their eyes, my being in Paul's life ruined everything for them, especially Ruth, his daughter. Ben, Paul's son, was more on the fence, you know, acknowledging his father's decision to divorce from their mum and marry another. Although he never accepted it, he acknowledged, realising they all needed to move on with life.'

'So, neither of them has been in touch with you since your real identity was established?'

'No.'

'And you can accept that?'

'Yes, easily. To them, it's merely a name change; I'm still the other woman, the destroyer of families.'

'That's being a bit harsh on yourself, don't you think?'

'No, not really, I am accepting everything has changed, so why not move on with my life?'

Her answers are quite to the point, self-critical in places, maybe indicating a lack of remorse for her impact on Paul's family.

'Anyway, reading your book, your wife became the other woman, and she, with her new lover, tried to kill you, is that about right? How do you feel about that?'

There's that deflection again. 'We're not here to talk about me; we're here to talk of your events, your feelings, and what you need to manage the here and now to help you rebuild a new life.'

She looks distant again, falling silent once more. I keep the pressure up a little. 'How do you feel about trust?'

'Huh, trust. That's just a word that means different things to different people.'

'I ask it in the context of trust with people; do you think you can trust a person again?' This is a deep and broad question, and I want to explore where it may lead us.

She pauses before replying, looking directly into my eyes. She has beautiful blue eyes; some would describe them as ice-cold, but to me, they are as blue as a summer's day, warm and inviting. My task is to try to work out what it is that's going on behind those blue eyes so they can make everyone else see them as a summer day again. Her beauty on the outside hides an inner turmoil and anger; I can feel it. I can sense that what she is going through was how I felt when I realised that my wife was cheating on me with my friend and, ultimately, finding out what they had planned to do to me, plotting the perfect murder. In my case, I decided their fate and dished it up; could that be it? Does she want revenge? Or did she already get it; did she have a hand in Paul's suicide?

'I don't know, can you?' Her reply, snapping me out of my thoughts, is a clever answer and deflection wrapped up in one.

'Yes, I think I can. It's taken some time, but I think I can trust again when I find the right person, that is.'

'To be honest with you, it'll take a lot for me to trust someone completely again, but one thing I'm sure about is that I'll never trust blindly again; it will have to be earned.'

'Then that is a good place to start. It shows you've not given up on mankind completely.' I smile at her, hoping she feels the warmth I'm trying to portray, but she doesn't respond. Continuing but touching on something closer to home, 'Do you think you can trust your mother, Angela? Believe what she says to you, as unfortunately, her limited time will make it impossible to earn your trust.'

'You do like to throw the odd, unexpected punch, Martin Nicholson.'

'To keep our conversation broad and on topic, but you get what I mean?'

'Yes, I do. I suppose I'll have to believe her. Anyway, why would I not trust what she has to say to me? We are mother and daughter trying to reconnect, and I already know the worst of her.'

'I suppose, but ironically, what you've just accepted is that you will trust some people blindly more than others.'

'Touché, monsieur.'

'It's a good start.' Looking at my watch, it's almost seven. 'Shall we break for dinner? I have a table booked for us downstairs.'

'If you don't mind, could we order room service? It's just that I don't want the hassle of dressing for dinner and being on the alert in case we're spotted.'

'Oh, er, yes, we can do. I'll grab the menu, and well, yes, we can dine here if you like?'

'Thank you. and we can carry on chatting without fear of being overheard,' she adds, smiling back at me.

'True.' I stand to collect the menu from the side table, quietly pleased with her suggestion to dine here and her willingness to keep the conversation flowing.

16

Emily

Martin's Hotel Room

Using his washroom while he clears the dinner plates away, I catch myself in the mirror. I'm a little tipsy now with the half bottle of red wine I've consumed, and my mind is wandering. He is handsome, intelligent, and witty, and for the life of me, I cannot see what his former wife failed to see in him. He is charming and always polite, well, when he's not engrossed in his work, that is, although now, I am his work, and I wish he could be more engrossed in me rather than his notebook. I catch myself again shaking my head slowly as I watch myself in the mirror, eyes locked, not moving. I'm not sure about that thought; the wine, the loneliness, the want to be held, to be touched, to be wanted. Yes, I miss it; I miss the company of a man I want to spend time with.

After washing my hands, I gently slap both cheeks slightly to bring me back to the now. Get a grip, girl; he doesn't want you, and really, you don't want him; you just want someone to be with, someone to extinguish the loneliness at night, that empty bed.

Placing the towel down, I return to the bedroom and see him down low on his haunches, rustling through the mini bar. 'Still thirsty, are we?'

'Oh, yes, well, since coming out here, I've become quite partial to Bourbon,' he replies, holding two miniature bottles above his head for me to see. 'Do you fancy one?'

'No, thank you. But, maybe a vodka, if there is one there?'

'Of course, one second. Haha! Eureka.' He stands and turns to face me, two small bottles in each hand. 'Here we go,' offering me the two vodka miniatures. 'I'll get glasses and ice.'

Taking the bottles from him, I decide to sit on the sofa rather than return to the desk, come improvised dinner table. He follows me with the ice bucket and two large, crystal-cut glasses, electing to sit beside me. As he settles into the sofa, he fishes out a large ice cube, deposits it in a glass, and passes it to me. I twist the top open, and as I pour the vodka over the ice, he looks at me.

'Sorry, I should have asked, would you like something to mix with that? Orange juice, maybe?'

'No, neat is good for me, thank you,' I reply, smiling back at him.

'Sensible, why pollute the taste of a good spirit.'

We clink our glasses and take a sip of our drinks. The vodka is a brand I'm not accustomed to, and it's a little harsh for my palate; I cough slightly.

'Umm, maybe I should get that mixer?' he suggests,

'No, it's fine, thank you, I just need to redirect my taste buds slightly.'

He nods gently as he takes another larger sip of his bourbon. 'So, what do you think of America?'

'Although I've not had the chance to see much of it, I like what I've seen so far. Everything is so much bigger and brighter, and the people are nice and polite.

Although, the food portions are enormous, and I do like the Mexican options with most meals, even breakfast.'

He nods, then asks, 'What are your plans after your mother passes?' His directness and topic changes, at times, unsettle me, no, not unsettle, catch me off guard more like; is that a tactic or his manner?

'I'm not sure. I don't need to return to the UK, as I mentioned earlier, as I can run my business interests remotely for a while. So, I don't know, maybe see more of America. You're based in California now, aren't you? You may like to show me the delights of California.'

'Yes, I could. The Golden State, I could do that; in fact, it would be my pleasure.'

'The Golden State; because of gold or the weather?'

'The former. The gold rush of the mid-1800s brought thousands of optimists and opportunists to the area from all over the world. Lives and fortunes were made and lost for many back then.'

'Not unlike now, I suppose, no different to anywhere in the world. Paul used to say...' and I pause, thinking carefully about my next words. 'I'm sorry, I have to stop doing this, bringing him into my conversations. He chose his path, wanting to be gone, to leave me. I have no obligation to continue referring to his existence as such.'

He is a little surprised by my comment. Finishing the last of his bourbon, he twists on the settee to look at me, 'There is no need to apologise; he took his life for his reasons; that was his choice. You may feel resentment and anger following his suicide, but what is done is done; we cannot change what has passed. We learn from it, rebuild, plan our future, and move forward.'

He has no idea of my role in Paul's death, and if he did, I don't think he'd be talking about planning a future.

"*Our future*", he said; does he mean that literally or metaphorically? I'm fed up with trying to think of what to say next, so I need to be careful with my word use to avoid tripping myself up. I look into his eyes, and then instinct takes over. I lean into him and kiss him softly at first, and as he doesn't pull away, my lips move to entice his.

He reacts, and we kiss passionately. On impulse, I fling my left arm around his shoulders and, putting my hand behind his head, pull him into me. He matches my actions, and as we close, I feel a cold sensation on my thigh. 'Oh, argh.' I pull back from him and look at my lap, my vodka glass tipping on its side as I twist, spilling its cold contents on me.

But this doesn't stop him. His arms come around me and pull me into him. Our lips meet again, this time in a passionate frenzy. I twist fully to face him now, drawing myself up onto the settee, onto him. His hands are firm behind my head, releasing my ponytail, his fingers becoming entwined in my hair. My god, I'd almost forgotten what this feels like, and I want more of it. I start to unbutton his shirt, and for a brief second, he stops, pulls slightly back from me and squarely looks at me.

'Are you sure you want to do this?' he asks.

Just his asking makes me want him even more. I throw myself at him, and he falls backwards awkwardly against the arm of the settee, but that doesn't faze him. He kisses me back with such depth and passion; I know I really want this. He moves, turning us on the settee, and without any sign of effort, he stands, lifting me, our mouths never breaking contact. I feel the muscles of his arms tighten their hold on me as my weight bears on him, and he takes steps towards the bed.

All thinking has stopped; I'm just in this for the now. I want him.

17

Martin

My Hotel Room

Waking, I hear her soft breathing beside me and feel the warmth of her hand on my chest, and a wave of concern washes over me. What have we done? We shouldn't have done that; I shouldn't have done that. This is going to complicate things now; why did I let that continue? I've compromised our professional relationship with a person I believe is still vulnerable. I haven't broken any professional ethics, as such, as I'm not a licenced practitioner, but I still shouldn't have crossed that bridge. I'm torn now. Do I apologise and continue as though nothing happened, or could this be something more serious just starting between us?

She stirs ever so slightly, her eyes slowing opening, looking up at me. 'Good morning,' her simple whispered greeting.

'Good morning,' my cautious reply, as I'm struggling to find other words to say.

'Thank you, I really enjoyed last night,' she replies, again in a soft whisper.

How do I reply to that? You're welcome? Not at all? Anytime? Stupid. I shouldn't have let it happen in the first place. Before I can reply, she continues.

'I'm sorry, I didn't mean to… well, you know. I think, what with the wine, your company, and me wanting to feel desired again, it all just kind of overtook me. I'm sorry.'

Now I really am struggling with what to say; I've never slept with a woman who has apologised to me the following morning; actually, it is usually the reverse, well, in my younger days anyway. Instinct takes over.

'There is nothing to apologise for; we enjoyed each other's company,' and as I say the words, I know I'm not being totally honest with her, which makes me feel uneasy. She is probably one of the most genuine people I've met in a long time, and now I've let this happen.

She wriggles up beside me, placing her arm across my chest. My word, though, she is so beautiful, and I did enjoy being with her last night and now.

I need to control this and manage both our expectations. She is still vulnerable; she has not yet resolved all her inner issues, and I need to tread carefully. Rejecting her now would be the right thing to do, but doing so, even gently, could actually re-ignite feelings of abandonment, reinforcing in her mind that she's not wanted. Believe me, she's wanted; I want her. I tip my head down to her and gently kiss the top of her head, causing her to snuggle into me even more. I'm torn. Looking over Emily to the clock beside the bed, the time is seven thirty-four, and there is much to do today.

'Emily,' I whisper, 'We should get up and get ready; it's going to be a big day for you and your mother, an opportunity to be in touch with each other without external pressures.'

'I know, but can't we just stay like this for the time being… another five minutes, please?'

'Of course.' I tighten my arm around her slightly, feeling awkward inside as I do it. Why am I feeling like this? She is wonderful, consenting, and free of ties; why can't we simply enjoy ourselves together?

The answer is simple: I am here to write a book about her life and, at the same time, help her address her anxieties and inner issues. This is not about two consenting people enjoying themselves; we came together for a business reason, and somehow, I need to address this with her and put us back on track. But I don't want to put a wedge between us; I really do want her. Should I drop the book plans and explore a relationship with her instead?

What am I thinking? No, of course not; I need this just as much as she does. From my perspective, her life story could put me back on top, back into the circles and connections I had when my story came out. It's not like I've really lost all the connections I made, but it is challenging to stay on top when there is so much more talent and ambition climbing the same ladder and snapping at your ankles. I genuinely feel there is a movie to be made of her life; if not, then some television rights to be had, so long as I stay focused and strategic. Having a relationship with her now could jeopardise this; I should have resisted and pushed back from her first kiss last night, but I wanted it too, and I still do.

Can I have both the book and Emily? I can try.

'Would you like to take the shower first?' I ask.

'We could shower together,' tickling me lightly as she says it.

'Whilst as tempting as that sounds, unfortunately, it will delay us?' and I kiss her forehead.

'I know, but it would be nice though. No, you go ahead, I need to dress quickly and return to my room; I'll shower there, then meet you downstairs in, say, thirty minutes?'

'OK, that sounds good. I have the rental car, so we can drive over to the hospital when we're ready; no fixed times to work to; I suspect we'll be on your mother's time schedule today anyway.'

'Yes, I guess so. To be honest, I was surprised with Mum yesterday, upset even, but today is a new day, a chance for a clean start; I can put yesterday behind me.'

As I release my arm from around her, peeling the duvet back slowly, I reply, 'That's the spirit,' and as I say it, it sounds awkward, almost sterile, like something a team coach would say to a young player. 'I'll see you downstairs shortly,' and I make a hasty escape to the bathroom.

18

Emily

The Pontin Institute

The drive over to the hospital was uneventful, mainly small talk between us. Martin did, however, propose I spend most of the time today with Mum to reconnect while he sits to one side and observes, leaving at times so we can have personal moments alone.

After checking in at Reception, we are directed through a pair of secure doors. At the foot of the staircase, Martin suggests that he'll take a table and chairs outside on the patio area, just off to our right, leaving me to find Mum on my own. Following the signs upstairs, I locate Mum's private room, and as I enter, two nurses are present, one tidying away Mum's breakfast that looks hardly touched as she walks past me leaving the room, and the other, by her bed, plumping up several pillows behind Mum.

'Good morning, Mum. How did you sleep?'

'That has to have been the best night's sleep I've had since you were born,' smiling at me, raising her arms. 'Good morning, darling.'

I walk across to the bed and embrace her, but I must have hugged her a little too tightly as she winces, quickly withdrawing her arms, the pain evident on her tired face. 'Oh, I'm sorry, Mum, did I hurt you?'

'No, no, it's fine, don't worry, sweetheart.'

'Do you need some painkillers?' as I look over my shoulder to the second nurse as she is leaving the room.

'No, I'm probably already taking too much, but if I don't take them, then I'm a different, short-tempered person; the pain can be excruciating at times. The doctor and nurses here are little loves, and my pain control is well managed.'

'Oh, good, I see.' I relax a little. 'Are you OK if I sit, Mum, and we chat for a bit?'

'Yes, of course. Pull up a chair. I love how you call me "*Mum*"; I've never had that before.'

Lifting the chair and looking back at her, I notice her wince again as she tries to move a little in bed.

'How bad is it, Mum?'

'Pretty bad. I know I haven't got long; I can feel it, but they won't tell me anything.'

'Mum, don't think like that. You're in a good place now, and maybe we can get you fixed up.'

'No dear, no,' shaking her head. 'The stuff I took is making my body slowly die from within; that was always my plan; if it didn't work there and then, it would get me eventually. You see,' wincing again, 'I never thought I'd see you again, and I wasn't going to end my days in an execution chamber, and so, I decided to leave this world on my terms.'

'Oh, Mum, I'm so sorry.'

She coughs and winces again, wriggling slightly to find a more comfortable position. 'What are you sorry for? You didn't know anything about what had happened to you or me; you're a total innocent in all of this.'

I am, well, of this anyway, but I do have other things I'm not so innocent about. If only she knew what really happened, but I'll never tell her; it'll stay with me, and she'll never find out.

'I know, but still, Mum.'

'Listen, Emily, while we're on our own, I've been wanting to ask you. I get what Mary is all about and what she has been doing for us, but who is this, Martin? What is he doing?'

I suppose this was going to be asked at some point. 'He's a writer; he's going to write a book about my life experience.'

'Why?'

'There is a public interest in my story, and there is also a therapy aspect as well, I suppose. He has helped many people who have experienced serious trauma.'

'What, by writing a book about it? Is this a business thing for him? Is he looking to make a buck out of what happened to you?' She coughs into the handkerchief provided by the Warden, his distinctive monogram in the bottom corner flashing as she lifts it to her mouth.

'Er, yes and no. It will allow me to confront all the issues head-on and, at the same time, provide me with a release.'

'Oh, are you sure? I tell you, there is something about him; I can see it in his eyes; it's almost like I can smell it on him. Be careful with him, Emily, I don't fully trust him.'

I'm glad Mum doesn't know what happened last night then; it would be beyond awkward.

'Mum, no, you can maybe sense he's been through something himself; well, he's been through a lot, actually. I've checked him out, read his book, reviewed his web page and the references he's provided.'

'That doesn't mean a lot; it's easy to create and then wear a mask, a disguise, making it harder to see the real person behind it. I've seen a lot of that in my time, believe me. Just be careful, darling, I have a feeling not everything is as it seems with him.'

'It's OK, Mum, everything will be alright.'

'No, I'm telling you, there is something about him; there is some darkness around him. Be careful.'

I'm not sure if it's the drugs or the pain, but this feels strange; I don't know why she would say this about Martin after only meeting him for the first time yesterday. She reaches forward to hold my hand and squeezes it.

'I know the worst in men; I've seen it, and I feel it in him. Be careful, Emily.'

She's obviously referring to her time with Barry and probably doesn't know how to trust a man again. To placate her, I reply, 'I will, Mum, I promise.'

The second nurse returns to the room. I look at her and ask, 'Is there any chance I can have a chat with the doctor looking after my mother?'

'Yes, Ma'am, Doctor Schlossenberg will be along shortly.'

I stand beside her, facing away from Mum, and quietly whisper to her, 'I mean, without my mother present, there are a few things I would like to discuss.'

'Ah, of course, one moment, I'll escort you to her consulting room.' She turns to Mum, 'Now Angela, shall we see about getting you out of this bed and enjoy some of our lovely Texas sunshine? My colleague will be along in a moment, and we'll help you into a wheelchair.'

'I'm not a cripple,' my mother snipes back, and the nurse ignores her bitter tone completely.

'We know you're not, but we wouldn't want you to fall and injure yourself; no, that wouldn't look good on us, would it?'

'Huh,' is Mum's reply, followed by a loud tut.

'I'll just take your daughter to see the Doctor, then I'll return with my colleague in a few minutes; is that OK with you, Angela?'

Another tut from Mum, turning away to look out of the window.

Looking at Mum, I say to the side of her face, 'I'll meet you outside on the patio by the garden, Mum.'

'Yes, whatever. Oh, OK, I suppose.'

After leaving the room with the nurse, the first thing I do is apologise for Mum's attitude and manner.

'No, don't you worry about it, Ma'am; we are used to it in such cases. Now, let's get you to Doctor Schlossenberg.'

'Thank you. Grace, is it? Sorry, I just noticed your name badge.'

'Yes, Ma'am. Grace, named after my grandmother.'

'It's a beautiful name.'

19

Martin

Grounds of the Pontin Institute

The secure grounds and well-maintained gardens are quiet, affording us the opportunity to be away from everyone else, from prying eyes and eavesdroppers, to talk privately and candidly. As we stroll on grass strips between rose beds, heading down to a small apple orchard, it feels like an appropriate moment to ask Emily some hard questions.

'What have the doctors said about your mum's condition?'

'There's nothing they can do; this is end-of-life care, palliative. Mum knows this; it's been explained to her also.'

'Have you discussed where she might want to go? I mean, to end her days; does she want to go back to the UK or…?'

'No, I've not asked her yet, but to be honest, I don't think she has any preference. If you think about it, where is home for her? Her house in Crockett was sold to pay off her legal costs; she has no other family here or in the UK; there's only me now.'

'Do you think she'll want to stay here then, in this hospital?'

'I don't know, I'll have the conversation with her. She knows she hasn't long, so here is as good a place as any.'

'OK. Do you want me to speak with the administration team here and arrange it?'

'No, thank you. Let me discuss it with Mum first, and then I'll make any arrangements.' She looks up and across the gardens. 'It's nice here, it's quite peaceful.'

'It is,' I reply. Emily is also resigned to her Mum's fate. Instinct takes over, and I lift my left arm, bending it so Emily can link with me. She sees it and smiles slightly, passing her arm through it, at the same time releasing a deep breath as we continue to walk slowly.

'Thank you for being here,' she says.

'You're welcome.' As the clock is running down, my business needs come to the fore, so I have to ask her, 'I know what a precious time this is for both you and your mum, and I feel awful for asking this, but do you think there is any chance I could talk with her, to get some background for your book?'

She continues walking beside me, contemplating her response. I continue, 'I know my timing is a tad cruel and insensitive, but we don't have long to interview your mother and record her experiences and personal thoughts.'

'I thought the book was about me?'

'It is, but your story is your mother's story also, and it should be told. And now, with the Presidential Pardon, it would be remiss not to address it in your book; the readers would expect it.'

We walk a few more steps, Emily thinking of her reply. She looks up at me, 'Alright, yes, I see that; I'll ask her this afternoon. I'd like to spend some time talking together first. Is that OK?'

'Of course, yes, absolutely. You two need to be in each other's company first to bond again without interference.'

We continue slowly into the orchard along the lines of apple trees bearing fruit. The heat of the day is rising steadily, another beautiful clear blue sky overhead. Contrails from an aeroplane, miles above us, scar the sky, carrying scores of unknown life stories high above us, each with new futures and old pasts.

'When do we start the book?' she asks.

'As you saw yesterday, I've already started. I've been collecting background and taking notes as you've been talking with others. We should formalise this soon, though, talk through what happened, your thoughts and feelings, etcetera.'

'Yes, of course. But if you want my mother's input, we had best focus on that first. We can talk about me later, back at the hotel, maybe over dinner?'

'Yes, that'll be nice.' This is one of the things I like about Emily: her forthrightness and ability to get straight to the point. And now we're having dinner together, which I kind of half expected her to suggest after last night; the continuation of our relationship looks to be mutually agreeable.

We turn at the end of the orchard and walk along the far edge, turning again to head back through the orchard in the general direction of the hospital wing. She continues to link her arm with mine, and we talk of other things, of Texas, of California, of likes and dislikes, and at times, she makes me laugh with her quick wit and charm. Before we know it, we're back at the patio area and garden doors, just as a nurse is carefully pushing Angela outside.

'Hi, Mum,' Emily calls out as she abruptly releases my arm and heads to her.

I raise my right hand in a small wave and say, 'Hi,' but Angela is locked onto Emily, quite rightly.

As they chat, I wait for a convenient moment to make my apologies and leave them to continue talking. Walking back into the hospital wing, a nurse attracts my attention. 'Excuse me, Sir, I have a message from your colleague, Mary. She sends her apologies; she is unable to visit today; she has some urgent matters to attend to; she hopes you will understand.'

'Oh, right, no problem, yes, thank you.' I look at her name badge, and continue, 'The ladies,' gesturing across to them outside, 'seem fine together; I think Mary's work is probably all done now anyway, but thank you, Grace.'

She smiles slightly, then returns to a serious expression, 'Yes, Sir, but…' she hesitates, then decides not to say anything.

'Yes, but what? It's OK, please, go ahead.'

'Well, it's just that… Mrs Collins, Angela, mentioned to her daughter that she had the best night's sleep last night, but that's far from the truth.'

'Really?'

'Yes, Sir. She had night terrors and bad dreams. We were not sure if it was her pain level becoming unbearable or something else, but she was getting very, er… well… very agitated. We ended up sedating her with quite a strong sedative and painkiller mix. I know she won't want her daughter to know this, but I don't think she has long left with us. I'm sorry, Sir.'

'No, no, thank you for letting me know.' She is clearly uncomfortable telling me this. 'And by agitated, do you mean aggressive?'

'Yes, Sir.'

'OK. I'll mention it to her daughter later. We'll let them have the day together first.'

'Of course, thank you, Sir. It's only right her daughter knows.'

'Thank you, Grace.' The nurse turns to leave, picking up a small cloth-covered tray as she departs the room.

I look back at them on the patio, chatting together. So, that's the second time I've heard she hasn't got long. I'd better get into game mode sooner than I thought I would need to if I want any first-hand input from Angela for Emily's book. I'll mention it to Emily tonight at dinner; we can make a plan then for tomorrow. We agreed today was for them, with no interruptions from me. However, this could result in a full day lost on an ever-reducing calendar. The problem is that we don't know when her last day will be; it could be as soon as tomorrow.

I rejoin them out on the patio, and as I do, Angela keeps a fixed stare on me as I sit at a nearby table. Emily sees this and interrupts her mother's gaze, 'Mum, do you like gardens and gardening?'

Her question is a little strange, but it's probably the first thing she can think of in the spare of the moment; Emily has seen the way her mother is looking at me, and to be honest, I'm uncomfortable with it also, it feels like she is staring me down, looking into me, not at me.

Angela responds with, 'Sorry, the gardens, yes, they're nice,' seemingly only half hearing the question, but it does the trick. Angela is now looking at Emily, and as she does, I notice her expression change, as though a cloud has moved from in front of the sun.

They continue talking of smaller things, their likes and dislikes, and I start to feel like a voyeur or unwanted witness, uncomfortable sitting away from them but watching and listening. I turn my attention to my notebook and begin to scribble a few things down, minor points, then move into planning some of the book's chapters, keeping my ears tuned for anything they may say that could be of interest.

Angela briefly comments on a couple of things that could be the start of something, but Emily moves along so quickly that, given her lack of experience in journalistic tendencies, she misses the opportunity to leverage these comments and expand on what lies behind them. I note them down to help with my interview planning later.

Emily talks of school days, friends, holidays, and the brighter parts of her life; she doesn't mention Duncan or Julia, the couple who stole her from Angela, or her husband, Paul. Angela has tried to pry a little, but Emily deftly deflects the subject in her responses. This is something I'll need to work on with Emily, as she remains in a protective mode at all times, a guard that she'll need to lower to let me in and for her to confront her torment.

After an hour or so of talking, Emily suggests they take a walk through the rose beds, mimicking our route of this morning, and as she stands, it spurs me into action.

'Shall I see about some refreshments for when you return?'

Emily turns to me, 'Yes, please, Martin, that would be wonderful, thank you,' smiling at me. As Emily turns back to her mother, I quickly glance at Angela and see her staring at me again, almost scowling;

it's quite unnerving. Is she also in protection mode on behalf of her daughter or mad at me for being there, observing their intimate time together?

Emily walks around to the handles of Angela's wheelchair and, releasing the brake, pushes off towards the rose beds. I watch them as they slowly move away and decide the best thing is to leave them alone this afternoon, not be that awkward observer, and use the time to work on some of the background events for inclusion in the book.

I stand and go in search of some refreshments, leaving my light jacket over the back of the chair for my return but picking up my notepad and messenger bag, the essentials of my living.

20

Emily

Grounds of the Pontin Institute

After about twenty minutes, I look up at the patio area and see Martin talking with a member of staff as they set out our table.

'Shall we return to the patio for tea, Mum? It looks like Martin has them arranged.'

She twists her head slightly to her left, away from Martin, as though she doesn't want him to hear her, not that he could at this distance, 'I don't like him, this Martin. You're better off without him, believe me.'

'Mum, you hardly know him; how can you be so concerned about him? He is nice, pleasant, and a gentleman. He is thinking of me in all this.'

'I doubt that; he's thinking of himself. But it's not the book; there is something about him, something I've seen in others, in prison.'

'Mum, we've been over this already.' Is she losing her short memory or becoming fixated on him? 'There is nothing to worry about.' If she finds out about last night, I dread to think what she would say to him and me. Anyway, last night was my doing, my decision; I don't want to be lonely anymore.

I turn her wheelchair, and we head slowly towards the patio. Looking up, I see that Martin has arranged a selection of tea, coffee, and some small cakes and cookies laid out on our table and has returned to his table beside us.

Pushing the wheelchair to the table, I lock the brake and retake a seat beside Mum. It looks like Martin is about to leave us, but I want him to hear what I need to ask her and get straight into it.

'Mum, I've spoken with the senior doctor here, and the medical team, and they have been clear with me, and I believe with you, that what we are dealing with is end-of-life comfort rather than treatment to prolong life. Grace, the nurse, also told me you had said you didn't want any treatment that would extend your life given the pain levels you are suffering.'

'Yes, dear, I know, that's what I said.'

'Well Mum…' and I'm struggling to ask this because it seems so accepting, so conclusive, as though we have given in, '…where would… I mean, do you want to travel somewhere else; is there somewhere you'd prefer to be?'

She reaches across to me, placing her hand over mine. 'It's alright dear, it is, really. This is what I wanted, to die outside of a prison wall. Having you here is a bonus, something I could never have anticipated, but here you are. So, here is good enough for me.'

'Mum…' my emotions, which I thought I could control, start to take over. I feel a deep urge to burst into tears, and I dare not say another word as I'm on the verge of breaking down in front of her, and I know I need to stay strong for her. My eyes start to water, to tear, and she sees it.

Squeezing my hand more, she speaks quietly, 'Now, don't be doing that, we haven't the time for such things. Come on dear, let's enjoy life for now while we can, shall we?'

Out of the corner of my eye, I see Martin nodding slightly, so I know he heard us. He moves his chair back and stands, turning to us. 'Ladies, I'll take my leave from you this afternoon, I have some work to do and calls to make, and I don't want to disturb you any more than I have already. Please enjoy the refreshments; the Hummingbird Cake is especially delightful, I'm informed. Emily, when you're ready to leave, please call my mobile, and we can head back to the hotel together. Now, if you'll excuse me.'

Collecting his jacket and slinging his bag, Martin turns to head off into the main building. 'Yes, of course, thank you, Martin,' I reply to him, whereas Mum rolls her eyes and reaches out for one of the small cakes.

Watching him leave, Mum grumbles to herself, and as I look back at her, she is trying to lift the teapot. 'Damn it,' she scorns.

'Here, Mum, let me.' Taking the teapot and focussing on pouring hot tea into one of the cups, 'You could have been more polite, Mum, with Martin.'

'Why? He's not my friend.'

'Mum, don't be so cold.'

'Just saying it as it is; I don't want to waste what little time I have left. Can you pass one of those cookies as well, please?'

21

Emily

Resident's Bar, The Merlin West Hotel, Waco

Walking into the bar beside the restaurant, it surprises me that some men take evening dinner still wearing decorated boots, denim, and their Stetson hats, no doubt very expensive ones at that.

Martin is sitting on a stool in the middle of the bar, chatting with the bartender. As I approach him, he notices me in the mirror behind the bar and spins on his stool to greet me with a broad smile and standing. 'Hello, would you care for a drink before we dine?'

'Yes, please, that'll be nice. What are you having?'

'House special, an Old Fashioned.'

'Sounds great, yes, I'll have the same, please,' and he orders two more.

He's dressed down a little now for dinner, leaving his more formal attire to one side, in preference for jeans with a light blue and white check shirt, typically blending in with most of the male patronage in the bar.

He leans into me slightly, 'I thought we could dine here this evening for ease. It's been another long day for the pair of us, or, if you would prefer, we could dine out? I just thought, after last night, you might like the quieter approach.'

'Yes, here is good, thank you. I'm still struggling a little with the jet lag and the heat of the day.'

'I've reserved us a private booth over by the far wall,' he gestures to the other side of the bar as he continues, 'So we can talk without too much interruption and not attracting attention; is that OK?'

'Yes, that is fine,' smiling back to him.

After a few minutes of watching the bartender prepare our cocktails, the two drinks are placed in front of us, and Martin asks that they be put on his tab. The bartender acknowledges Martin's request, turning and tapping information into a display screen behind the bar. As Martin is picking up both drinks, I notice the bartender looking into the mirror, watching me, and as our eyes connect, he winks slowly. I don't know why, but this makes me feel very uncomfortable. Even though he probably doesn't mean anything by it, and is just flirting, it has a feeling of menace, and it chills me.

Martin has both drinks and turns towards the booth, 'Shall we?' indicating towards our waiting table.

'Yes, of course,' welcoming the opportunity to leave the bar.

I take the lead, and he follows me as we cross the room. Martin lets me sit first before placing the drinks down on the table and taking a seat beside me in the booth. He raises his glass in a toast, and we clink glasses before we each take a drink of the cocktail.

'Um, that's quite nice, a little different to what I've tasted before, but very good,' I say to him as he places his glass back down.

'The bartender's personal twist on a classic, he makes it with Bourbon and a rich demerara sugar syrup, completing it with a secret ingredient I've not yet managed to pry out of him. Very tasty but quite potent, so be careful, you may fall for my charms again,' he says, looking directly into my eyes, sporting a smile and a slight wink of his right eye.

Another wink, although this one I am comfortable with, as it's playful and from Martin. I look over to the bartender, who is now distracted with a female customer, both leaning in over the bar, and talking as though they know each other.

He continues, 'How was your time this afternoon with your mother?'

Looking back at Martin, 'It was good, I suppose. She has been through so much, and clearly, she just wants to forget about what has happened and end her days as peacefully as possible.'

'Can she do that? I mean, if I were her, I would be bitter and twisted and want to rage at the world.'

'I think she was, but after all the years of feeling that way, she now considers it was all wasted; the lost time, effort, and energy when she could have been doing something more proactive.'

'More proactive; like what?'

'I'm not sure, her choice of words, and I don't think she knows either, but the internal frustration and anger has taken its toll on her, that is clear. And, given all the emotional and psychological stress she has been through, she trusts no one.'

'What, not even you?'

'You know, I'm not sure, possibly not; after all, she doesn't know me. She has even warned me of you, but to me, that's all just part of her "*trust-no-one*" approach she has adopted and lives by.'

'Oh, so she doesn't like me then?'

'It seems that way, although I don't know why.'

'Ah, well, that makes my next question a little more awkward then.'

'Oh. What is it?'

'Well, in pulling together a plan for your book, it seems to me we should include something from Angela in either the prologue or epilogue, as her story is so entwined with yours, especially now after the Pardon.'

'You're right, of course, I can see the merit in it, but I don't think she will go for it.'

'Are you willing to ask her? You could indicate it is for you and your journey, facing the reality of what happened, and that it will allow others to appreciate the impact it had on your mother's thoughts also; an opportunity for her to have her final say before…'

I nod ever so slightly, 'All I can do is ask; I can't promise anything.'

'If she is willing to do this, I, we, will need to talk with her sooner rather than later, like tomorrow, if possible.'

'Why the rush? Do you know something that I don't?' As I ask him, he moves uncomfortably in his seat, taking another sip of his Old Fashioned.

Placing his glass down again, he softly clears his throat and looks at me, 'I was talking with one of the nursing team at the hospital today, a nurse called Grace, and she told me they don't think your mother has long with us. Your mother is saying one thing to you, probably to protect you or lessen the impact, but the reality is that she is suffering badly and is on strong painkillers and sedatives to help her sleep. She has been agitated and aggressive with the medical team, probably borne of frustration and pain, but they have seen this before and consider her days are coming to an end quicker than expected.' He pauses, the concern on his face genuine, 'I'm really sorry to let you know like this.'

'No, please, don't feel sorry, I need to know these things. There are a few things I must work out with Mum before… well, you know, so knowing helps me appreciate the limiting timeframe we have.' From his body language, he wasn't comfortable telling me this but thought I had a right to know. 'Did they indicate how long we have with Mum?'

'No, sorry, just in their experience, it's not long.'

I take another sip of my cocktail. 'What is it you need from Mum, for the book that is?'

'Some details about the run-up to your abduction, the months after that, why she came to the US, how her husband, Barry, was with her, his death and the trial, and then naturally her thoughts upon hearing you were still alive and wanted to reconnect. We have most of this as official record but not her personal side to everything that happened.'

'Oh, so not much then,' I smile at him. He wobbles his head slightly from side to side, almost as if weighing up what he's just said.

'Umm, it does seem quite a lot, I know, sorry, but…,' gesturing the two of us, 'we have time on our hands, whereas unfortunately your mother doesn't. We can filter through what she tells us at our leisure and weave into your story after… well…'

'Yes, quite. Well, with so much to get through and so little time to collect it, we had best get started tomorrow… so long as Mum agrees, that is.'

'So, you're OK with this?'

'Yes.'

'Will you ask her in the morning?'

'I will.'

'Thank you.' He nods while picking up a menu. I can understand the urgency he's injecting now; he's dropped a few hints here and there, and now this. He must think it's important that we get her side of the story while we can. Remaining looking at his menu, he adds, 'I'll be ready first thing in the morning and await your call.'

He is very organised and likes to plan. Driven. Focused. I think I like that approach as it cuts through all the flowery conversations and dancing around the subject that I've experienced with others, others that I wish would have just got to the point, others that I came to realise in the end, I should not have trusted so easily and so blindly.

He's right, of course; we have time, but Mum doesn't.

22

Martin

Hotel bedroom

Dinner was enjoyable; Emily is delightful company to be with, with a natural beauty that commands that second and even third look from most men. It's easy to see what her husband saw in her, why he had to have her for himself, why he would risk his relationship with his grown children just so he could be with her. Her being herself is what made me crumble last night when I knew I shouldn't have.

Working with her this evening subtly over dinner, I tried my best to keep away from mentioning anything too emotional and steer the conversation into more background topics of schooling, employment and friendships, but this last one seemed a little raw, with a couple of subtle deflected responses from Emily; something I'll need to explore when we really get into it.

The white image of plain paper on my laptop screen won't fill itself, and is begging for content, and the keys wait patiently to be directed to create words forming sentences and chapters. The structure of her book I have clearly planned, but the way in which I want to tell the story is likely different to the way she needs to tell it. For her to gain the benefit of the cathartic release of her inner thoughts, her doubts and fears that she holds close within her, she needs to say it in a way that are meaningful to her. It's my task to then to interpret and craft that into marketable book and hopefully, more.

The nurse's comments this morning regarding Angela's night terrors and disturbed sleep still ring in my ears. Logging into the web page and entering the cloud platform, I view the images of Angela's room. All is quiet and peaceful. The static images in shades of grey are the result of low light levels in her private room and the absence of movement. With the volume turned up to a maximum, I can just hear her faint, laboured breathing. Every now and again, from her writhing slightly in bed, it looks like she feels discomfort. She's probably heavily sedated after what the nurse said so that she can at least sleep and, no doubt, allow the nursing staff to have an easier night.

Running the recording backwards and stopping it intermittently, it has captured video and audio without interruption; so long as my hacking into the hospital system remains undetected, I should be able to collect more background, covertly recorded, to allow me to aim more pertinent questions to Angela. I'm surprised at the hospital, though, installing such a system in private rooms; they obviously don't consider patient confidentiality a high bar. With nothing further to observe now, I close the link again.

My plan for this evening is to write out a play script for tomorrow, to direct the conversation topics to get the most out of the interview process, for that's what it is, a question-and-answer session based on a predetermined script, but it must never feel like that to the interviewees, it needs to feel more natural.

Emily did mention one thing, though at dinner, without any lead from me. She was surprised at how calm her former father, stepfather, well the man purporting to be some kind of father, was in prison when she visited him. It was almost like he knew the day would come when he would be found out and incarcerated, and he was strangely at peace with it. When she told him she was travelling to see her dying biological mother, his reply of "*Oh, I'm so sorry to hear she's unwell!*" rattled her. She couldn't believe the depth of his callousness, not even a hint of an apology or sign of remorse. From what I've read online and in reports I've managed to access, he does seem like one cold piece of work; his sociopathic tendencies fuelling how he lives his life the way he wants and nothing, other than his wife, counts for anything, that is, nothing beside Emily, or Kate as they called her. Emily never saw it in them; they were the model citizens, the perfect doting parents. Was it all a sham, a charade? Or did they really love her?

This relationship with her then "*parents*" and what happened with her husband have created trust issues within Emily, and it's easy to understand why. However, I do need her to trust me; we need to be honest with each other for this to work. I need to find out her inner thoughts and feelings, but whenever she has shared any of these with a loved one, it has somehow backfired on her. She was guarded in some of her responses this evening, and I'll need to work carefully on that.

It's interesting how Angela has taken a dislike to me already, even though we've hardly spoken, and I've been nothing but polite and courteous. Emily said Angela could "*see*" something in me, sense that something was wrong about me. Uncanny, as yes, there is plenty wrong with me, but I keep it locked up, hidden from all, buried deep inside that at times, I forget what I've done and what I'm capable of. It's an interesting concept, though; can she sense a killer's presence? Can a killer spot a fellow killer? Does she have psychic tendencies with the ability to read someone for what they are? No, I do not believe in all that mind-reading mumbo jumbo. You can save that for the kiosks at the seafront and theme parks, but clearly, she is sensing something.

I thought this evening would be a replay of last night, that Emily and I would spend the night together. However, her day with her mother had been tiring, and all she wanted to do was retire to her room, reflect on what had been said today, and rest. Jet lag was mentioned again, although I would have thought that should have passed already. It's probably better this way; it remains a one-night thing. We can't let a relationship interfere with the work that needs to be done, and I don't want to risk any kind of bias in crafting the book about Emily's life. I want it to be independent, honest and provocative, hard-hitting where it needs to be. If, after the book is finished, Emily wants to be with me again, then I'll welcome her with open arms, even though critics will try to tear us apart when it becomes public; but at least I know I'll have done the right thing by her.

Me and the right thing; oxymoron at its best. No, I believe I do the right things; it's just that my methods are unconventional with definitive outcomes, ones which are more direct and permanent.

Taking a deep sigh and staring at the screen, I'd best get on with it and start typing question one: *"Why don't you like me, Angela?"* I chuckle to myself as I place my finger on the back delete key. I need to be sensible now.

23

Him

Wolf Rock Ranch, 15 Miles Outside Waco

She is very good-looking; I really like what I see. Her charm, her cute English accent, her young, shapely body, and that long blonde hair; she is just what I've been looking for; she's perfect. I want her.

No, come on, I need to be more assertive. She will be mine.

All those positive, self-confidence-building social media websites keep telling me to take control of my life, to act positively, to take assertive steps to achieve what I want from my life… and that's what I want. I want her.

I will have her. I will have her for me.

Replaying news clips over on my laptop, I select close-up scenes to freeze and print colour images of her and pin them to my project board alongside the downloaded magazine articles I already have of her.

I will have her.

She will be mine.

She far outshines all the other guests I've had, even though they all come to accept in the end that I am the best thing for them. Like any bronco, it takes me some time to break them in, but we get there in the end.

When Emily Collins moves in, I wonder what *she'll* think of her? It's going to be interesting watching them trying to outdo each other for my affections. Ha.

Yep, I like what I see in this Emily Collins, and I want more of her.

24

Emily

Angela's Hospital Room

Our drive over to the hospital this morning was uneventful, the same as yesterday, other than Martin driving a slightly different route, which shaved off a few minutes but relied on a rather dusty track for about half a mile or so.

Martin is now waiting for me, and hopefully us, in the garden patio area again. I've the task of convincing my mother to talk openly with him present, allowing him to ask questions and take notes. This may prove difficult as she has taken a dislike to him for some reason.

On entering her private room, Mum is already up and sitting in her wheelchair, a nurse trying to cover her legs with a light blanket. 'I don't need this,' she is saying to the nurse, 'Take it away.'

The nurse, seemingly flustered, replies, 'I'm sorry, Angela, it is hospital policy; when you are being moved around in a wheelchair, we cover your legs; the gown you are wearing is not appropriate clothing for you or others when you're in public.'

'Others? What others?' Angela replies, just as the nurse, struggling with Mum, notices me enter the room fully.

Grace looks to me, ‘Good morning, we’ll be ready shortly. We’re just having a difference of opinion on modesty this morning.’

Mum bites back quickly, ‘Nonsense, it’s not my fault the gown doesn’t cover up everything. Huh, modesty.’

I walk up to them and take the blanket, ‘It’s OK,’ I say to Grace, ‘Leave it with me.’ She smiles slightly, thanks me, and leaves the room.

‘Look, Mum, it’s not the nurse’s fault; she is applying policy, and she is looking after you, you know, wanting to make sure no one is offended, most of all you.’

‘I’m the one who is offended! Making me wear this stupid gown that barely covers my ass. Huh. Others, I ask you! They are not the ones getting prodded and poked, being treated like a guinea pig in a lab!’

‘Mum, don’t be angry, please don’t get worked up. No one is doing that to you; they are treating your symptoms. Now, let’s put this blanket over you so we can leave this room and go outside.’

‘Why do I want to go outside? It’s hot out there! I’d rather just stay in here.’

Mum is clearly in an agitated, confrontational mood this morning and won’t welcome the ask I have of her for sure. I place the blanket on her bed and sit down on the edge of the mattress. ‘What is it, Mum? Why are you so upset this morning?’

‘I don’t know. The pain, I suppose. I can’t walk far at all; I struggle to make it to the washroom. I’ve got someone cleaning up after me, and it’s degrading. It’s embarrassing!’

‘No, Mum, it’s not. They are caring for. If you can’t do it, then they are happy to help; you have to think of it like that; no one here wants to harm you.’

'Poppycock! What would you know about it?'

'Stop it, Mum.' Her attitude is frustrating me, and I react, 'Well, you did this to yourself. Remember, you were the one who tried to kill yourself, and you've succeeded in doing it, just slowly. So, accept the help or lie there in a pool of your own mess – which would you prefer?' That stopped her instantly. She is staring at me, neither flinching nor blinking. Have I gone too far with her already? I never thought I had it in me to say that to her, but her being cantankerous and offensive to people helping her will only go so far with me.

In a quiet voice, she replies, 'You're right, darling, of course you are. I'm sorry.'

'It's not me you need to apologise to, is it?'

'No, I suppose not.' She lowers her head slightly.

I feel like I have the upper hand slightly now. 'Do you need any more pain medication, or can you cope?'

'If I have any more, I'll fall asleep again, and I don't want that. I want to remain awake as long as possible.'

'OK, well, you only have to say when it becomes unbearable, alright?'

'Yes, I will. I'm glad you're here.'

'So am I. Now,' seizing the moment, 'I have something important to ask you, and I want you to think about it before answering, and whatever your answer is, we'll respect it.' She remains looking at me without comment, and I continue. 'I've mentioned that Martin is writing my story and at the same time helping me come to terms with what has happened to me, and it'll help me develop some coping mechanisms.' Again, she remains silent. 'He... No, we think it would be beneficial to talk with you to get your personal thoughts on what happened in your own words, which will help provide some background to what happened to me. Will you sit with us today and talk us through your thoughts and feelings?'

Her silence and fixed stare at me are unnerving; did she hear me?

'Mum? Is that something you can do for me?'

'I'm thinking about it; you said I could.'

Her reply shows she is still as sharp as a pin. Instantly, I feel a sense of regret for asking the question. The thought of having to put her through it all again when what precious little time she has left shouldn't be wasted on the past. I have my future ahead of me, so I get that my talking about it will help me, although it won't help Mum with the weeks or days she has left, far from it.

She's had a terrible time, but my reconnecting with her brings some hope, some peace for her, surely. I remain looking at her, and she at me, her thoughts running through her mind; I wish I could read them and fully understand what she is thinking. She breaks the silence.

'Emily, I'll do this, but I'm doing it for you and for me, not for him. There is so much you don't know that maybe you should. And if it will help you, then I'll do it. It could help me, too, I suppose. So, yes.'

I don't know if I'm relieved or not with her acceptance now. I feel guilty for asking her to do something she shouldn't or probably wouldn't do if someone else were asking. But one thing she said is true: there is more to learn, and I should know as much as possible about what happened. So, I'll take this over the guilt. 'Thank you, Mum.'

'I suppose you want to start straight away?' she asks.

'Yes, please, if that's alright with you. Martin is out on the patio anticipating you would agree.'

'And why does that not surprise me?'

I look at her, deciding to ignore the question, pick up the light blanket from the bed and hold it out to her. 'Shall we?' I ask.

Throwing up her hands, 'I surrender. I'll take the blanket. Come on, let's get on with it.'

25

Martin

Hospital Patio Garden

Emily, smiling and nodding, emerges through the open patio doors, pushing her mother forward. I take Emily's actions as an acceptance that Angela is willing to talk us through her life events and how they start and end with Emily. As they approach, I stand and welcome them both. Emily manoeuvres the wheelchair around the table to place Angela in the shade of a large oak tree.

'Good morning, Angela, how are you this fine day?'

'Tired, sore and grumpy.'

'Ah, that good?' I reply as I don't know how to respond to her negative manner. I can appreciate the negativity, but she is now at least a free woman, and that should bring some levity. 'It's a beautiful morning, though,' as I smile at her.

'That may be, but I don't have too many mornings like this left, do I?'

'No, I suppose not.' This feels like it's going to be a tough conversation. I look at Emily, 'And how are you, Emily?'

'I'm good, thank you. Mum has agreed to talk with us about what happened and how it affected her; that's right, Mum?' she asks, not sure if she is looking for reassurance or providing direction.

'Yes.'

Such a short, curt reply, indicating her displeasure but her acceptance to at least start the process.

Emily takes a chair beside her mother, and I sit down opposite them. 'Well, there's no time like the present. Shall we start?'

Emily looks to Angela, who gives another curt but straightforward 'Yes'. I lift my canvas messenger bag from beside the table and open it, withdrawing my laptop, notebook, pen, and my trusty digital voice recorder.

'Are you going to record this?' Angela asks.

'Yes, if that's OK with you? It helps me reflect on our discussion and the emotions involved, giving context to responses and descriptions; useful for facts and for when I'm writing about feelings.'

'Whatever,' replies Angela, shaking her head and lowering her eyes whilst swatting her right hand across her lap.

Emily looks at me, raising her eyebrows above a small smile, almost in submission and asking for my forgiveness. I reply with a brief smile. 'OK, let's start at the beginning. How did you meet Barry?'

We talk for nearly an hour about general background, meeting her husband, their wedding, employment, home building, the want to have a family, month after month of failing to conceive then going to seek medical advice, the subsequent tests, and then the realisation they couldn't conceive. To overcome the infertility issue, they considered a fertility treatment option using an anonymous sperm donor, and approached a specialist private clinic, resulting in Emily's conception and birth.

Reaching this point, I consider it a good time to pause for a comfort break and refreshment. I stand and leave them to order some tea for the three of us.

Inside the lounge area, I order a large pot of tea for three and some local made cookies. As I wait, my attention returns to them sitting outside, across the patio area. They are talking, but I am unable to hear the discussion. Then, suddenly, the change in Emily's body language is intense, with Angela pointing at her, jabbing a crooked index finger towards her. Emily's face portrays shock, and she quickly stands, knocking over her chair and stepping away from Angela, her gaze never leaving her. Emily stops and raises her hands in front of her as if she is pleading. This doesn't look good; I'd better get out there to see what's happening.

Stepping out onto the patio, Angela sees me approaching and, in a raised voice to Emily, pointing to me, she remonstrates, 'And he can go fuck himself!'

'Whoa! Whoa!' with my hands held up in passive gesture in front of me, switching my eyes between the two of them. 'What's going on?'

'Fuck you! Make yourself useful and get me back to my room. Bloody writers, you're all the bloody same,'

'Hey, now, that's not called for, Angela. There's no need to get abusive,' I reply.

'And what do you know about it? You've never been through anything like I have.'

'I think you'll find I have and that I can genuinely empathise with your experiences.'

'I'm not looking for empathy. Just piss off!'

Her aggressive tone and use of profanity are the complete opposite of how she was not five minutes ago when I left them. Has Emily said something to upset her, touched on a raw nerve?

Emily is standing about three yards away, her arms crossed in front of her with her right hand up, covering her mouth as though she is preventing herself from speaking.

'What happened?' I ask them both, but neither responds. I look at Emily, 'Emily?'

Lowering her hand, 'She… she… I don't know. I'm not here to be spoken to like that. That was vile.' Switching to her mother, 'You know it was, that was not called for,' she says directly to Angela, who doesn't take her on.

Angela, still in her wheelchair, is staring at the table, her hands clasped in her lap like she isn't a part of what had just happened.

'Angela, what upset you?' I ask, but she shows no sign of registering my question. 'Angela?'

She is almost comatose, as though not here. Grace briskly walks out onto the patio. 'Angela, it's OK, nobody here is looking to harm you; this is a safe place.' She drops to one knee beside the wheelchair. 'Are you in pain? I can help with that.'

'Yes, I am. Take me inside.'

'Please,' adds the nurse, 'We don't forget our manners, especially if we want something, Angela, you know better than that.'

'Sorry. Please,' Angela adds.

'That's better.'

As they leave and head back into the building, I walk up to Emily, who turns from me with arms still folded and takes a couple of steps towards the garden before stopping. As I reach her, she says, 'Uh, good manners for the nurse but not for me. The bloody ungrateful…' she stops herself.

I put my arm around Emily's shoulder to offer some comfort, but she pulls away from me, shrugging me off. 'Emily?'

'Oh no, look, I'm sorry, but she can't just be nice one minute when you're there, then the next, be vile to me when we're on our own.'

'If anything, I would have thought the opposite would have occurred. I suppose it could be the pain; I should have considered shorter, briefer conversation slots; maybe I've overdone it; it's my fault.'

'No, I'm not buying that; there was something else behind what she said; I'm not sure what, but there is definitely something.'

'Did you say something that prompted her to react?'

'No, well, at least I don't think so, I simply thanked her for helping us, then asked her about my stepfather, Barry, and her mood changed, then she just erupted. She didn't flicker an eyelid when she mentioned him to you, but she went for me when I asked about him, calling me all kinds of vile names and swearing at me. I don't know what it was.'

'OK, OK. Let's leave it for now; she obviously needs to get some rest and some further medication. I have some tea coming. Would you like to sit with me? We can talk?'

'No… thank you. I think I'll just take some time to myself.'

With that, she steps onto the lawn and walks out into the gardens, slowly pacing with her arms still folded in front of her. I watch her turn into the orchard at the end of the trimmed lawn and decide to leave her to her thoughts. Returning to the table to collect my things, I notice that my voice recorder is still recording. I click it off and then fish out my headphones from my bag, connecting them to the recorder. I run the recording back to the last ten minutes or so and listen for the moment when I leave them alone.

Reaching the point of Angela's change, it follows an innocuous question from Emily, "*Did my stepfather, Barry, want me?*". Emily is correct; it was a query about Barry that caused Angela to flip out. There was no apparent reason to turn on Emily, and I can appreciate why Emily thinks there is something else to this. For now, giving Angela the benefit of the doubt, I'll put it down to her pain and discomfort and just bad timing.

But is there something more? Something about Barry that caused Angela to react as she did to the question. My mobile phone rings, distracting my thoughts. Looking at the screen, it's Mary. One of the staff is approaching with a tray and tea for three; I thank them and answer the call, 'Hi, Mary.'

26

Emily

Hospital – Angela's Room

She's been resting for a couple of hours now, and the nurse has indicated it's okay for me to sit with her as long as I don't disturb her. My walk through the gardens helped calm me down, and Martin is right; she was more than likely in pain, disoriented and frustrated with her health and her lot. Talking about how they met and came to have me would have been the happy days of their relationship, which all changed when I was abducted. She killed Barry after being so badly treated by him following my abduction, and she probably realised this was to be the next part of our discussion but didn't want to go there and relive it. However, this is an important part, well, for me, that is, as I want to know everything.

Her vicious tongue in those few minutes left me wondering why I'm here at all, but looking at her now, I know why. We only have each other now, in these short days remaining, and I can rise above her mood swings in the knowledge she is carrying so much pent-up frustration and anguish. It's not Martin's fault, and I'll apologise for my behaviour with him; I know he was only trying to comfort me. She just caught me off guard, and I'll be sure to not let it happen again.

Mum stirs a little in her sleep, then falls still again, propped up on pillows, held in a bed with the side rails raised, the soft beeping of machines to either side of her.

Barry must have been pretty relentless in pushing her to the point that killed him with a kitchen knife. To me, her situation was clearly one of psychological and emotional coercion, manipulation and torture by him, excessively bullying and tormenting her. Going too far that day, he pushed her to her limit, and she cracked, reached out for the knife, and attacked him a frenzy, releasing all those years of bottled-up anger, regret, denigration, wounding, hurt, and lost love.

Should it have happened? Hell no. There were failings all around her, including from her friends who should have rallied to support her but instead chose to join in with the blame and finger-pointing, the vocal character assassinations that would have fuelled Barry even more. Why didn't she just leave him if it was getting that bad?

She stirs again, this time opening her eyes slightly, looking around the room before deep sighing and closing them again.

'Hello, Mum. I'm here.'

'So, am I, still, it seems,' she replies with eyes remaining closed.

I wish she wouldn't be so negative all the time. I speak softly, 'I'm not sure what happened earlier, Mum; did I say something wrong?'

'Why? What happened earlier?'

She opens her eyes again and shuffles slightly against the pillows, trying to become a little more upright and failing. Is that a truthful reply? Is she unable to recall what happened, or is she trying to ignore it and brush over the whole thing? Taking it at face value and wanting to move on, I ask her, 'How are you feeling?'

'Well, I'm still breathing.'

'That's a good thing, Mum, it is. I think it best you rest for the remainder of today, and we can carry on tomorrow.'

'Oh, that's right, we were talking with your writer friend, weren't we.'

'Yes, but he's not a friend; he is a professional acquaintance.'

'Umm, if you say so. We're on our own now, aren't we?' she asks, tipping her head slightly and looking up again at me.

'Yes, we are.'

'Good. Look, I haven't got long. I'm tired, and I'm ready to go. What is it you so desperately want to know from me?'

'Mum, please don't keep talking like that. You should try to make the most of what you have.'

'Of what I have? You mean the final pain-ridden few days of a crumbling old murderer who can only reflect back on a life of regret as she has no future ahead of her. Really?'

'I can appreciate your feelings and emotions, but I don't want to hear this and have this as the lasting memory of our remaining time together. You need to accept you are not a murderer, that you were driven to it, and now you are a free woman, a mother, who has the good fortune to reconnect with her long-lost daughter. You can see the benefit of changing your mindset, surely?'

She sniffs and grimaces at the same time; I'm unsure if that's because of her condition or a reflection of her disdain for what I just said.

'Change my mindset? Huh. When I change my mind, all hell breaks loose. I should have learned to live with my lot and accept it for what it was.'

'What does that mean?' She is looking off to some distant point as though staring through the wall of the room to a place known only to her. Her breathing is feint, the sallow grey skin of her face painting a picture of a tormented life. She raises both palms and places them over her face as though a child playing peek-a-boo, but I'm sensing she is coming to terms with something that she is recalling and possibly wants to shed. Her painfully thin arms lower again, and her skeletal, gnarled hands rest on her lap.

She looks at me; the coldness in her face, especially her eyes, is chilling to the point of almost terrifying; it's as if another being has entered her body and is now in control.

'I did it. It was me.'

'Mum, we know it was you that killed Barry, but we can put that behind us now and move on.'

'No. It was me. I planned it.'

27

Him

Hospital Car Park

Well, this is fortuitous; I never thought it would be this easy. She is half walking, half running away from the building. Looking at my watch, 15:27; I start the timer before swinging my van around and head to cut her off just inside the line of trees that shrouds the approach to the hospital car park, a good place to conceal my actions, so long as another vehicle doesn't pass in the next minute or so. Fortune favours the bold.

I pull up the van beside the road, and, leaving the engine running, I push the button that automatically opens the side door. I hear the satisfying soft clunk as it locks into the open position. Peeling my ski mask down from a hat to face covering, I open the small bottle and drip the liquid into the cloth in my left hand. Checking the wing mirror, she is approaching me down the left-hand side of the van, perfection at its best; it's as if she knows exactly what to do.

Climbing between the front seats, I ready myself in the back, ready to receive my guest. I can just make out her position by craning my neck to look into the door mirror. As she passes the back quarter of the van, my timing is faultless; I reach out, wrapping my right arm around her neck at the same time as I place the cloth in my left hand tightly over her face. She tries to scream and kick out, but it's useless; I have all the advantage here, as I always do; when will they learn to accept resistance is futile.

Pulling her into the van, her legs kicking out, she starts to slow, and after about fifteen seconds, she falls limp, allowing me to fully pull her inside and press the rear button for the side door to close.

Switching on the internal light, I work quickly, fitting the prepared zip ties to her ankles, bringing them tightly together, and then her hands behind her back. I reach up for the larger zip tie hanging on the small hook and wrap it around her knees, feeding the tail through the little plastic teeth of the clasp and pull; that satisfying little zip sound confirms the tie is working correctly, bringing a smile to my face. Quickly but clinically, I pat her down and find her cell phone; turning it off, I smash it with the hammer to shatter the screen, then prize open the side using a screwdriver as a lever to remove the sim card, cutting the card in half with my small shears before returning the tools to their designated silhouette positions on the tool rack. Collecting the remnants of her cell phone and card, I open the plastic container of heavily salted water, place them inside and re-seal it. Carefully placing her head on the cushion and making sure she is on her side on the mattress, I pull up her knees slightly into a fetal position, then pack the rolled-up towel into the space between her back and the mattress to prevent her from rolling as I drive. Picking up the black cotton sheet, I unfurl it over her as an interim shroud in case anyone should chance a peek inside.

Resting back on my haunches, I press the stop button on my watch to gauge my performance; fifty-six seconds, my fastest time yet from start to finish, beating my long-standing personal best of fifty-nine seconds. Practice and experience always pay dividends. Removing my ski mask, I breathe in deeply, hold, count to ten, and then release it.

Moving forward, returning to the driver's seat and donning my sunshades. I slip the gear control into drive, indicate to pull away from the curb, release the brake, and slowly move forward, emerging from the tree cover and into bright sunlight. Seamless. Anyone would think I'd done this before.

28

Martin

Hospital

When Mary called earlier, I updated her on what had been happening but decided to leave out the part about Angela's outburst; there will be nothing gained from it other than Mary wanting to drive up here and offer further support to Emily, support I don't think she needs as I can assist her from now on.

Sitting at a small desk in the corner of the main visitor lounge, I've been playing back the discussion from this morning over my earphones, moulding key parts into typed script on my laptop. This provides some good background context to Angela and Barry's relationship before Emily was taken.

My stomach rumbles slightly. I reach for the missing cookie that accompanied my coffee, the one I'd eaten an hour ago. Looking at my watch, I'm surprised it's already gone three in the afternoon and that I've missed grabbing some lunch. I thought Emily would have returned by now from her walk; she's been alone in her own thoughts now for a few hours.

Picking up my cell phone, I press her number on speed dial. A few seconds pass while it tries to connect, and then it trips automatically to voice message without ringing out, and I speak.

'Hi, Emily, it's Martin. I was wondering if you've had lunch or would like to meet me in the cafeteria here at the hospital; I'm going to grab a quick sandwich and head there now. If you do, I'll see you there; if not, shall we meet at, say, five in the reception area and head back into town together? I'll be working in the visitor lounge this afternoon until then. Catch you soon.'

As I end the call, it dawns on me that she probably won't get the message; she is either in a remote part of the hospital or has decided she wants some peace and doesn't want to be disturbed. I close my laptop and drop my things into my messenger bag, slinging the strap over my head as I stand. Depositing my cup and small plate on the table near the coffee machine, I head towards the cafeteria. Turning out into the corridor, walking towards me is the nurse who assisted with Angela this morning, and I slow as she approaches.

'Hi, erm, I'm sorry, I never got the opportunity to thank you for your assistance this morning, forgive me.'

'It's no problem, Sir, we're here to help,' replying with a pleasant smile as she continues to walk past me.

As we pass, I turn and ask, 'Oh, sorry. I don't suppose you have seen Emily, Angela's daughter, or know where she is? She went for a walk in the gardens a few hours ago and…'

She looks back at me. 'Yes, Sir. She is sitting with her mother as she rests in her room; well, she was still there about thirty minutes ago when I last looked in. They were quietly talking.'

'Ah, good. OK, I'll leave them to it. It's good they are chatting again. Thank you.'

She smiles again and continues on her way, and I turn and head to the cafeteria. Hopefully, they are back on good terms again, and we can progress tomorrow with the next part of Angela's story and what happened to her when Emily was taken.

29

Angela

Hospital Room

Sitting upright in my bed, I look around at what could be my final earthly surroundings. The room is plain, clinical, clean and sparsely furnished, but it's far better than that place I was in last week, and the room service here is far superior.

I told her the whole truth, not for her, but for me. My time here is done, and anyway, I only did what she told me I needed to do, to think of my future, and I am, whatever it may be. In telling her the truth, my conscience is now clear. If there is a maker up there, I can meet him or her, in the knowledge I've confessed to all my mortal sins on earth and faced my demons before it was too late; well, I think it's best to play safe, just in case there is actually something in the hereafter.

She was shocked, of course she was, and now she probably won't want to know me or see me again. I have no problem with that; after all, it's not like I know her or owe her anything. Yes, she is my bloodline, but does that mean that I should be beholden to her for the remains of my life? No, I don't think so. Her being found alive was proof enough to all that I wasn't involved in any infanticide incident, and the allegations were all baseless. Her turning up as she did played out perfectly for me to get a Pardon and be released from prison to live out the final days of my life in relative comfort, well, the best comfort I can achieve under the circumstances.

Will she do anything with this new information? No, I doubt it; anyway, if she did, I would just say I was delirious due to the extreme pain and medication and didn't know what I was saying to who or when. But if he found out the truth, this bloody author hack, Martin, now that would be something else; he would have a field day with it, causing me some real upset in my final days if he put his mind to it. But it's going to be up to Emily to tell him if she ever will; he won't hear it from me.

Looking up at the clock on the far wall, it's just gone five, and it'll soon be dinner time; I wonder what today's dinner is? I can't recall what was on the menu this morning; ah, well, the surprise will make it all that more interesting.

30

Martin

Hospital

That's the third time I've called her and been directed straight to her voicemail. Her phone battery could have drained, or she's still angry from earlier and taking longer to come to terms with what Angela said on the patio; she was clearly upset by it.

Flicking another glance at my watch, it's showing nearly five-thirty. It's unlike Emily not to be in touch, to let me know what her plans are, and my message was clear about meeting here at five, assuming, that is, that she has listened to it. I can appreciate that she may still be angry with Angela, but she should at least let me know her plans, especially since I've been here all day. We are supposed to be a team working together.

Picking up my bag, I decide to go to Angela's room to find out what Emily's plans are for the evening, to see whether she's coming back to the hotel with me or staying here with Angela.

Walking through the hospital corridors, the nursing staff are busy serving the evening meal to patients, and I pass them without any acknowledgement or recognition. On approaching Angela's room, the door is fully open. As I enter, Angela is sitting in her wheelchair, her back to me, looking out of the large window over the gardens.

'Hello, Angela. Is Emily here.'

Without turning or looking at me, she replies, 'Does it look like she is?'

Clearly, she is still in the same bloody-minded mood; the curtness of her reply without even registering my presence is, at best, ignorant and, at worst, offensive. Brushing it aside, I continue, 'I guess not. Do you know where she is?'

'I'm not her keeper.'

'No one ever said you were. I just want to catch up with her, and it would be nice to know where she is as she's not answering her phone.'

She shrugs her shoulders, 'She left here a few hours ago, no idea where she is now.'

'Oh. I see you've calmed down then,' and as soon as I say it, I regret it; I don't want to give her the satisfaction of me rising to her attitude.

She tuts loudly and continues staring out of the window. Nothing further, no engagement. She simply sits there, quietly in her own thoughts.

I quickly check the washroom off her room, but it's empty. As she's not engaging with me, I leave and walk back through the hospital, exiting through the security door into the entrance reception area. There's still no sign of Emily, and one last try at dialling her mobile phone yields the same instant trip to voice message. This is not like her; Angela must have upset her even more this afternoon, more so than this morning. I approach the reception desk and leave a message in case Emily shows up looking for me. I don't like doing this, but I decide to leave the hospital building, cross the car park and climb into my rental car.

As I exit the car park through the tree-lined entrance, Emily is at the forefront of my thoughts; it's not like her to be so detached and disconnected. Through the hands-free facility, I call Mary to ask if Emily has been in touch with her today, but she hasn't. Mary asks if everything is OK, and I simply play it down, suggesting Emily's phone battery has probably died, and I am on my way back to the hotel, expecting to find her there. Mary asks me to keep her updated before I cancel the call.

Emily doesn't know anyone else here that I can think of, other than maybe Ernesto, our driver the other day, and so I try him. He replies, similar to Mary, that he has had no contact with Emily today, nothing since dropping us off at the hotel after our time at the prison.

In twenty minutes, I'm back at the hotel and check in with Hotel Reception to see if there are any messages for me, then use the house phone to dial Emily's room, but again, there is no answer. As I take the elevator up to my floor, my mind is torn between whether I should worry about her or leave her alone; she is an adult with considerable self-confidence and has more than likely taken some quiet time for herself.

As I put my keycard to the door handle, the camera and video recording in Angela's hospital room come to mind; if Angela and Emily argued again this afternoon, it'll be recorded, and I can play it back.

Placing my laptop on the desk, I open it, and whilst it is connecting to the hotel Wi-Fi, I grab a chilled bottle of beer from the refrigerator and hang the expense. Kicking off my shoes and placing my phone and wristwatch on the desktop, I plug in my noise-cancelling headphones and log into the cloud site hosting the security video from the hospital; they really should have this more secure.

Leaning back in my chair, sipping at the beer, I rewind the video file until I see Emily enter the room, then press regular speed play. The volume is down low again, and I crank it up to a level where I can hear them both speaking clearly.

Emily is trying, but Angela hasn't really calmed down; she is just as cantankerous as earlier today in her replies to Emily. Lifting the beer bottle and taking a long pull of its contents, it is Angela's words that almost choke me, "No. It was me. I planned it."

Sitting bolt upright, I stop the video and run it back at three times speed, then press play again. I must have misheard her… "No. It was me. I planned it. I arranged for you to be taken." There's no mistaking it; she is crystal clear. Leaving the video to run, the scene unfolds before me in glorious high-definition monochrome, and it's easy to see why Emily fled the room, wanting time to herself. I can't believe Angela said what she did; what possible motive could there be to be so cruel to her own daughter, her own flesh and blood. Is she just being vindictive, or did that really happen? Did she really plan Emily's abduction?

The statements about Barry, how he was after Emily was taken, and her role in his death, the evolving route to his murder are unbelievable. I'm stunned. I want to have this out with Angela, but clearly, I can't; I'm not supposed to know. She doesn't know about the security camera and audio pickup in the room, that's obvious, and I shouldn't have hacked my way into the system. She could make my life very uncomfortable if she were to say something to the hospital or the police.

My business head registers the scoop for what it is, but my heart aches for how this will have affected Emily; the visible hurt is clear.

Leaning back, I pick up my mobile and try Emily again, but I get the same result: straight to voice message.

Leaving another short message, I place my phone down and grab another beer. This nugget of information was totally unexpected, and I need to exploit this knowledge for the book; this is a significant revelation and will provide a perfect sales opportunity; the book lifting the secret of what happened, the story now has a unique revelation needed to promote the book and boost sales; but how do I get the information legitimately so I can use it? The only two people in the room were Emily and Angela; one of them needs to let me in on the secret so I can exploit the hell out of it.

There is another route to the information; if Angela is being truthful, then the Leydens were in on it with her; they would have negotiated with Angela to take Emily. Could I get to them and get one or both of them to reveal this information to me? But they had the opportunity to do this already during the police investigation and the trial but chose not to disclose it; why? Why did they decide to leave Angela's part in this out of the police investigation?

I need to contain this bombshell until I'm ready to release it on the world through my book, but that's going to be difficult, especially if I can't get a hold of Emily.

Looking up, I see my reflection in the mirror over my laptop, and I'm appalled. Sales, promotions, revelations, scoops… how can this be more important to me than Emily?

This confession will be hurting her badly, and she needs my support.

Where the hell is she?

31

HIM

Wolf Rock Ranch, Outside Waco

She is even more beautiful in real life than I ever imagined; I've now found the woman I always wanted. I knew I would get her, that she would come to me.

I'll let her settle in first before I start getting serious with her. Yeah, I should do that, seeing as she is my house guest; I won't push her just yet as I want her to submit to me and not resist. Treat your lady well, and she'll look after you, Pa used to say.

Placing her on the bolted-down bed and handcuffing her right hand to the bed frame is a real pleasure; the touch of her soft skin and the tiny light blonde hairs on her arms are amazing. Coupling her right ankle to the shackle and chain fastened to the foot of the bed frame, I begin to relax as I know she is now safely in my care, and I step back to admire her form. The urge to touch her again overtakes me, and I place my hand on her thigh, sliding it up and down slowly, caressing her skin. Biting my lip, I move my hand slowly up beneath the hem of her summer dress, and as I do, the quiet one reacts, grunting loudly from her corner, followed by a "No!" and rattling her chains.

'Shut up!' I shout back at her and turn to kick her leg but miss. She's only jealous now that I've brought some real competition home, but she won't be jealous for long; I've got a treat for later. She cowers back to the corner, curling up on the mattress and pulling the blanket over herself. She's broken my mood now, which is just as well as I don't want to rush this. Emily Collins will eventually want me to touch her; she'll beg me to please her. I won't force myself on her, no, not this one; she is special, and when she's ready for me, it's going to be magical; yeah, real magical.

I have all the time I need with her to make this happen. No one saw us; no one knows I have her. I had my last visitor for nearly five months, and no one came close to finding her. In fact, her disappearance didn't get much airtime at all, just like the others; my research and homework helping me select ones who are not going to be missed much. However, Emily here is different; she is a celebrity, and she will be missed by someone, which makes this all the more exciting, as they'll never find her.

I'll stay calm, go to work tomorrow as usual, do nothing out of the ordinary, return home at the normal time, and then work with Emily over the nights ahead. If I play this right, this one will satisfy my needs for a long time, well, until I get bored of her, and when I do, then she can go join the others out in the woods, but I don't expect that to happen for some time yet.

It's hard to believe how easy it was to get Emily Collins; I really thought I would need to work harder at it. Certainly, it feels like my luck is getting better; maybe it's all my positive thoughts and assertive actions that have brought this about. This mind training really does work; I can do whatever I want and win at it. Yeah, I can.

32

Martin

Hotel

There has been no word from Emily, and when hotel housekeeping confirmed she hadn't slept in her room last night, that's when I really started to worry about her.

Her phone is still not ringing out, and no one has seen her since yesterday at the hospital. Angela's revelations very clearly upset Emily, quite rightly, and she ran out of Angela's room in tears, but then what? Where did she go?

Returning to my room, I connect my laptop to the room's widescreen TV and hack back into the hospital security system, bringing all twelve available cameras up. Taking each camera in turn, I rewind the stored recordings to the time Emily left Angela's room and begin piecing together her movements. The image quality is good, high definition and full colour, so she will be easy to identify and follow.

Leaving Angela's room at 15:23, I pick her up in the corridor outside, half running, half walking, clearly upset. The next time I catch her, she is on a staircase, heading down to the ground floor towards the reception area. Then, selecting that camera, I see her cross Reception, pass the busy desk, and rush out of the front doors. One of the external cameras, pointing at the front doors, captures her as she exits the building and turns left. Switching to another camera, I see her crossing the car park, heading towards the main exit on foot, towards the trees on the approach road. Why go that way? Why leave on foot? It's hot, and she'll not have much luck trying to flag a cab down out there on the main road.

She's probably not thinking straight after those shocking revelations from Angela and what was said afterwards between them; I can appreciate why she needed some space, but to leave like this, then not be able to reach her by phone, and for her then not to return to her room last night is a genuine concern. Do I call the police?

No, I can't. I'm hacking hospital systems, and that will not go down well at all with them. No, she's fine, I'm sure she is. She'll get in touch when she's ready.

Pushing back from the desk, I stand and walk across to the large glass window, looking out over the main street below and towards the park square beyond. No, I can't rest my mind; I'm not easy with this; something may have happened to her, and I'm probably the only person at this time who even knows something may have happened; it's on me to do something positive, to take some action.

Returning to my laptop, I rewind the external camera videos and watch them again. There is nothing unusual or out of the ordinary, just Emily crossing the car park, a couple getting out of a parked car, and a white van driving past her on its way out of the car park. She walks into the tree line and then is gone from view. I try two other car park cameras, but they don't show anything related to her, both aimed in different directions, filming other sections of the car park and parts of the front gardens.

I rewind the two recordings and play each again, but this time at half speed, watching the screen carefully for any sign of something of interest, but nothing jumps out as extraordinary. The only vehicle moving is the white van. I pause the video and zoom in on the side of the van; there are no markings, no company names or brand logos, just a plain white van. Pressing play again, the van passes Emily, and as it turns into the trees, I catch a glimpse of something on one of the rear doors and pause the video again. Zooming in, it's hard to make out what it is. Pressing play again, the van drives into the tree cover and disappears from view.

Emily is walking down the far footpath towards the trees, following the route of the van, then she disappears from view also, and I press pause. Nothing.

Returning to the other external cameras, I replay them and watch again, this time at half speed. Then, just in the upper corner of one of the recordings, I notice the white van leave the tree line after turning out onto the main road and pulling away just beyond the garden fence line; I press pause. Again, nothing unusual in that.

Leaning back in my chair, I have both images paused on the large screen in front of me. Tapping my fingers on the body of the laptop, I look at the respective time stamps; Emily enters the trees at 15:26:50, and the van is on the main road outside at 15:28:23. The van should have been out on the main road at a similar time to Emily entering the trees as it was already in front of her and driving away. Did it stop before leaving the tree screen?

I rerun the video of the van out on the main road and note there is little traffic around, not enough to have the van waiting to exit for more than a few seconds. Sitting upright, this might now be something. The times are all running from a central clock, not a clock on each camera, so they are all synchronised with each other. This van was in the trees longer than it should have taken to exit the hospital grounds. It must have stopped for about a minute or so.

Did Emily get inside the van? Was she forced into the van? Has she been taken? No, it can't be, not again.

Shit, yes, she could have been, it would make sense of the timings, but they would have had to be quick. Now, what do I do? I can't bring the police into this, not yet. Nervously clicking my fingernails on the tabletop, I have to do something; nearly eighteen hours have passed since she was on that video, and no one has seen her or heard from her, and her phone isn't working.

What can I do?

I can't do this on my own; I need some help, but from who? There is no one I can turn to.

Nico. He can help me; he has access to all kinds of resources I don't; he'll know what to do.

33

Nico

London

My mobile phone starts ringing, and as I remove it from my pocket, I see it is Martin calling on an encrypted messaging service. I hold up my right index finger to stop the meeting and click answer. I speak first, 'I thought we agreed, no contact unless it was an emergency. Is this an emergency?'

'Nico, yes, I think it is, and I have no one else I can turn to for help.'

He sounds anxious.

'One moment.' Pulling the phone to my chest, I speak to the people around me. 'Gentlemen, give me the room, please.' They stand and depart without comment, and as the door closes behind them, I lift the phone again and speak. 'Are you OK, Martin?'

'Yes, I am, but a friend of mine isn't. I think she is in real trouble.'

'She? Umm, what have you got into now, little brother?'

'Nico, look, I don't have the time to go into this now; the clock is ticking. I need urgent help with video recordings and enhancing video images so I can make out some details. You see, I think my friend has been kidnapped, and I need some leads to track down who took her.'

'Kidnapped, really? Are you still in the States?'

'Yes.'

'Then, go to the police or the FBI, let them handle it.'

'I can't, Nico; at the moment, I am the only one who thinks she has been taken, and I know this because I've illegally hacked into a hospital server to view security footage.'

'Oh, tut, tut, little brother. You should not be getting yourself involved in such matters; you are a writer of books. Remember, you are not a private detective or criminal mastermind like me.'

'I know, but trouble seems to find me wherever I go. Can you help, please? It's urgent.'

He sounds desperate, desperate enough to turn to me for help. 'Yes, of course, I can help my little brother. I know someone. Are these videos in digital format, and can you upload them to a cloud site?'

'Yes, and yes. What is the site address?'

'I'll send you the link. Just upload them and tell my contact what it is you need; they will get it; they are the best in the business.'

'Thank you, Nico. Look, I'm really sorry I called you, but I had no choice. She is a special friend, and I really need to help her quickly.'

'This is not a problem; whatever you need, I will provide. But before I do this, the police and Feds, they will remain out of this, yes?'

'Yes, correct, they have to, or I'll be in deep trouble with them myself. No police or Feds, you have my word.'

'Then OK, I'll send you the link, and you communicate with them directly; it is a secure connection on the dark web. I will call them now. If you need anything else, you must let me know.'

'I will, thank you, Nico.'

'OK, little brother, I'll make my call and send you the link. You stay safe.'

'You know I will,' and he closes the call.

Trouble does seem to follow my little brother around, but he always lands on his feet and comes out on top. Scrolling through my contacts, I find X4, press call, and give him my instructions, offering a premium fee if he drops what he's doing immediately and sorts this out quickly for me. Then, I type in the website link from memory and send it to Martin via the encrypted message service. I'll leave it with them; Martin is resourceful, I am confident he will manage, and I know he will call me if he needs more help from me.

So, he has found another special someone; I hope she is better for him than his last wife. I thought that going out to America would help him start afresh and stay away from trouble. He has made himself a future out there, away from my world, but every now and then, it seems our paths cross, not on a family front, but more on a business front - well, in the sense that I can use my contacts to assist him.

Perhaps I should have a chat with him about joining me in my enterprises; they are becoming more diverse, and many are now legitimate, needing someone clean to front them. Martin could do that for me. Yes, that's it; when all this latest crisis is over, we'll have a good talk about setting him up here in the UK; there is that internet business I've acquired, and he could develop that further, especially with the contacts he will have made in the publishing media world.

Putting my phone away again, I press the intercom and ask for my colleagues to return to the room. I don't want them to know about Martin, well, not yet anyway; for the time being, my little brother will remain a ghost. If my enemies find out about him, it could put him in danger; they will see him as a pawn to be used for leverage or revenge. There is always someone out there who thinks they can wear the crown, take over the empire I have built, and become king, but that isn't going to happen, not while I'm sitting on the throne.

34

Emily

The Ranch Room

My head is spinning; I'm disorientated; I'm thirsty and feel nauseous. What happened? Opening my eyes, the light is dim, and as I raise my hands to touch my face, my right arm is yanked backwards, chained to something behind me. My left arm is free, and reaching across, I pull at the chain, but it's solidly fastened. Everything comes rushing back to me; I was grabbed and pulled into a van. My god. I sit up quickly and realise my right leg is also chained to something. Blinking repeatedly to clear my eyes, I start to look around the dim room and realise I'm chained to an old bed frame; it's hard to focus on anything, and I rub my eyes with my left hand, hoping to clear my vision.

'It's no good,' says a quiet female voice from somewhere in the room.

'What? What the hell is going on?' Who are you? Why am I here, chained up like this?'

'He took ya, like he took me.'

Screaming out 'Arggh' as loud as I can while pulling at the chain to my right wrist doesn't help free me.

She replies with a loud 'Shhhh, for god's sake, don't make him angry.' Her Texas accent clearly discernible. 'It's best he's not disturbed. If he gets angry, he won't think twice of thrashing ya with his belt. Be quiet, please, or he'll blame me, and I'll get a beating, too.'

My eyes just make out a slight movement in the shadows in the corner of the room opposite me. She's in here with me. 'Are you chained up as well?'

'Shhh, yes, I am,' she whispers, 'I'm chained to an iron ring on the wall.'

I stop moving, realising it's pointless pulling at the chains; I'm never going to snap or free them. 'Who is he?'

'I don't know.'

'How long have you been here?'

'I've no idea, but it must be months. I should have counted the days and weeks.'

The room falls silent; there are no sounds of the building or outside, and then I hear her start to sob ever so quietly.

Whispering in reply, 'I'm sorry, I'll stay calm. What is your name?'

She sniffs, and I see movement as she slowly shuffles forward into a small shaft of light halfway between us. As she moves, I hear the soft ticking of chain links passing through the iron hoop. She is wearing a t-shirt and shorts, with dirty white sports socks, her hair pulled back and tied in a ponytail; she looks much younger than me. 'Kelly, Kelly… Brown. What's yours?'

'Emily Collins.'

'You English?'

'Yes, the accent gives me away, I guess. Do you know where we are?'

'We're on a ranch, and from the state of it, it's not a working ranch; it's too run down. He takes me outside now and again, usually about sunset, and when I look around, I can't see any other lights or hear any traffic, nothing. We're miles from anywhere. I think he does it to let me know it's pointless screaming. There is no one around to hear me but him.'

'And now me, Kelly, you're no longer on your own with him; I'm here.'

She starts to cry, quietly sobbing, and I can just make out her lifting her hands to cover her face. Through her palms, she replies, 'Thank you.'

This whole scene before me is terrifying. He takes women and chains them up; what kind of sick person does that? Kelly is fragile; the poor thing has spent months here with him. No one knows we're here, so it's up to us to do something to escape.

'Tell me about him,' I ask her as I continue to look around the room.

She wipes her face and looks at me, sniffing before she replies. 'He's not that bad, really.'

I wasn't expecting that, 'What the fuck, Kelly, he has you chained up in the middle of nowhere. That's not right, Kelly; he's kidnapped you and now me.'

'No. Yes, well, what I mean is, he only beats me when I don't obey his rules; if I follow his rules and I'm good to him, he treats me well.'

'But Kelly, no, this isn't right, you know it isn't. He shouldn't have us locked up here. Don't fall into some kind of false illusion; he is bad, and this is wrong. We need to get out of here.' I move on the bed, and the stainless-steel chains tinkle quietly through the bed frame. 'This is not a good place to be, Kelly.'

'Guess not.'

'You know it's not. He took us; we didn't come here voluntarily, and sure as hell, we didn't give him permission to chain us to a bed and a wall.'

She is quiet for a few seconds, then replies. ‘Yup, you’re right.’

‘Yes, I am. Now tell me everything you know about this man; we need to find a way of getting out of here.’

35

Martin

Hotel Room

I've uploaded the video files to the dark website Nico provided and included instructions on what I need in the text communications between me and X4, whoever this is. That's all I know them by, and that's all I'll ever know; there are no questions about identity, just stating what needs to be done, and X4 hopefully getting it done.

It's been nearly an hour since I spoke with Nico. I should not have involved him in this, but I had no choice; I needed this kind of specialist help and couldn't get it from the police; in fact, if I had gone to the police, firstly, I would have been kept at arm's length and not involved any further, and secondly, probably arrested and locked up for illegal hacking. But I want to be in on this; I want to know if someone has taken her, whoever they are, and what they want from her. There has been no ransom request that I'm aware of; although, if there had been, I would have no idea who it would have gone to, other than the police directly, and I'm confident that hasn't happened, as they haven't come calling.

I'm staring at the black screen and the white font of our messaging. The cursor is slowly blinking in a steady rhythm, reminding me of a ticking clock. Each tick could be the countdown of one less for Emily. What do I do if

X4 comes back with the information I want, the name and address details of the van owner? I still can't just hand it over to the police; this is getting deeper by the hour. I'm getting more involved in this matter and its outcome, whatever it may be. But what if they come back and report nothing, that there is no information? No, they've got to come through for me; they must.

If we were in England, Nico would give me some people to help, I'm sure of it; in fact, he would probably just take over and see it through to resolution without me, wanting to keep his little brother away from such things. But I'm out here, in Texas, I'm Johnny on the spot, and I need to sort this out. Even though I've never used one, I'm confident there will be some way to get my hands on a gun out here; maybe X4 can assist me in locating one. The screen beeps as a new message post appears, and I read it slowly and carefully:

> *"X4: Van is carrying false plates, and no obvious markings. Managed to get a couple of reasonable images of the driver from different cameras on the road outside, merged the images and run them through facial recognition programme. A 73.6% probability the driver is a man called Job Gunnarsson, local to the area. He was born in 1988 in Texas, only child, reports of both parents passing when he was in his early 20s. His current registered address is Wolf Rock Ranch, Southwest of Waco, four miles off Route 35. Gunnarsson has a registered white van. He has a prior for sexual assault as a youth in 2003, served 2 years in detention, nothing since. No gun registration showing but that doesn't mean he's not armed. No*

sign of anyone else in the vehicle but only have limited info. Anything further?"

At 73.6% probability, could this be him? That's a sizeable margin for error. I need to be sure I'm not going off on a wild goose chase, wasting precious time. This Job Gunnarsson could be completely innocent, with no involvement at all, just visiting someone in the hospital. Then again, the van is on false plates, and there is that time delay when the van is in the trees; it has to be him. It can't be a coincidence that he's there on false plates in an unmarked white van, and she's gone missing, and he has a prior for sexual assault. Damn it; it has to be him.

I ask X4 for the coordinates of Wolf Rock Branch, and he provides them. It's up to me now. Do I need a gun? Where the hell am I going to get a gun from? Who is going to give one to an unknown Englishman? Shit, I don't even know how to use one.

Ernesto: he might help me. He's the only person I know out here who carries a pistol and is trained to use it. Will he help me? What I'm thinking of doing is no doubt illegal; he might not want to get involved, then I'll be stuck as he will have the knowledge that Emily is missing and I'm trying to do something about it without informing the authorities; he could call the police and tell them of my intentions. Maybe that's what I should do, just call the cops, let them take over, and ride out any fallout that comes from hacking the hospital systems. But it'll take hours just to get them motivated, and then all hell will break loose; every agency around here will get involved, and how on earth do I say I know it's Gunnarsson without exposing X4 and then Nico? I need speed if I want to get her back alive. There's nothing else for it; decision made; I need Ernesto.

Wasting no time, I look up Ernesto's cell number on my mobile and press the call button; he answers on the second ring.

'Mr Nicholson, are you in need of some more driving work?'

'Hi, Ernesto, of sorts. Listen, are you on your own at the moment and not using the loudspeaker?'

'Yes, Sir, I am driving currently with my Bluetooth hands-free earpiece in; we're not overheard. What can I do for you?'

'This is very sensitive. Can I rely upon your absolute discretion to keep this matter confidential?'

'Yes, Sir, you can. Please wait one while I pull over.'

As I pause, waiting for him, my mind is racing, wondering how I'm going to ask him for what I need. He is a reliable sort with a family, and I don't want to get him into any trouble, but he is the only one I can think of to assist me out here.

'Yes, Sir, please, go ahead.'

'Well, there is no easy way to say this, so I'm just going to say it, and I hope you appreciate why I'm asking you for this help.'

He replies, 'You need my help, Sir?'

'I do, Ernesto, and this has to remain between us.' I take a deep breath, 'Emily Collins is missing and…'

He cuts in, 'Missing Sir? As in lost or…?'

'Taken, I believe, kidnapped, well, I'm pretty sure she has been kidnapped and being held against her will.'

'Wow, Sir, are you sure? Are the police involved?'

'I'm pretty sure, and no, the police are not involved yet; it's complicated. I think I know who has taken her; don't ask me how. I know you'll have to trust me on that, but I'm going to need your help.'

'Yes, Sir, anything you need.'
'Ernesto… I need a gun.'

36

Emily

The Ranch Room

I can hear heavy footsteps from a room next door, the wooden floorboards conveying the sound through the timber-framed structure. I look over to Kelly, and she has retreated back into the shadows of her corner. He's been out all day and the meagre water ration and sandwiches he left us with have me hungry and thirsty now. The room is getting cooler now; at times today, it was getting ridiculously hot and stuffy, making me tired and weary.

In a whisper, I ask Kelly, 'Will he come in here with more water and food?' but she doesn't reply; maybe she's not heard me. As I speak again, the bolt on the outside of the door is drawn across, and the door creaks open, letting in a rush of yellow sunlight. Illuminated particles in the air, captured in the low sunlight, seemingly give him a glowing, mystical presence, a theatrical entrance almost.

Involuntarily, I start to shake, even though I'm trying to control my emotions. His silhouette portrays the menace of the man.

'Good afternoon, ladics. Did y'all havc a good day? I hope y'all played nice together.'

I'm not sure whether I'm supposed to answer him or not, so I decide to follow Kelly's lead. He speaks out again.

'I said, did y'all have a good day? I hope y'all sleeping and not ignoring me?'

'No, Sir. Yes, Sir, I was sleeping a while, awake now, Sir,' Kelly replies.

'That's good. And what about you, Mrs Collins? Ya awake now?'

'It's Miss Collins, I'm not married,' instantly, I know my defiant reply is a mistake.

'Ooh, hold on there. Kelly, now see, we have a feisty one here. What do ya think? Does she need some of my special treatment?'

'No, Sir, she's fine, Sir, just confused, Sir. She doesn't know ya like I know you, Sir.'

'Haha, and you do know me, don't ya gal?'

'Yes, Sir, I does. Miss Collins here just needs to learn about respect from me, Sir, I can teach her.'

'That she does, girl, that she does. Now you be giving her an education, and I'll be back with some supper.'

'Yes, Sir,' Kelly replies.

His silhouette turns, and he steps away from the door frame, disappearing from the porch area to return, I presume, to the main house, allowing more light to stream in, illuminating more of the room now for me to scan. His footsteps quietly diminish the further he pads away from us. I can see Kelly plainly now, upright on her knees on the mattress in the corner, her back against the wall. The bare floorboards and timber-clapboarded walls are the same shade of ancient, old, dry, and dusty. Looking up, the roof appears to be boarded also, with the odd shaft of light piercing through tiny openings.

'Emily,' Kelly quietly says, 'Ya need to show him some respect, or he'll beat on ya.'

Whispering, I reply to her, 'Respect? He's kidnapped us and has us chained up; I wouldn't treat an animal like this. He won't be getting any respect from me.'

'Please, Emily, please. He can be real nice, y'know, kind, but real bad when deserving.'

'Deserving?' We don't deserve to be chained up in here or deserve to be treated like this. I would say it is him that is deserving of some treatment.'

'No, no, please be quiet, I know what he can be like. It ain't worth fighting him. He'll beat ya down until ya do what he says. If you act up now, he'll blame me for not teaching ya some manners.'

I can sense the concern in her voice. Her approach has changed, becoming compliant and submissive, no doubt following his mistreatment of her and her fear of receiving some form of retribution from him. I won't yield to him, though; I'm stronger than that.

He's left the door open, confident we haven't broken free of our chains. 'Where is he now?' I ask Kelly.

'He'll be out back looking to fix us up some food.'

If he does this every day, then this is how we escape; we just need to find a way of freeing ourselves from these chains so we can walk out of here. I slowly turn my head around, scanning the room for anything I've not spotted in the gloom. There is very little in here save the bed, Kelly's mattress, the bucket we use, and the old fireplace built of bricks and mortar. There is a broad, cracked timber beam above the fireplace with three large rusty iron hooks protruding out about six to eight inches, possibly to hang something in front of the fire, but they look rigidly fixed and, at the moment, well out of my reach.

I hadn't noticed it before, but there is an old glass and timber frame window in the far wall, opposite the fireplace, with timber shutters on the inside. A square timber beam is across the inside of the shutters, slotted into two more L-shaped iron hooks; this looks to be acting as some kind of window restraint or locking device. The window could be an escape, with the timber beam useful as a weapon or lever if only we could reach it. There is nothing else of any interest in the sparse, plain room.

His footsteps are coming closer again, his boots menacingly padding across the room next door, growing steadily louder and clearer. He's in the door frame again, this time with a tray held out in front of him. Silhouetted again, I can't make out any of his facial features. He is wearing a baseball cap and appears to have collar-length hair that falls down onto his broad shoulders. I'd say he's about six feet tall and muscular built.

He enters the room and turns towards Kelly, placing the tray down on the floor in front of her. As he turns sideways, I see him in profile, registering a rough, short beard and moustache and thin spectacles resting on a prominent nose. His back is to me now, and he looks like he's whispering something to Kelly. I can make out that she's replying to him, but it's impossible to hear what they are saying.

He stands upright, turns, and heads back towards the door frame, spinning about to look back into the room and at me, putting his face back in shadow. A glint of sunlight catches the lens of one of his spectacles and dazzles me for a second.

‘Now see, good girls get a treat. Y’all enjoy your supper now,’ and with that, he walks away again, his footfall disappearing to nothing.

Looking over to Kelly, I whisper, ‘What did he mean by that?’

‘He asked me how ya had been today, and I said good, nothing to report.’

This shocks me. ‘What? Nothing to report. Are you… his spy?’

‘No, Ma’am, but he said if I was to make sure ya were good, we would get a treat for dinner, and he’s good to his word, always has been. We have fried chicken, greens, corn dogs, coke, and a slice each of pecan pie. He’s never treated me this good before; ya must make him happy.’

‘I make him happy, me?’

Kelly replies as she raises a piece of fried chicken to her mouth, ‘Yes, Ma’am. Let’s get closer so we can share.’

Kelly picks up the plastic tray and shuffles forward on her knees, her chain quietly drawing through the hoop on the wall until it snatches taught when it reaches its full extent. She places the tray down on the floor and, sitting in the sunlight, continues to eat. She seems weirdly pleased and is ravenously biting into the boxed food while drinking from a large paper cup. ‘It’s good. C’mon, ya need to eat.’

She has a point, but I don’t want to eat it if it’s being seen as a treat; I refuse to be trained like a dog. But watching her, the urge to eat and drink gets the better of me, and I shuffle to move off the bed. My leg chain is longer than I thought and tinkles through the bed frame, but my right-hand chain snags in the headframe. I stand and wiggle the chain so it frees from the snag, and I can slide it down the post, allowing me to sit on the floor in front of her, although my right arm can't reach any further forward to the tray, so I twist and lean, lifting my cup with my left hand. Taking a sip through the plastic cup cover, the sweetness is refreshing, and I start to gulp it down.

'Slow, Emily, make it last,' Kelly whispers. 'No free refill here.'

The sun is moving across the door frame, leveraging light slowly away from behind Kelly. As the light is gradually fading, we sit quietly eating chicken and greens, basking in the pleasant warmth of the sun on us both. I can just make out some soft, distant birdsong but nothing else.

Looking at her close-up, she is young, much younger than I first imagined. Pretty, with her blonde hair in a ponytail, she is slight in build, leading me to ask, 'How old are you, Kelly?'

Biting into a corn dog, she looks at me, 'Seventeen, still, I think. I don't know if my birthday has passed or not.'

Her hazel eyes and sweet smile soften me. She shouldn't be here; no one should. I need to get us out of this, as no one knows we are prisoners or that we are here. With a bit of luck, Martin will be missing me by now and has already contacted the police, for I know my mum won't be missing me, and she definitely won't contact the police. My mum, no, not any longer; she's just my biological mother. She's Angela now to me. We have nothing in common other than some genes, and I don't want there to be anything else. To me, she is just as bad as Duncan and Julia; no, she is worse than them; she is a murderer.

As I finish the last of my so called supper, I watch Kelly tidy the box cartons and cups, placing them inside each other and neatly returning them to the tray. As I look at her, she looks up at me, smiling, 'He likes it when I keep the place tidy. I don't mind.'

37

Martin

Hotel Room

It is just after midnight when Ernesto knocks on my hotel door. When I provided him with the basics over the phone, he didn't hesitate to change his schedule, drive home, speak with his wife, pick up his kit, and drive straight here. Explaining everything to Ernesto; he is with me; I needed to be honest with him to earn his trust. I stressed this could be dangerous, and his reply, "Really? As I know what danger is," filled me with confidence that I had the right man with me.

Opening the door, he nods simply to me and steps in, passing by me while carrying a large green holdall and a military camouflage rucksack on his back. By the time I close the door, he has placed the holdall beside the desk and is removing the rucksack.

'I wasn't sure what we might need, so I brought everything.' He stands upright and turns to me, 'Are you sure you want to do this, Mr Nicholson, Sir?'

'I am, and it's Martin from now on.' I step forward with my right hand outstretched, 'Thank you for doing this with me, Ernesto.'

'I'm happy to do this for Miss Collins; if she is in trouble, then I will gladly remove the trouble.'

He turns and bends to unzip the large green holdall at his feet. 'Have you any firearms experience, Mr…, Martin?'

'No, nothing of any real substance, nothing like serious firearms.'

'As I thought, then I have just the thing for you.' He takes a large towel from his bag and spreads it out over the desktop. He then extracts a wrapped pistol from his bag, undoing the cloth it's wrapped in, and withdraws it from its camouflaged holster. 'A tactical revolver, Smith and Wesson Model 327 TRR8. Simple to use, holds eight, .357 Magnum rounds; just aim and squeeze the trigger.'

As I step forward, he holds it out to me. 'It's quite big,' and as the weight transfers to my right hand, I add, 'and heavy.'

'Yes, Sir, simple and very reliable. It packs a punch and is very effective at close quarters, the kind of thing we may be faced with. It has some recoil, though, so if you have to use it, try to use both hands in a firing stance.' He demonstrates a pose, which I copy. 'However, I am not expecting you to use it; it's for your self-defence only. I will take any active role needed.' He turns and removes another pistol, places it down on the towel and then pulls out a machine gun-type weapon.

'Wow, what is that?'

'Colt AR-15. 5.56 NATO round, semi-automatic slash automatic rifle. Coupled with this,' lifting the other pistol, 'My personal choice of sidearm, the Beretta 92FS; these do what I ask of them.'

I'm stunned at what I'm looking at. 'You really have come equipped.'

'Yes, Sir. I also have NVGs, night scope, and some flashbangs.' He sees my curious look and adds, 'Sorry, night vision goggles and scope. These M84 stun grenades help disorientate personnel in a closed environment.'

I know Ernesto has had extensive military training and field experience, so I'm convinced I've picked the right person to rely upon, but this feels quite extreme to me. 'Isn't this all a little over the top, Ernesto; do we need such… firepower?'

'Well, we don't know what we're going up against, and Sir, this is Texas.'

38

Emily

The Ranch Room

The room is steadily growing darker as the sun settles behind the horizon. Kelly is gently humming to herself as she picks at the dirt under the fingernails of her left hand.

'That's a nice tune, Kelly. Something your mother taught you?'

'No, Ma'am, my mom left when I was small, can't rightly remember her now. One of Daddy's women friends used to hum it when she was brushing my hair. Janie, yep, Janie, she was called.'

'Is it just you and your father then?'

'Yeh, of sorts, Daddy has his women callers come round now and again; otherwise yeh, just the two of us.'

'Is he a good man, your father? Does he look after you?'

'In his own way, if ya know what mean. I'd feed myself, keep busy looking after the house and food and stuff, off what money he gives me, and I does the washing and cleaning.'

'Are you still at school or college?'

'No, Ma'am, I ain't, not been for a long time. Gotta look after Daddy, y'know.'

'Oh, I see. So, he'll be missing you, will he?'

'Awh, I ain't so sure 'bout that. Probably missing me buying his liquor and stuff. He's always worried I'd go find me a boy and leave him.'

Poor thing, it doesn't sound like a fulfilling upbringing, with little love and support for her. It wouldn't surprise me if her upbringing somehow brought her to this place, snared by Him outside, her being easy prey.

'I'm here now, I'll look out for you.'

'Mighty nice of you, Ma'am, but I'm good. Anyway, I'm the one that needs to look out for ya,' and I see her nodding her head in the low light, her teeth displaying a smile.

There is a loud thud from next door, and immediately, Kelly scuttles off to her corner, saying over her shoulder, 'Remember, be real nice to him; that way is best all around. He's awake now.'

Her change in actions and tone terrify me; she is clearly expecting him to come in here. I move back to the bed and climb back up onto the bare mattress. Sitting up as best I can with my back against the iron bars of the bed frame, I look out at the orange sky, hoping that Martin has things in motion and the authorities are searching for me, for us.

Another resounding thud, followed by something being dragged across the floor, then someone talking in a deep voice, but I can't make out what is being said. I cast a quick glance over to Kelly now, and I can't see her anymore, hiding deep in the shadows like the first time I met her.

A deep belly laugh followed a very clear "*Yes siree, let's do this*".

Kelly whispers, 'Remember, be real nice to him.'

The footsteps crossing bare floorboards get louder and closer, and then he's there, standing in the doorway silhouetted by the dying light, hands on his hips. 'Papa has come for his sweet thing.'

Shit, what the fuck does that mean. He steps into the room slowly, menacingly moving closer to the bed I'm on. I instinctively pull my knees up and curl up as tight as I can, pulling my dress down over my shins.

'Nah, Miss Collins, not yet, ya waits your turn, lil'missy.' Turning to Kelly, 'Come on then, sweetness, time to give Papa his treat. He turns and heads to the corner where Kelly is. I hear chains softly rattling as they are pulled through the iron hoop, and within seconds, he's back in the partial light, holding a length of chain in one hand.

'Remember, we have a guest this evening, and ya've already had ya treat, so it's time t'play nice now, y'hear.'

Quietly, submissively, Kelly replies, 'Yes, Sir, sure thing, Sir.'

He yanks the chain, and the snatch of it has Kelly wincing slightly. 'C'mon now, girl, ya know it's not good to keep me waiting.' He turns, throwing the chain over his right shoulder as though he is about to drag her out of the room. Kelly stands and comes into the light where I see her. She looks back at me with an awful, forced smile, 'It's me tonight, I got this. He said you are special.'

'Kelly, don't go,' I call out after her, but she disappears around the door frame as I say it; it's not like she has a choice in the matter. I listen to his boots on the floor, fading as he moves further away, and for a few seconds, what could be her soft feet padding after him. No, this can't be happening. A door slams shut, and all is quiet.

Just as the last light ebbs away, a small lamp flickers on in the far corner of the room as though it's on a timer or is solar-powered, and the low light level in the room has activated it. The lamp emits a very low light, but it does actually help illuminate the gloom a little. Looking around, I must figure a way out of this; I, we, cannot rely on Martin or the authorities arriving anytime soon to rescue us, not if Kelly has been here for months and we are as remote as she says we are.

I slide off the bed, and moving my tethered limbs slowly, I look for the best way to maximise the length of the chains to increase my reach capability. Pulling to their extreme, the thick leather straps strain at my wrist and ankle, and my twisting and straining start to rub and irritate my skin at the contact points. It's useless; no matter what I try, I'm still a few feet away from either the hooks in the fireplace or the window bar keeping the shutters closed. I return to the bed and try to lift the frame, but floor bolts restrain it solidly without any noticeable give or movement.

Climbing back on the bed, I sit with my legs crossed, again looking around for something, anything. Outside, night has fallen, and I can clearly see stars against a jet-black canopy through the open door.

Distant sounds reach me from beyond the room; it must be Him with Kelly. The deep roaring and the occasional shout of "Yes" indicate it's Him, but I can't hear a peep from Kelly. The bastard! I'll kill him when I get free of this, yanking my arm against the chain.

What can I do? There must be something. The very thought of him touching her and then wanting to touch me horrifies me. I feel tears start to form, and as one breaks to roll down my cheek, I wipe it away quickly with the back of my hand and loudly sniff, determined not to be weak, to remain strong, resolute. I will get out of here.

Another loud thud from within the building, then nothing. I listen hard, but there's not a peep of human noise. I start to become aware of background noise from what I presume are bugs outside, crickets, or something, getting louder, these now drowning out all other sounds. I have my bra on; maybe, if I remove it, it could extend my reach a little and close that gap to the fittings I want. I start to wriggle slightly, moving my free hand behind my back, then stop. What the hell? This isn't going to help me; what can I possibly achieve with a bra strap? However, I need to continue thinking innovatively and consider what I have at hand, looking for anything that can help. I tip my head back on the bed frame and close my eyes.

Another loud thud wakes me, startling me into consciousness; I must have dozed off while sitting upright, waiting for her to return. My neck is stiff and aching, and as I move my free hand to rub my neck muscles, there is a clear, short, crisp bang, like metal on something solid, and all the animal noises cease instantly. Total silence.

Then the footfall returns; slow, solid, determined. I hear him talking, although quietly, mumbling something, his voice competing with the drag of chain across the timber floor. Looking towards the open door, out to the stars and freedom, the sounds grow louder until, without notice, he fills the doorframe once again, this time with an old kerosene lamp in his right hand, swinging low near his knee.

'Oh good, I see ya still awake, Miss Collins. Kelly here,' as he tugs at the chain at hip height with his left hand, 'has been a real good girl tonight, very good in fact, so there'll be more treats for ya ladies tomorrow.' Kelly stumbles into the doorframe, almost dropping to her knees. Her ponytail released, with hair wild in the light of the moon; she keeps her head lowered as she shuffles past him into the room.

'A real good girl; Papa is pleased.'

It's sickening listening to his voice; I feel like I want to vomit and fight the urge to let my stomach empty. He follows her in, back to her corner, and whilst his body blocks my view, I hear the chain being fed back through the hoop on the wall. Silhouetted by his lamp placed in front of him as he addresses the chain, I strain my eyes to make out any detail that could help me. I have already decided he had better not touch me, but if he does, I'll try to wrap my chain around his neck and pull hard. He must have a key on him, so if I can render him unconscious, we may have a way of escaping, at the same time locking him up in chains for the authorities to come and arrest him.

'There we go, now get some rest, sweet thing, ya earned it. Here, a blanket; it's going to get cold tonight unless ya want to keep Papa warm,' laughing loudly at his own voice.

He steps back, and as he turns, swinging his arm around, I catch a fleeting glimpse of his face in the light from the kerosene lamp. I wish I hadn't. It's one of those faces I know will be etched in my mind forever. He sees me looking directly at him.

'Now then, what do we have here? Are ya still playing nice, Miss Collins?'

I want to scream at him, but I'm mindful of what Kelly said and that I'm still his prisoner, his hostage, chained to this bed with no escape... yet. 'Yes, I'm still playing nice. Thank you for dinner this evening; it was tasty and welcome.' I swallow hard, fighting back both my bile and the vitriol I want to scream at him.

'Ah, now, well, I see ya being much nicer this evening. I'll have a special surprise for ya tomorrow night, Pumpkin,' followed by a sickening wink and shallow laugh. 'Here, a blanket for ya to keep warm.' He tosses a rolled-up dark blanket onto the foot of the bed from a few yards away, wisely keeping his distance from me. I need to get him closer and draw him in.

'And what surprise will that be?' I ask, trying to disguise any tremors in my voice. I'm absolutely terrified of being near him, never mind conversing with him. Can I do this?

'Patience, Pumpkin, patience. It won't be a surprise if ya know what ya getting. Ya had best get some sleep,' and he winks again.

He turns for the door, and as he leaves, he begins humming a tune I recognise; it's the one Kelly was humming earlier. The door closes behind him, and the bolt slides across once again. I let out a slow breath, and my hands start to shake wildly now. I no longer need to maintain a calm front.

'Ya did good there,' Kelly says to me from out of the dark corner.

Considering what she has just been through, I'm surprised she wants to speak, let alone reinforce my actions with encouragement.

'He'll treat us good tomorrow,' she adds.

I close my eyes and drop my head backwards to rest on the bed frame, my legs now shaking to accompany my hands and arms.

'Ya best use that blanket; it's gonna get cold real quick.'

Kelly seems to have accepted her fate, not wanting any additional stress or hassle. She must know we are living on borrowed time, especially her, as she has seen him up close and can easily identify him. Shit, I've seen his face too.

39

Martin

Woods, Outside Wolf Rock Ranch

By the time we reached the woods on foot, daylight was just starting to break on the horizon. Ernesto took us on a circuitous route to avoid any other likely occupied buildings and ensure we were in our hold-up position with the sun rising behind us before breaking the horizon. I never thought I'd be dressed up in camouflage gear with a painted face and hands, but Ernesto insisted that he wanted to maintain the element of surprise following initial surveillance of the ranch. I argued with him on the way over here, as I believe time is of the essence, that every minute that passes could be Emily's last, but he calmly replied grimly advising that if we rush in, it could be ours also. He's right; it's sensible; while we know of Gunnarsson, we still don't know for sure if it is him who has Emily, and we don't know if he's acting alone or in some group or gang; the only way to find out what we could be walking into is to conduct surveillance.

The buildings that make up the ranch are about three hundred and fifty yards from our position. Ernesto has been studying them through the scope he has set up on a small tripod, describing their almost derelict condition to me, and he thinks he has identified the likely building where any hostage would be held.

I bite down on an energy bar just as he places his left hand on my arm with a 'Shhh, movement ahead.'

I have a small pair of binoculars, and I lift them to my eyes. As I focus them, I see a male carrying a handled toolbox to a white van parked at the side of the main building. 'That could be Gunnarsson,' he whispers, 'but at this distance, impossible to confirm his I.D. Keep eyes on the male; I'll look for any other movement.'

As I watch him, he places the box in the van, looks back at the building, and then climbs into the driver's seat. 'It looks like he's leaving,' I whisper.

'OK, but there could be others.'

The van pulls away from the building, kicking up dust as it drives off into the distance on the dirt road. Within a few minutes, the van is lost in a cloud of rising dust that gradually diminishes to a speck on the horizon before disappearing behind a distant rise in the land.

All is quiet, and we remain still. Two hours have passed since the van drove off. There is no other sign of life in the place, not even a dog or any livestock; it seems even birds are staying away from this place.

I break the silence. 'Shall we go in?' I ask Ernesto.

'Not yet. Just because we haven't seen others, it doesn't mean they are not there,' replying without breaking his watch through the scope.

'He could have just gone to work. He has a maintenance job in town, and if he is on his own, then this is the best time to find out if Emily is in there.'

'But…'

'But, with respect, it is. We're not a hundred percent sure it was Gunnarsson who took Emily, so this gives us a chance to check out his place, and if there are no signs, we can withdraw and think of Plan B.'

He looks at his watch, 'It's nearly ten fifteen. I'd rather we observe the place for longer, but you have a point. OK, look, I'm going to make my way across there and go in. I want you to stay here, and if you see or hear anything, fire off a warning shot into the sky. Got it?'

'Yes, but shouldn't I come with you as backup or something?'

'No, you're better off here; if it all goes south in there, I know to shoot anyone that's not Emily. You stay here and watch my six.'

'You're six?'

'Yeah, watch my back.'

'Got it.'

40

Emily

The Room, Wolf Rock Ranch

The sound of doors closing, an engine starting, and then a vehicle driving away breaks the silence, waking me from my half-sleep. I can already feel it's going to be another hot, dry day; the temperature is slowly rising, and soon, the room will be stuffy once again.

'He's going to work now; we're on our own again for the rest of today,' Kelly says from her corner. She slowly shuffles forward into a shaft of sunlight coming between cracks in the window shutters.

'Is there only him?'

'Yes. There's no one else.'

I reach for the bottle of water at the bottom of my bed and take a long drink. As I lower the bottle, Kelly speaks again.

'I'd save some of that if I were you; that's all we got, a bottle each.'

'Bloody hell, one bottle each. It was hot enough yesterday, and it feels like it's going to be hot again today.'

'Yes, Ma'am, it'll be hot today and tomorrow too. This is our summertime, and it can get awfully hot and dry around here unless we get a storm.'

'What time does he return?'

'I don't rightly know what time of day, but it's usually late afternoon, not long before sundown. He said he'll have a special treat for us tonight; I wonder what it is?'

She seems excited by the thought of this special treat from him, which astounds me; I think she's forgotten what it's like to be free and do your own thing. I don't know; maybe it's because she's had such a tough childhood that any sign of affection or compassion is special for her, more meaningful and acceptable.

'Kelly, will your family not be missing you?'

'No, guess not, I have no real family left to talk about.'

'What about close friends? Will they be out there looking for you?'

'Nope, no real friends to speak of either.'

This could be why she appears submissive when he's around, why the smallest treat or show of compassion is appealing to her. When it comes down to it, though, will she back me up or him? I need to be sure she's with me when I make my move. Why am I even thinking like this? Of course, she'll want to get away from all this.

'What are your plans for the future, Kelly?'

'Don't rightly know, I guess, I never really went to High School, well, not after the first year anyhow. Maybe I'll get me a job at the supermarket or down at the Willowbrook Mall. Yeah, down in the Mall, at one of those fancy clothes shops. That way, I'll know what to wear out on a party night.'

'Oh, where's that? Where's the Mall?'

'Hou

ston,' she replies with a beaming smile and wide eyes. Then she lowers her head and mumbles, 'But more likely I'll end up on a ranch like this one, ya know what I mean?'

'What, married to a rancher?' I ask her.

'Yep, well, a ranch hand, more like.'

I'm glad she answered the way she did; I was hoping she didn't mean locked up like this. 'Well, that's something to aspire to, to look forward to. I can see you working in one of those shops. You can dream of that, and no one can take your dream from you.'

'Awh, Emily, that's so nice. You think I can get me that job if I want it?'

'Yes, of course; if you put your mind to it and never give in, it can happen.' I need to give her hope, something to aim at and live for.

'You really think I can do that?'

'Yes, Kelly, you can. You just have to believe in yourself and work at achieving it.'

'Yeh, I can do that. I can do that.'

We fall silent; I sense she is thinking of this, dreaming, maybe. After a few minutes, Kelly starts to gently hum that sweet tune again. We now have some hours without him being around, giving us a perfect window of opportunity to escape if only we could cast off these chains. The weakest part of my binds has to be the thick leather straps around my wrist and ankle, to which the chains are fastened. I shuffle forward and sit over the edge of the bed, dangling my legs just above the wood plank floor. Looking around, I desperately look for something to use to work my way through the leather, but there is nothing sharp in here and nothing remotely of use at hand.

I slide off the bed and twist to get on my knees, my arm pulling against the restraints to my wrist, and lower my head to look under the bed frame. The iron frame is old and rusty for the most part, and I feel along the edges of the angle iron sections, testing for the sharpness of any jagged edges. Running my fingers carefully along the iron, I find a small length of metal that feels more corroded than other parts, and the edges are rough. I try to lie down and wriggle under the bed so that I can run the leather strap around my wrist along the iron edges, hopefully cutting into the leather, but the shortness of the chain prevents me from getting the leather strap low enough to meet the rough steel edge of the frame. As I struggle, moving my hand left and right, trying to find some extra length in the chain, Kelly lowers herself to my level and speaks.

'He'll get angry if ya damage those leather straps, and he sees it.'

'Hopefully I can cut through this, free us and then we can get out of here before he returns this evening.'

'But what about the treat you're getting tonight?'

Her question shocks me, and I stop moving. She's not interested in escaping; she wants to still be here when he returns.

'No, Kelly, we need to escape. He's not going to let us go.'

'But he will… he let the others go.'

'What do you mean, the others? What others?' As I ask, I slide back out from under the bed and look across at her, sitting on the floor with her legs crossed in front of her.

'His other women.'

Her calmness in saying these words astonishes me; she's saying it as if it's a normal, everyday thing he's doing. Other women?

'What do you mean, has he had other women chained up like this with you here?' asking the question but not really wanting to hear the answer if it's in the affirmative.

'Yep, three. There was Shona, then Jackie, then Ellie. Yeah, Ellie was the nicest of them; well, she wasn't as nice as you,' smiling at me as she pays me this surreal compliment.

Fuck. There is no way he's letting these women leave here alive. He's a serial kidnapper, and… and… I don't want to think about it. 'Look, Kelly, we need to get out of here today. Are you going to help me?'

'I'm… I'm not so sure. You're nice and all, but if ya leave, he'll get real angry, I mean *real* angry. He says you're a guest in his home, and I know he likes you.'

'Do you honestly believe he let them all go free?'

'Yep, that's what he told me… and I believe him.'

She's either super naïve or she's under his spell. Whichever it is, I'm not staying around to find out what treat he has for me tonight; I'm getting out of here.

'Look, Kelly, I want to leave, but he's keeping me chained up here, keeping both of us chained up. This isn't right, is it? If we were his guests, he wouldn't treat us like this, would he? Come on, you've got to see that at least.'

'He's always been good to me; he calls me his good girl, you've heard him say it. I'm his favourite girl. He lets them go because he wants only me. I don't think I want to leave here.'

Looking into her face, I feel she means it; she doesn't want to leave. I haven't time for this. I need to work on my escape. I turn from her and crawl back under the bed, hopelessly yanking at the chain again to make it longer so I can get the leather strap against the rough iron edge. I'm on my own; it's down to me. When I get out of this, I'll free her, and then it's up to her to stay or go. But I am not going to hang around waiting for him to come home. I need to put as much distance as possible between me and this place. Rubbing the leather strap against the iron frame isn't going to work; I can't get enough of the leather to the steel edge, but now I have a new energy in me, a new determination to get out of here. I need to find another way.

But something tells me I need her with me. I need her help, and she must know of something that will be useful to our escape. I just have to win her over.

'Kelly, remember your dream job, your perfect job in the Mall, and all those beautiful clothes you'll be around; you want that, don't you?'

'I do.'

'Good; tell me some more about this Mall and the shop you want to work in.'

41

Martin

Wolf Rock Ranch

It feels strange lying here, watching Ernesto crossing the open ground in front of me, adopting a prone and alert posture, like he's hunting or stalking an animal. Using the scope on the mini tripod Ernesto left with me, I scan the ranch buildings, looking for any movement. There's nothing. It is slowly getting hotter, with the sun now higher behind me, and I can feel it heating the back of my neck. Pulling back slightly from the scope, I turn my baseball cap around so that the peak is covering my neck, and instantly, I feel the cooling relief. Watching in front of me, every now and again, Ernesto drops to his knee whilst lifting his weapon and scanning the buildings through his gun scope. Each time he rises, I presume he also sees no movement, and cautiously, he edges ever closer to the main building.

Way off in the distance, the silence is broken intermittently by a faint cattle call, while in between, there is nothing other than the sound of the warm breeze pushing along the occasional dried leaf or scrub, with little swirls of light sand moving across the dry ground. It's an eerie atmosphere but weirdly peaceful at the same time.

In a final sprint, he reaches the side of the main building, the ranch house, and I watch him slowly step up onto the porch deck with his weapon in firing position up at his shoulder; he moves carefully towards the front door, lowering himself down below a window as he crosses in front of it. He stands beside the door frame and reaches for the door handle; he throws the door open, briefly stepping aside, then enters quickly.

Nothing. It's all quiet, save for the breeze.

Within about thirty to forty seconds, he is back outside on the porch, moving along to the smaller attached building. He lowers himself again in front of the shuttered window and then makes the same move with that door, flinging it open, checking, and then entering. Again, all remains quiet. I move the scope slowly from side to side, switching between the outbuildings and the main building, staying alert for any movement. There's nothing.

Letting out a deep sigh, I start to think that this is more than likely the wrong place, and maybe it wasn't Job Gunnarsson after all. I quickly turn the scope up toward the access road to check that no vehicles are approaching, and all is still; there is nothing to be seen. I slump back from my alertness. Gunnarsson has simply gone to work; I have the wrong man; it's not him, and I've wasted precious time, time that Emily may not have.

Where the hell is she?

42

Ernesto

The Room, Wolf Rock Ranch

Entering the room, light enters from behind me, and automatically, I flick on my flashlight attached to the AR, instantly illuminating in front of me an old iron bed frame and mattress with a woman seemingly chained to it, lying still.

'Emily?' I whisper, but there is no response. 'Emily?' this time louder.

The woman stirs on the bed and rises slightly, lifting her head and shoulders from the bed, shielding her eyes with a chained hand. She is dishevelled and disoriented.

'Who…?' she croaks and coughs, pushing herself more upright with her left arm, 'Who are you?'

'It's me, Ernesto. I've come for you.' Flicking the switch to safety, I tip the AR so that the flashlight illuminates my face; a tactical error, but she needs to know it's me.

'Ernesto? No, you're not Ernesto.'

I realise then that I'm smeared in disruptive camouflage cream, and I use the sleeve of my shirt, dragging my forearm across my cheeks to try to remove some of it, unsuccessfully. 'Emily Collins, it is me, Ernesto. Martin is here also; he's outside. Remember, I collected you from the airport with Mary, and we went to pick up your mother. We've come to rescue you.'

At that, she sits fully upright, her eyes widen, and shouts out, 'Ernesto, thank God, thank you. Quick, he could be back at any time. Can you get these chains off me? I can't free myself; I tried, but I can't get them off.'

Unclipping the AR from the shoulder sling, I place it down on the bed with the flashlight pointing at her and take a step forward to look at the restraints.

Running my fingers around the wrist restraint and across the padlock, I quickly realise that cutting the leather won't free her; I'll need the bolt cutters in the bag I left with Martin to cut the padlock or chain. She won't want to hear this, but I have to tell her I need to go back outside.

'Emily, look, I'll need to…'

'NO!' she screams out, and in that split second, I register she is looking over my left shoulder with sheer horror on her face.

I spin on the spot, twisting lower and around, spiralling, and at the same time, I raise my left arm above my head; my right hand is reaching for my Beretta in its holster strapped to my right thigh. My moves are well practised, and as something slices along my left forearm, my right hand is low across my belly, bringing the Beretta to bear on the assailant. The single shot echoes around the room, smashing the silence, the bullet striking the target mid-body.

'NO!' Emily screams again, followed by 'KELLY!'

I know adrenalin is masking the pain of the injury I've just taken, and I continue to rotate, firing a second shot into the assailant, this time hitting the target, centre chest, as they stumble backwards.

The body falls backwards and hits the floor hard, and something clatters across the wooden floor.

'KELLY!' Emily shouts out again.

I drop to a prone position and scan the room thoroughly. Inside, I'm berating myself, quietly saying, 'Stupid, stupid, I should have checked the corners.' I was too focused on Emily to check around the room properly, as I should have done.

'WHO THE HELL IS KELLY?' I shout out to Emily.

'Kelly. She's a prisoner here, like me. Is she hurt?'

I know she's more than likely already dead; two close-quarter shots from my nine-millimetre would be more than enough to kill an Ox.

'If she's a prisoner, why is she attacking me?' and as I ask, whoa, the pain in my left arm starts to reveal itself. 'Argh, fuck,' I call out as I bring my left arm into my stomach and cradle it above my right arm, still primed in case I need to take another shot. 'Why attack me?'

'I… I don't know. I don't know, Ernesto. Check she's alright, please. She's only a kid, help her.'

A kid. Oh my god, what have I done? I stand and holster my pistol, then pick up the AR with the flashlight. Turning, I shine the beam down onto her body, and clearly, I know she's gone; I've seen the dead many times before.

'Help her, please, Ernesto.'

I know it's pointless but go along with Emily's request. Placing myself between Emily and Kelly's body to screen Emily's sight of her, I crouch to check her pulse. There's nothing, as I expected; the gunshots would have inflicted massive trauma at this close range. Lowering my head, I close my eyes, and then quickly, professional training switches me back into operational mode. Get a grip; these things happen. I look again at her; her right hand is open, and a few feet away lies a large Bowie-style hunting knife with a shiny steel blade. The first thought is relief; such a clean blade minimises the risk of infection, but this thought surprises even me, how I'm thinking about myself before anything else. I move the AR so the light shines onto my left arm, and I see the blood-soaked sleeve, with blood trickling below my shirt sleeve, across the back of my left hand. I need to stop the bleeding, stabilise, and then dress the wound. Come on, man, you know what to do. I stand and turn back to Emily on the bed, now with her knees raised up and pulled in tight to her body, sitting, looking at me.

'I'm sorry, Emily,' shaking my head slowly, 'No, she's gone… she's dead.'

Emily screams out, then covers her face and begins to cry. I need to move now, get her mind back on this rescue. I need to first aid my wound, get Emily free, and get us the hell out of here before Gunnarsson returns.

Placing the AR down again on the bed, I remove the sweaty camouflaged bandana from my head and hold it out to her, 'You need to open this out, twist it into a bandage and strap it around my arm over the wound, tight. My medical kit is with Martin, so I'll dress it properly when we get outside.'

She doesn't move.

'EMILY!' I shout at her, 'Snap out of it! I need your help, NOW!'

As she lowers her hand and reaches for the bandana, the loud boom of a gunshot just outside the door reverberates around the dry timber walls. Emily falls back down onto the mattress, and I turn, quickly lowering myself again to make myself a smaller target whilst simultaneously drawing my Beretta and aiming it towards the open door.

43

Martin

Wolf Rock Ranch

There is no mistaking that sound, two gunshots in quick succession. Shit. Was that Ernesto shooting, or is someone shooting at him? There must be someone else here, an accomplice.

Do I go to him or wait here? We didn't discuss this option, shit. My head is spinning. I must do something; he could be hurt and need my help. I roll onto my left-hand side and extract the revolver from the holster strapped to my right thigh. Aim and squeeze, that's all I have to do, he said, aim and squeeze. Eight bullets, eight shots. You can do this, Martin, come on.

Looking through the scope one more time, I still can't see anyone else, no signs of life. I stand slowly and start to cross the open ground, keeping low like Ernesto did, my revolver pointing out in front of me, aiming in the general direction of the buildings. My breathing has changed to heavy, short panting, and I can feel the adrenalin kicking in, my heart pounding.

As I approach from the side of the main building, I see a figure come out of the front door of the house carrying a long gun, possibly a shotgun. I drop down and take aim, but I know I couldn't hit him from here, not at this distance, not with this. The man in denim and a check shirt is moving towards the attached building, the one Ernesto entered, and is raising his gun in front of him as he moves slowly, closing in on the door. This person must be with Gunnarsson and is now after Ernesto; I can't waste any time. Registering I'm more or less outside their peripheral vision, given the angle I'm approaching at, I take a gamble and stand, moving forward quickly, reaching the porch deck just as he nears the open door where Ernesto entered. He's about ten yards in front of me as I raise the pistol in my right hand, try to steady it with my left, aim along the barrel using the sights as Ernesto indicated and squeeze slowly.

The gun mechanism moves gently, the hammer drawing back slowly, until I feel the pressure change on the trigger, and the hammer slams forward, striking. The loudness of the bullet firing shocks me, the recoil causing me to move my aim off the man. Looking at him still standing there, I clearly missed him, and now he's aware I'm on to him. He starts to turn, bringing his shotgun to bear on me. Quickly taking aim back at him, I release a second shot as he turns full-on to me, pointing the shotgun in my direction.

The second shot hits him in the left shoulder, knocking him off balance, causing him to spin, and firing off the shotgun into the sky. It all seems to go into slow motion; I drop to one knee, mimicking Ernesto's position as he crossed the ground earlier, preparing to take a shot if needed. I take aim again, this time slowing my breathing, exhaling, then squeezing the trigger softly. Boom. I see the almost instant hit in his body mass, and he falls backwards and drops to the floor, his shotgun falling from his grip, clattering off the raised deck, and landing in the dirt below. I got him.

The buzz I'm feeling is enormous. Wow. I'm the hunter, and in meeting my match, I bested him. He's down. I stand slowly and tentatively step forward, my gun trained on him, lying there in case he moves again.

'Martin,' I hear Ernesto shout out from the door, 'Is that you?'

Relief, he's still alive. 'Yes, it's me. I've hit him, he's down.'

'Is it Gunnarsson?'

'No, I don't think so.'

'Be careful, make sure he's down. Stay alert, there may be more. I'm coming out the door now, don't shoot me.'

'OK, got it, you're coming out.' I step forward slowly, keeping the revolver pointing at him as he lies there motionless. Upon reaching him, I realise it's not a him, but a woman, maybe in her mid-forties, just as Ernesto comes out of the door pointing his assault rifle down at her.

'Good shooting, Martin. You saved me from being shot in the back. That was close, thank you.'

'Who is she?'

'No idea, but she was sure out to get me,' gesturing towards her shotgun.

I look at Ernesto and see his bloody arm, drips hitting the wooden boards and splattering in oven-dry dust, turning it a dull mud colour. 'Have you been shot?'

'No, it's a knife wound. Some girl called Kelly in there; she came up behind me, cut me, so I had to put her down.'

'What about Emily? Have you found her, is she here?'

'Yes, she's in there,' flicking his head back toward the door. 'She's alive. Look, I need to get the bolt cutters to free her and my first aid pack for this arm. I'll go get the kit. You go in and see if you can calm her. She's not in a good place. Don't worry about Kelly; she's dead. Leave her but keep that gun handy just in case. Here,' uncoupling the flashlight from his AR, 'Take this with you; there's not much light in there.'

He steps over the woman, dropping off the porch deck and picks up the shotgun. 'Pump action; she could have done a lot of damage with this. I don't know how I missed her when I cleared the house. I must be getting too old for this shit. You did good, Martin,' he nods to me, then turns away.

Ernesto heads off to our lying-up position and our kit, and while I turn away from him to enter the room, I holster my revolver and flick on the flashlight.

As I walk in, I quickly arc the flashlight around the room. The light catches Emily curled up on the bed, her legs pulled in tight to her, her arms wrapped around them, pulling them in tighter. She's rocking slightly and sobbing, and I see the chains she is in.

'Emily, it's me, Martin. You're safe now.'

She lifts her head to look at me, squinting. I turn the flashlight away from her just enough that she remains within the cone of light from the flashlight but not directly in it. However, the bulk of light now illuminates a body on the floor with a small pool of blood coming from beneath it. This must be Kelly.

'Martin.' Her relief is obvious. 'Get me out of here, Martin, please?'

I look at her restraints and see the padlocks to her wrist and ankle fastenings. 'We will, Ernesto has just gone for the cutters to get those padlocks off.'

I pull my water bottle from the side pocket of my combat trousers, unscrew the lid and offer it to Emily. She shakes her head, not wanting it. My mouth is as dry as the dust in here, and I take a long pull on the water before refastening the lid and putting the bottle away again.

Looking across to where the body lies, I say loud enough for Emily to hear, 'Ernesto said she is called Kelly.'

'Was. She's dead. Ernesto shot her.'

'I'm sure he only did what he had to. What happened?'

Looking back at Emily, she keeps her head bowed, 'I'm not sure. She was tied up over there in the corner, in chains, a prisoner like me; she's only a kid, seventeen. But when Ernesto came in, he spoke to me and tried to undo these chains; I don't think he saw her in the dark, and… then she… she just jumped at him from her corner. It was so quick; I called out, and she lashed out at Ernesto with a big knife.'

I look back at Kelly lying on her back, both arms splayed out, and see the knife but no chains. 'She's not in chains now. Where did she get the knife from?'

'I don't know! I don't Know! She was definitely chained up. He chained her to a hoop on the wall. I saw it, I heard it. He treated her badly… she's, she's been here for months, she said.'

I lift the flashlight slightly to illuminate a steel hoop on the wall with a length of stainless steel chain looped through it. Walking across to inspect it closer, I see that the end has a wrist shackle like Emily's, but it's open, and there's no padlock. What the…?

Turning back to Emily and approaching the bed, she starts to sob. 'She was only a kid… the bastard.'

I hope she's referring to Gunnarsson and not Ernesto.

'Emily, you're safe now; let's get you out of here.' I place the flashlight down on the mattress and embrace her, wrapping my arms around her, wanting to scoop her up and carry her away.

From outside, Ernesto calls out, 'Martin! It's me, Ernesto, I'm coming in, OK?'

Shouting over her shoulder, 'OK. OK. Come in.'

As Ernesto's frame fills the open door, the room darkens again, 'I have the cutters. Here, cut her free.'

I release Emily to reach across the bed to him, and he slaps them into my hand. 'If you can't cut the padlock, then try cutting the chain; we can cut the bracelets off when we get out of here.'

Ernesto picks up the flashlight and directs the light to her wrist. I open the cutters, place the jaws over the padlock loop and try to close them. I try with all my strength to close the handles of the cutters together, but the steel is too strong; the cutting edges of the jaws do not make any impression on the padlock loop. Ernesto sees me trying to do this and instructs again.

'OK, probably hardened steel; try cutting the chain near the bracelet. You will have to do this, Martin, I can't, my left arm is fucked up.'

Moving the cutter jaws to the chain, I close down hard on the handles, and I feel the steel jaws ever so slowly sinking into the steel link as the handles gently come together until the chain link instantly snaps and the handles close.

'Great, good job, now for the ankle chain, same thing, cut the chain near to the bracelet,' Ernesto instructs again, and I follow his directions.

The chain snaps quickly, and Emily is free of her restraints. She jumps up to embrace me, throwing her arms around my neck and kissing me.

I look at Ernesto and see his smile and return a smile to him. He winks at me.

'Come on, let's go,' he says in a calm voice, Ernesto's experience showing through; he's still on a mission. This time, I scoop up Emily and head towards the door. Ernesto is already there looking outside before we exit, scanning to make sure we are alone. 'Clear,' he calls and steps out onto the porch deck.

As I leave the room, and we come out into brighter light, Emily sees the body of the woman I shot lying motionless, the two bullet entries clearly noticeable from the blood loss across her check shirt and the decking. Emily shrieks and buries her head into my chest, and I pull her in tighter to me, trying to instil confidence and protection that I have her now, and she's safe.

We move quickly across the open ground, and my mind flashes back to Fell View Cottage and the scene I left behind me when I killed Tanya and Craig, not knowing how it would turn out. I was resigned to my fate, accepting what I had done, but luck or good fortune played in my favour that night when a third party intervened; Hatzis. Hatzis turning up when he did was enough to put him in the frame for the killings. Carrying Emily over the uneven ground, I start to sweat and breathe heavily as the sun beats down relentlessly. But I won't get that same good fortune here; there is no one else around that can take the blame for this, become culpable for shooting Kelly and the shotgun-carrying woman, and for sure, I can't let Gunnarsson roam free as he'll come looking for Emily, especially if he thinks Emily somehow did all this; he will come for her again.

I can't allow him to do that, and I'm saying over in my head, *"No police"*.

As I reach the spot where we laid up, Ernesto is already collecting our equipment, removing any trace of our presence.

I slowly lower Emily to her feet and hand her the remainder of my water. My mind is made up; it's now time for me to take control of the situation.

'Ernesto. Take Emily out of here, get her back to the hotel or somewhere safe. There is a loose end I need to tie off.'

He stops and stands upright, looking at me, ever the warrior, with kit and guns adorning his body. 'What are you talking about?'

'I can't leave Gunnarsson.'

'Yes, you can. We get out of here, call the police, and they come over and arrest him.'

'You know we can't call the police; we've been over that, and I can't leave him free to come after Emily again. He has to be stopped.'

Emily looks up at me, taking hold of my hand, 'What do you mean, stopped?'

'I must stop him; I have to put an end to this. He'll hold you responsible for what's happened, and we cannot provide twenty-four-hour protection for you, not knowing when or how he'll come for you again. Kelly is dead, you're free, and I shot and killed his partner or whoever she is. He is going to be one pissed-off cowboy when he gets back to the ranch this evening. At the moment, I have the advantage; he doesn't know what's happened yet, and he won't be expecting me.'

'No, you can't do this, Martin. Tell him, Ernesto, tell him.'

I look at Ernesto, and I can see it in his expression; he knows I'm right, but I'm nailing this now before he speaks, 'Ernesto, you're wounded; you need to get that arm looked at properly, and Emily needs to go with you. I have to stop Gunnarsson before he goes on the rampage. You know this makes sense. You know I'm right.'

'How are you going to get back into town? Shall I come back later for you?'

'Ernesto!' Emily shouts at him. 'No, he can't do this!'

Ernesto turns to Emily and calmly replies, 'He's right, Miss Collins. Martin is right; Gunnarsson is a wild one that needs putting down. Look how easily he got you; he could do it again. I would bet he's done it before; you said Kelly was his prisoner, too. We can't go to the police, but he has to be stopped.' He turns to me, 'Martin, let me do it; this is my territory, and I have the training for this.'

'No, my mind is made up. You need to get Emily safe, get yourself some medical attention, and I'll clean up here. Now go before he comes back and finds us all still here.' I bend down and take another bottle of water and some food packets; this could be a long day.

Emily grabs at my arm, 'No, you can't do this, Martin. No! Anyway, why can't we go to the police?'

I turn to her, grabbing the tops of both her arms in my hands and holding her tightly. 'Emily, you have to trust me. We haven't the time to discuss it here, so you're just going to have to trust me.'

Turning to Ernesto, 'No, thank you, don't come back. I'll drive back to town in his van, leave it somewhere remote, set fire to it, whatever. I'll call you when I'm ready. Bring me some clean clothes and wash gear to get cleaned up before I head back to the hotel. That good? Does that work for you?'

'Sure thing,' he nods.

Emily swivels her head between us as we talk.

I continue, 'I'll need your pistol and the shotgun.' You keep the machine gun; it's too much gun for me. Both pistols have been used, so I'll need to create a narrative as I clean this up. I've got to stage this so that Gunnarsson is accountable for the deaths of these two women.'

'Roger that.'

I turn to Emily again, 'Emily, help Ernesto with this equipment, will you? Keep an eye on him and his wound.'

She starts to reply, 'But…'

'No buts. The decision is made. You can do this; you have to be one of the strongest women I know, and I want you to now look after my friend here. I'll see you later this evening… I promise.' I lean down to her, placing both palms on her face, pulling her into me and kissing her.

'Jeez, later, guys,' Ernesto quips as he removes his pistol and holds it out to me. 'Both guns are clean, no serial numbers. You have six rounds in the Smith and Wesson, and there's ten left in this,' handing me his Beretta. 'Same thing, point and squeeze the trigger slowly. However, this here is the safety catch, here to shoot, and here for safe. Got it?'

I nod, 'Yes, got it.'

'Now, the shotgun, just pull this forestock all the way back, then slide forward to chamber the next cartridge,' and an empty cartridge flies out as he seamlessly transits the forestock back then forward along the barrel. 'It's now loaded and ready. The safety is here,' indicating a slide lever on top behind the trigger, 'Red dot indicates it's ready to fire; got it?' clicking the safety on again.

'Yes, got it.'

He hands me the shotgun, then picks up the spent cartridge and passes it to me. 'Clean everything down as best you can; if you leave any empty cases around, clean them as well. There will be blood from me in that room and probably on the porch; all that needs cleaning away. Might be best to torch the place.'

'OK, I got this.'

Emily steps forward and softly, in my ear, whispers, 'You remember Paul's death? A shotgun is quite versatile when things need cleaning up.'

I look at her quizzically, wondering what she means; versatile? She notices my confusion and adds, 'You'll work it out,' and rises up on her toes and kisses me again, this time on my right cheek. 'I'll see you later this evening. Be careful.'

'I will,' I reply. She smiles at me, and even with her hot, dirty, and dishevelled look, she remains stunningly beautiful and encouragingly but surprisingly resilient. 'I will see you both later.' Looking at Ernesto, I add, 'Look after her for me.'

'You have no worries on that front.'

'I'll contact you when I'm ready to be collected.'

'Roger that.'

They turn to head back the way we came, and I watch them for a couple of minutes. Emily looks back, and I wave them off.

Now, I need to clean this up and set the scene, so that nothing comes back on any of us; it all has to land at Gunnarsson's feet, somehow.

44

Job Gunnarsson

Home, Wolf Rock Ranch

Tonight is special; I've been waiting for this, planning this, she will be mine. It's been on my mind all day; my god, she is the best one yet. I can't wait any longer; she's driving me crazy. Watching the hours tick by has been annoying. I've bitten my nails to nothing in anticipation, but the hours have passed, and now I'm nearly home. She will want me, that I'm sure of, this dress I've bought her, and this fancy French wine will make sure. Kelly and the others are proof that I can turn a mountain lion into a pet cat, one that respects me and my kindness; most do in the end, and then when I'm tired of them or a new one comes along, they get taken out to the woods.

My previous guests have been good, some more than others, but I'm expecting the best from this Miss Collins.

Approaching the ranch, I see she is not waiting for me on the porch. That's unusual. She's always there to welcome me home after a day's work. I slow the van and sound the horn to let her know I'm home, but she doesn't come out; is she sick?

Stopping the van outside the house and killing the engine, I step out, walk around, open the side door, pick up the dress and the wine, and head towards the porch. As I step up onto the dry planks, I see a large, wet patch outside the side door, the door to my room; it looks like someone has been washing it down. I've never known her to scrub the porch; has she tried to empty the slop bucket and messed up? She'll pay for it if she's been in there; she knows that's my room, and only I go in there. Looks like there's gonna be some discipline needed tonight after all. Putting my hand on the door handle of the house, a sound from my room next door turns my head. Now, Kelly knows not to make any noise; she knows what she'll get, so I suppose it's my new girl; still a bit of respect needs teaching then. I can wait some 'til I'm ready to eat, and letting go of the door handle, I turn towards my room to go see my new girl, see if she's ready for tonight.

Stepping slowly toward the room, heavily stomping my boots down to build her excitement, to tease her like, I call out, 'Hello, Miss Collins, ya ready for ya treat tonight? I got something real special here, special f'sure. We gonna have some fun tonight, little Missy.'

Opening the door, the darkness inside slowly escapes as the low sun creeps around me, highlighting the outline of the bed in the middle of the room, allowing me to see her lying on the bed, her shape under the blanket.

'Awh, ya cold? Well, Papa's here to warm ya up.' I step in, and as I do, a quiet voice from my right whispers, 'This way, Job.' I turn to my right to see who said it, and this thing is coming out of the shadows, heading towards me. Wham!

45

Martin

The Room, Wolf Rock Ranch

The shotgun butt hits him squarely in his face, and he drops like a sack of potatoes, dropping what he is carrying, causing a bottle of wine to roll across the floor, stopping at one of the bed legs. He's much bigger up close, and I'm going to struggle to move him, but I will move him. Resting the shotgun against the door frame, I bend down and grab the shoulders of his work jacket, but his jacket just slips from him; he doesn't move. Bending lower and placing both my arms under his sweaty armpits, I bring my hands together in front of him, across his chest and interlock my fingers. This is a man desperately overdue a shower and some soap, and he's a real weight. I half pick him up and half drag him to the foot of the bed and rest his back against the iron bed frame.

Everything else is cleaned up, and the scene is set for discovery at some future time; all I need do now is dispatch Gunnarsson and leave no trace of me behind. But before I do, I want to question him first to make sure there are no loose ends, and I also want to find out why Kelly wasn't chained up and had a knife; it's a loose end I don't like, especially as Emily believes Kelly was also abducted by him.

Binding his legs together, then his hands behind his back, I prop him up in a sitting position against the bed frame and place the prepared noose around his neck, throw the rope up and over two of the roof beams, and back down to rest on the floor near the entrance door. Pulling it taught and tying it off for the time being, all I need do now is pull down on the rope, and he'll feel the pressure around his neck and throat, a technique I'd read about to try to make him talk as I'm sure he'll resist. I fight the impulse to stuff a rag in his mouth or gag him, as, from the state of his smashed-up nose, I'd only suffocate him if I did. Anyway, there is no one around to hear his calls if he shouts out; no doubt, one of the reasons he likes this place as well.

I pat him down for his van keys but don't find any, although I do find a large Bowie-type knife in a sheath under his shirt, fastened to his belt, one similar to the knife Kelly had; I'll have that and undo his belt and pull it through the loops in his jeans to release the knife. I need to find those van keys so I can get back into town. Back outside, I approach the van, and on opening the driver's door, I see the keys are still in the ignition; that's very obliging of him. Opening the side door to check the rear contents, it doesn't take me long to recognise the snatch kit he has, the mattress, the zip ties, the tools on a rack, and the black sheet. So, he's a planner; he prepares for his abductions. If he is, then he'll have information on Emily somewhere, and if he does, I'll need to remove it so that she is not connected to this place and him; I'd best search the house again. Ernesto said Shotgun Woman came out of nowhere, which shocked him as he had searched the house and thought it empty. That being the case, there must be a hiding place or cellar in there somewhere that

Ernesto missed on his first sweep; this could be where he has information on Emily.

Before going into the main building, I check on him, and he's still out cold, blood from his broken, smashed nose drying down his front. He'll be out for some time, but to be safe, he is trussed up and unable to move. Leaving the room, I pick up the shotgun, as there could be another person, or persons, in the house, and this kind of firepower would come in handy.

Entering the main house, I am surprised by how sparsely furnished it is. The large stone fireplace still holds the ashes from last night, and the two chairs in front of it are rough timber fabrications, possibly made by him. There is a stove and a couple of old wooden larder units beside a rough stone sink, and the worktop is covered with an array of pots and pans. The floor is timber planking, the same as the room next door, devoid of rugs and floor coverings of any kind. Across from the fireplace, there is a single picture up on the wall, and stepping closer to it, it is of the Pyramids of Giza, with camels in the foreground. This seems so out of place here in the middle of Texas, on a semi-derelict ranch; is this a dream maybe of Shotgun Woman or him?

I check out the bedroom, and it is equally sparse with another old iron frame bed, a small cupboard and a small pile of clothes on a chair; nothing else of any substance, save for the wardrobe in the corner. There is a distinct lack of anything feminine, no mirrors or a dressing table, and noticeably, no bathroom in the building. This place reminds me of an old prospector's shack I'd expect to have found in the mid-eighteen hundreds.

So where was Shotgun Woman hiding? She would have been impossible for Ernesto to miss in these two barren rooms.

I reach out to the wardrobe and open the single door slowly. It contains a couple of floral dresses and a dark-coloured suit, each on individual hangers and shrouded in clear polythene dust covers, their Sunday best, no doubt. Leaning in gently, I part the hanging clothes and, with the muzzle of shotgun, nudge the back of the wardrobe; it is solid old dry timber, just what I'd expect. Closing the door and taking a step back, I notice the faint outline of arcing drag marks in the light dust on the floor, radiating from the left front corner of the wardrobe, resembling a door opening on a hinge. I pull at the rear right edge of the wardrobe, and giving it a sudden jerk, it moves, slowly opening to reveal an opening in the timber wall behind. I pull it open more until it's just enough for me to step behind and through. Holding the shotgun out in front, I squeeze through the gap and the narrow opening in the timber wall, stepping into another room.

This is it, the other room, the room that Ernesto missed. It's another relatively simple room, containing a double iron frame bedstead, but this has a side dressing table with an antique-looking porcelain water pitcher and bowl on top. On the floor, there is a large rectangular floor rug, heavily worn, with missing fringe tassels. Taking a couple of steps into the room, in the corner of my right eye, I register an old wooden desk, complete with a laptop computer and small printer, and turning fully, I see the wall behind me is covered in colour photos of Emily, comprising pages carefully torn from magazines and newspapers, computer prints and maps, and there are even photos of the hospital, the Pontin Institute, where Angela is; how did he know she was there? The contrast in room wall décor is intense. This guy clearly has a thing about Emily, and obviously, this was no opportunistic snatch; he had planned Emily's abduction.

Solving where Shotgun Woman was hiding has only generated more questions to ask him. Approaching the desk to inspect the laptop, I hear a groan, deep and painful, like a large animal in distress; if that's Gunnarsson, he sounds really close to me. Another groan, and as I slowly move across the room to the picture-covered wall, a small shaft of light flashes across my face. Closing in on the source of the light, I find a hole located between photos of Emily, about the size of a dime, a knot hole pushed through, and looking through it, the peephole lets me see into the room next door where I can see the bed Emily was chained to, illuminated by the lowering sun coming through the only door into the room. Moving my head slightly, I can see Gunnarsson's legs and notice him trying to move, fighting against the restraints I've put him in. The swine. Shotgun Woman must have been in here when Ernesto searched the rooms; that's why he missed her, and she would have seen Ernesto enter the room with Emily and Kelly, deciding then to make her move. She was out to kill him, but who was she? An accomplice to Gunnarsson?

It's time to get some answers from the beast next door.

46

Martin

The Room

Returning to Gunnarsson, I find him wrestling against the restraints, trying his best to free himself. He looks up at me standing in the doorframe, silhouetted, complete with his shotgun. His bloodied face and shirt make for a sorry sight, with contempt and anger in his eyes that cannot be mistaken. I know a killer's look when I see one' and having him cornered and restrained is a dangerous situation to be in, as he will want to use his aggression to escape and exact his revenge on me.

'Who the fuck are you?' he snarls before coughing out clotted blood onto the wooden floor beside him. 'Where is my Mama?'

'Your Mama? Your mother, I thought she died years ago.'

'That's what they all think, numb nuts. Where is she?'

'Well then, I guess she's the woman lying on the bed behind you.'

'Hey, Mama! You OK, Mama?'

'She won't answer you, Gunnarsson. She's already gone, dead. I shot and killed her. Me.' As I say the words, I jab my left thumb into my chest for exaggeration, and in hindsight, that was probably too provocative; his reaction is intense. He flies into a rage and begins to stand up, unbelievably lifting the bed he is tied to with his mother lying on it, ripping two bolts from the floor. I put the shotgun down and run into the room, pick up the loose rope end, slip the knot holding it, and pull for all I'm worth. The slack is gone in a second as the rope tightens around his neck, and the knot of the noose forces his head to one side. He groans as I put my full weight on the rope, having the effect of strangling him. After about thirty seconds, his struggle begins to quickly subside, and I slowly let off some slack in the rope. He slumps back down to the floor with a thud, the bed crashing down to the floor again at the same time.

He's coughing and spitting, then looks up to me, the evil in his eyes burning. 'I'll kill ya slowly. Then I'll roast ya over a fire like a hog on a spit. You are one fucking dead man, and I will eat your roasted flesh.'

I've heard enough and put my full weight on the rope again. Instantly, his head jerks upward, but this time, from his sitting position, the rope has a greater effect. His tied legs flail uselessly on the bare wood boards, his eyes wide open and tongue protruding from his mouth. I keep the rope tight, wanting to show him who is in charge here.

Just as he starts to lose consciousness, I release the tension on the rope, and he slumps back down against the bed frame, his head dropping forward, his chin resting on his chest. I pull a bottle of water from the side pocket of my fatigues and, removing the cap, take a drink before spraying some of the water over his head.

'Wake up, big boy, you have some answers I want.'

His coughing starts again, with his head bouncing up and down. Reaching down behind the door frame, I pick up the steel bucket of trough water I had prepared earlier and throw it at him, instantly thoroughly drenching him. He looks up at me again, and his stare puts me in no doubt he would kill me in a second if he could break free.

'Now we have worked out that Shotgun Woman on the bed there is your mother; who is that over there?' indicating to the lifeless body of Kelly.

'Fuck you!'

I quickly snatch the rope downward, yanking his head upward and to one side. He yelps out, his face contorted. Remaining calm, I look at him in pain, 'Look, there is an easy way to do this or a hard way; it's up to you.'

Releasing the tension again, he slumps back down to the floor. One thing is clear to me now, whilst I can torment him in this manner to get the information I need, I won't be able to send him on his way by hanging him; I'll never raise his weight fully away from the floor. It's then that Emily's comment about the shotgun comes to me; was she hinting that the shotgun would be the best way to dispatch him? Did she do that with Paul, or at least have a hand in his death?

He groans and curses again. I go to raise my right hand high again on the rope, and he starts to shake his head, mumbling 'no' repeatedly. It's having the desired effect.

'So, Gunnarsson, who is she, this girl, Kelly?'

'What's it ya?'

'I want to know so we can let her family know what happened to her.'

'She has no family to speak of.'

'There is always someone to inform. Now tell me what you know, or I'll hoist you up again.'

'Fuck you!'

I pull down hard on the rope, getting an instant reaction from Gunnarsson, but this time, he is trying to fight it. Reaching my left hand higher on the fully tensioned rope, I jump up and grab tight, and instantly, the rope responds, lifting Gunnarsson off his backside and slowly rotating him as he tries to hold some of his weight on his trussed up and bent legs. Somehow, he finds the will to straighten his legs and stand up, instantly dropping me to the floor, but I don't let go of the rope; this is the only thing keeping this monster under control now.

Quickly finding my feet, I jump up, reach higher for the rope and grip it tightly, then swing on the rope, lifting both my feet into the air. My full weight now pulling the rope downward on my side of the beam but upwards on his. Although my full weight is not enough to lift him from the floor, he is now on tiptoes, trying to relieve the pressure on his neck from the tightening noose. He starts to fade, and once again, his eyes are seemingly popping, and his tongue sticking out from his mouth, the colour draining from him.

As he starts to slip into unconsciousness, I wait another few seconds, then let go of the rope, landing on my feet as he drops to the floor once again, this time without any finesse, like a sack of grain falling from a cart. He must now be starting to realise this is not a good place for him anymore, that he can't escape the inevitable.

'We can do this all night long if you want, Gunnarsson, I'm in no rush.'

I can hear him struggling to suck in oxygen between bouts of coughs. Taking the bottle of water from my pocket again, I spray his face, and he responds by trying to take in as much water as possible.

'Now, who is Kelly?'

He is trying to speak, but his throat must be dry, constricted and damaged by now. 'She… she… is… my… daughter.'

'What? Your daughter? You kept your daughter a prisoner in chains? What kind of sick bastard are you, Gunnarsson?'

Coughing, he tries to speak again, 'It's… what… she… wanted. She wanted to do this... for me.'

So that's why she wasn't chained up properly, and she had that knife; it was subterfuge. She was in on this from the beginning. He is quite a piece of work this Gunnarsson; him, his mother, and now his daughter, all three of them in on it together. How can this even begin to become a thing?

'So, hang on, ha, forgive the pun; while Emily thought Kelly was another abductee, she was really acting as a jailor for you; is that right?'

'Fuck you.'

I snatch the rope down hard. He feels it straight away and grimaces at me as we eyeball each other, him trying to spit at me, but he has no saliva. I release the tension in the rope again.

'Why did you abduct Emily?'

'Why not? She is what I wanted, so I went out, and I got her, just like all the others.'

'The others?'

'Yeh, all of 'em.'

His calmness and matter-of-fact delivery are starting to interest me, especially given he must know what is going to happen to him. There is no way I'm going to let him live; I've killed his mother, Ernesto killed his daughter, but he thinks it was me, and ultimately, Emily needs protection from this animal.

'Where are these others? Did you kill them?'

'No, my Kelly did, when she was tired of them, or ya know, when she got real jealous of them, ya know what I mean?' He has mustered up something to spit in my direction and attempts to hit me. I sidestep it easily enough.

'Where are they? Did you bury them?'

'Nah, Mama and Kelly buried them out in the woods. I always say, *"Them that made the mess can clear it up"*. I just go out to get me another guest when I need one.'

It is saying something that this person can even make me feel sick.

'Is there anyone else involved in this, Gunnarsson? Have you any other accomplices?'

'Like I'm going to fucking tell you. Go screw yourself, fucking limey!' He tries to lash out with his bound legs but is short of reaching me by a couple of feet.

I don't think he'll give me any more information, and what I've got is more than I thought I would get out of him. The sun is settling on the horizon behind me, and it'll soon be dark. Time to finish this while I still have some daylight left.

Letting go of the rope, he sees his opportunity to make a move, but as he struggles to get to his feet, I step backwards and reach out with my right hand for the shotgun leaning on the door frame. As I pull it in and raise it to my shoulder, he manages to get to his feet. Although staggering because of the binds to his ankles and around his knees, he tries to jump forward toward me as I calmly take aim. Then, as he takes another small hop forward, I squeeze the trigger.

The boom echoes around the wooden room; I wasn't expecting the recoil to impact my shoulder as much as it did, knocking me off balance, and I stagger backwards. The blast hits him squarely in the chest, and he moves backwards, away from me, the blast physically lifting him, forcing him toward the bed and hitting the iron frame before slumping in a pile at the foot of the bed. The damage to his chest is enormous; I have never contemplated the effects of a close-up shotgun impact on a human body before. Blood and tissue seem to have flown out in all directions, and I realise I've just lost my chance of trying to make this look like a murder-suicide; there's not much more I can do now.

I clean the shotgun down of all traces of me and Ernesto, removing anything of any evidential value. Leaving Gunnarsson like that, tied up with a gunshot to his chest, indicates an execution-style killing, but I'm not going to fish around in what is left of him to untie ropes and his binds and risk further scene contamination. I was going to place Ernesto's pistol next to Gunnarsson when I had the murder-suicide plan, but now, I'll remove all the weapons to make it look like some kind of gang killing or something, the perpetrators taking their guns with them; I'll dispose of them on my way back into town.

Re-checking everything, I slowly step backwards out of the room and close the door behind me. Turning towards the main house, I stop and decide to reopen the door to the room; any wildlife around here needing a feed will be able to feed on him, making more of a mess of the scene for the police to deal with if they ever venture out this way.

Picking up an empty meal sack from one of the outbuildings, I return to the hidden room and take down all the photos and articles regarding Emily, putting them in the sack along with his laptop and printer; I can't leave anything behind that will link Emily to this place.

I'm sure I have everything now loaded into the back of the van that I want to remove from this place. The sun has fallen below the horizon, and the twilight is diminishing quickly. Before climbing into the driver's seat, I look back to the buildings; it's not gone entirely the way I planned it, but we got Emily out safely, and all three participants involved in or related to her abduction are dead inside that room. We've managed to keep a lid on her kidnapping and not involve the police, and no one has found out about my illegal hacking of the hospital CCTV system. Hopefully, when the police finally get here, they will believe this was some kind of deal gone wrong, or maybe Kelly had an unknown boyfriend that exacted some vengeance for some reason on the three of them; whatever they come up with, we need to be sure we are far from this place when they do.

As I start the engine, I still can't believe that Shotgun Woman was his mother and Kelly his daughter, and that they were all actively participating in abductions and killing of young women. I'm glad they are all gone now and that I had an active part in their demise, bringing about closure in this matter. The note I've left on the dressing table indicates the possibility of other missing women being buried in nearby woods. Hopefully, the police pick up on this and find their remains, allowing at least their families some kind of closure. The police will no doubt want to search for the note writer, but I'm hoping they will settle at closing the missing women cases without the desire to hunt me down; this is something I know creates a risk of me being tracked by the authorities, but it's the right thing to do for those women and their families.

Turning on the headlights and putting the van into drive, I release the parking brake and drive away slowly from the ranch. Turning onto the single access track, I glance a look backwards through the side mirror, and the ranch has already disappeared, consumed into the dark of the creeping night, hopefully never to be seen again by me.

47

Grace

Hospital

Entering her room, I look at her sitting up in bed, dozing, her chest rising and falling lightly in short breaths. I look at her; she's just another one, another of those frail people taking up a valuable hospital bed, distracting medical expertise from where it's best used and most needed.

And this one, she's different. She's a convicted murderer.

It's been nearly three days since she made her confession to her daughter, the one I watched after I'd finished my shift that afternoon via the video camera I'd placed in her room. Why must we spend valuable, highly trained personnel and resources to keep her alive any longer than she deserves? She was sentenced to the death penalty, and I'm going to ensure she gets it. She was found guilty by a jury and sentenced to death. Then, through the timing of events, she manages to avoid the lethal injection when her long ago stolen daughter is found alive. But I know the whole truth now, and I know she rightly deserves the death penalty.

Apart from her daughter, I'm the only one who knows about her confession, and no one knows that I know. A perfect opportunity, as the finger of blame, will never point at me.

Closing the door behind me, I cross the room to the window and quietly turn the handle to close the blinds. After she confessed her sins to her daughter, I thought her daughter wouldn't want to see her alive again after hearing what she did. Given that almost three days have passed, during which she's been in her room all that time on her own with no visitors, her daughter's absence screams volumes to me; she's made her decision to stay away from her evil mom. My goal is to arrange her dispatch from this place; after all, I am in the caring profession.

I'd say her daughter was hurt significantly enough not to return to her "*darling mother*" and, in all likelihood, will not miss her when she's gone. In fact, I don't think anyone will really miss her; maybe that author will, but he'll still write his book either way.

So, I'll put an end to this charade now; the best outcome for all involved, and at least I'll know that justice will have been served, justice as it was sentenced, carried out. I turn to her and see her eyes are open, watching me; it's as if she knows what is coming her way, as though she is reading my mind. Approaching the bed, I remove the nurse call button from her side and place it just out of her reach, then look at her, my smile portraying I'm here to care for her, but really, I'm super excited at the thought of extinguishing her life.

She'll be the third I've killed in this room, another one all alone, which will be my seventh in total, all dying of seemingly natural causes. My enjoyment comes from helping them escape their suffering, holding their hand as I administer the final treatment, whether they want to receive it or not. But this time, I'm dispatching one that truly deserves it, doubling the fulfilment I'll get from this, as she is not an innocent, and I will be doing a service to others; it's they just won't know it; my little secret.

Holding her hand softly, I rotate it to access the catheter already inserted in the back of her hand, and from within my tunic, I remove the already prepared syringe. She is watching me, her eyes following my every move. I push the end of the Luer lock into the receiver on the saline connector and twist it slightly but firmly, clicking it into place. I watch her closely, as I don't want to miss anything. Placing my thumb over the syringe thumb rest and two fingers beneath the finger flange, I smile at her, holding the knowledge these are her last few seconds, then very slowly start to depress the plunger.

She looks at me, and at first, I can see what looks like a concern in her eyes, the fear of what I'm about to do; this is the look that gives me the greatest buzz, the almost silent pleading to spare them. But then, slowly and unexpectedly, she places her right hand on my forearm, looks at me and says quietly, 'Thank you.'

I'm instantly annoyed; this is not the charitable act that she thinks it is, and I speak out when normally I wouldn't at this precious time, 'No! I'm not doing this for you; this is for me.'

'Yes, I know it is. My thanks are from one murderer to another,' she replies.

'But you're ruining it, I'm in control here, not you. This is for me.'

'I know it is. You are in control, but it's also helping me. I've had enough of life now and want to let go. I've confessed my sins. Thank you for doing this.'

I look down at the syringe and realise I have pushed it all the way in, and she has received a full dose, much more than is needed; it's too late for me now to pull back from this without alerting others. I am angry with her, but I need to stay in control and not show any further displeasure; I'll not give her the satisfaction that she is in any way winning here.

'I've been looking forward to this moment since you arrived, Angela.'

'Yes, I, I know, I see it in you.'

Her eyes close, and her head drops backwards onto the pillow. I lean back slightly and breathe deeply, watching her as her chest rises and falls, and I quickly reach forward, placing my hand over her palpitating heart to experience the exact moment when it stops. Her thin, frail body makes it easier for me to feel her heartbeat, which is starting to slow now, slower, shallower. This is a good death for her, far better than she deserves.

Then I get the rush, the satisfaction when I realise there is no beat left. I extract the curled-up stethoscope from my tunic pocket and listen to be sure. It's done; she got her lethal injection at the end, as she duly deserved.

While I achieved the outcome I intended, it wasn't all that I wanted it to be, and I expected to reap greater enjoyment. I should have been the one in complete control, but she denied me that. She really was a selfish bitch, always intent on getting her way, even at the end.

I can stay mad at this, or I can move on. This was only one, and while it had a novelty twist to it, I decide to accept it's not worth getting all worked up about. There will always be more.

48

Emily

Hotel Bedroom

The water is hot, and I've nearly emptied my shower gel bottle with the constant scrubbing, trying to remove any trace of Him and that place. I cried when Ernesto got me to his vehicle, and he comforted me, embracing me with his right arm, reinforcing that I was safe and leaving the horror behind me. But my concern quickly turned to Martin; he stayed behind on his own to clean up the situation and take care of Him.

Him. Ernesto filled me in on who he is, Job Gunnarsson, a man with a history, but Ernesto wouldn't tell me how they found out about Gunnarsson, how they knew it was him who had taken me, and how they found out where his ranch was, consistently replying that Martin will fill me in later.

Later, when Martin comes back to me, assuming he comes back, I'll be sure to get the full story from him.

Stepping out of the shower and wrapping a large white towel around me, I reach for another smaller towel and wrap my hair in it, twisting the towel into a kind of turban and flicking the loose ends over my back. Then, looking up at the obscured mirror, I wipe it to see my reflection.

I look tired, feel dirty still, and I'm worried about Martin; I want him here, now, safe with me.

As I dry myself, I think over the last few hours. Ernesto stressed I must remain calm, not get twitchy and call the police, that I have to stay patient, and that he has every faith in Martin. On the way back, we stopped by his cousin's home to get cleaned up, and his cousin's wife generously lent me some clothes. Calls were made, and his aunt and uncle arrived within ten minutes, with his aunt instantly tending to the wound on his arm with an aid kit she brought with her, and as she tended to Ernesto's arm, she quietly murmured what I presume were prayers or blessings. The wound was quite long and deep, and she expertly cleaned it, then started to deftly stitch the cut. Watching how she worked with confidence and without hesitation, I was convinced she must be a nurse or medical practitioner. Ernesto confirmed this after leaving them, saying that years earlier, she had also served in the army, in the medical corps. His uncle looked concerned, watching over me closely but saying nothing; it was clear Ernesto's aunt ruled the relationship and was in charge. Ernesto and his uncle stepped out back at one point, and no doubt Ernesto explained just enough to appease him, his aunt seemingly not wanting to know, well, not outwardly anyway. On leaving, his aunt hugged me and whispered something I couldn't quite make out, and his uncle nodded once to me without any words or sound. Ernesto embraced his cousin and his wife, exchanging quiet words, and she hugged me tightly, kissing my cheek. Ernesto's family clearly love him and trust him; to be honest, I wouldn't know what to do if I had a relative turn up after dark with a knife wound accompanied by a stranger, but they did, and it didn't phase them at all.

After drying, I slip on the cotton robe hanging in the bathroom and re-enter the bedroom, looking at the bedside clock just as the digital numbers switch to midnight. Where is he?

I want to call someone and find out what was going on, but Ernesto made me promise not to do anything. The inactivity, the silence, the not knowing, is eating at me. Switching on the television, I aimlessly skip between channels, not registering what's showing, before turning it off again. I open the refrigerator to remove a small bottle of gin and a can of tonic water when a knock on the door startles me, and I drop them both on the carpet. Standing still, looking at the door, I'm frozen, unsure of what to do; is it Martin or Gunnarsson? Has Gunnarsson come back for me?

Another knock, slightly louder, but this time followed by a familiar and welcome voice, 'Emily, it's me, Martin.'

Running to the door, I scrabble at the locking mechanism and door chain to open it quickly, and as I pull it back, Martin is standing there with a small, confident smile and his arms outstretched. As I fall into his arms, he wraps his around me, and I feel him deeply exhale, as though he knows he can now relax, that it's done, it's behind him. I look up to his face, and without further words, we kiss deeply. As I pull him tighter to me, I want him to know we are one, that I am grateful, and that I love him for what he has done for me.

Without any real thought, we slowly stagger backwards into my hotel room, and Martin closes the door behind him with a trailing foot, all the while we remain kissing. He bends and swings his right arm around behind my legs and sweeps me up, my hair towel falling to the floor as he takes me towards the bedroom. I want this. I want him. My saviour.

49

Martin

Hotel Room

My mobile phone, vibrating on the bedside cabinet, wakes me, shaking me from my dream. Through bleary eyes, I look at the clock, ten twenty-two; jeez, I must have needed that sleep. Swinging my left arm out to reach for Emily, her side of the bed is empty, and I sit quickly, scanning the room, looking for her. Soft humming emanating from the bathroom confirms she's safe and nearby. I turn back to my phone and pick it up, looking at the screen to see that it's Mary calling. I take a deep breath before accepting the call.

'Good morning, Mary, how are you?'

'Good morning, I'm fine, sweetheart, but I need to speak with Emily, do you know where she is? I've tried her cell a few times, but it keeps going to voice mail. I've left messages for her to call me back, but she hasn't returned them. It's important I speak with her.'

'Argh, yes, she's here with me, just in the bathroom. Yeah, sorry, Emily lost her phone the other day and hasn't purchased a new one yet. Do you want to leave a message with me, or should I get her now?'

'I'd rather speak with Emily directly, if that's OK with you?'

'Yes, of course, one minute, I'll just get her.'

Tapping the mute button on my screen and swinging my legs to the floor, I stand and feel my muscles ache as I approach the bathroom door to interrupt Emily's humming.

'Emily, darling, Mary is on the phone; she wants to speak with you.'

'Oh, er.' The door opens, and she is standing in a white cotton robe with her hair in a towel. 'What do I say?'

'Nothing. What is there to say? I just said you lost your mobile phone a few days ago and haven't managed to pick up a replacement yet. She won't know of anything else, promise. Just go along with the conversation, but it sounds important, and she's adamant she wants to speak to you.'

'Ah, OK,' as she takes the mobile from me and sits on the edge of the bed.

'Best you put it on loudspeaker so I can help if needed,' I suggest.

Emily looks at the screen, taps the speaker button, and then unmutes the microphone. 'Hi, Mary, I trust you are well. Martin just mentioned you've been trying to get in contact with me; sorry, I lost my phone. Is everything OK?'

Mary replies, and I hear her clearly. 'Well, no, not really, sweetheart. You see… well, there's no easy way to break this to you, but… well, your mother, she passed away late yesterday afternoon. I'm so sorry, sweetheart, you didn't get much time with her, but what you did have, I'm sure, will be a blessing to you. The hospital tried to get a hold of you last night, and then they contacted me. I'm so sorry for your loss.'

I look at Emily; she seems lost, stunned almost, not knowing what to say. I feign surprise at this news to

Emily, fully aware of what Emily knows about Angela, but Emily doesn't know that I know. I need to play a role here that I didn't expect to play, the unwitting but supporting partner. She will be torn over this news, conflicted with the knowledge Angela is dead and probably happy with that outcome, but having to pretend to Mary and others to come, including me, that she is heartbroken. It just seems this story of Emily and Angela is one of those that keeps on giving. How do I support her now, knowing what I know? But support her, I must.

'Emily, sweetheart, you there?' Mary asks.

We look at each other, and I nod ever so gently to Emily, outwardly expressing to her my sorrow and regret at this news. It seems that almost instantly, she feels alone again. I sit beside her on the bed, put my arm around her and pull her into me. She looks up at me, and I know that look, the look of I don't really care, and I understand why. I decide to speak up.

'Hi Mary, sorry, Emily has the mobile on loudspeaker, and I heard you.' I need to play along with this deception as well, 'Late yesterday afternoon, you say?'

'Yes, quietly in her sleep. The nursing team thought she was resting and left her undisturbed, but by early evening on serving supper, they realised she had already passed. They're not sure what time, but rest assured, it was peaceful.'

'Oh, I see, well that's a blessing, I suppose, it's good to know. Has the hospital said anything further?'

'No, not really. Naturally, they need some instructions, you know, the arrangements and all; maybe you could help Emily with this, Martin?'

'Sure, of course. I'll call them straight after this call.'

'Thank you,' Mary replies. 'The hospital did mention that Emily had not visited Angela recently; is everything alright there?'

Emily has still not spoken, so I take the initiative and steer away from providing a direct answer. 'As you can imagine, Mary, this is awful news for Emily; she is clearly upset here. Can we call you back later?'

'Yes, of course, of course, sweethearts, whenever y'all ready, call me. Would y'all like me to head up there and help with the arrangements and all or…?'

'That's kind of you to offer, but no, thank you, we'll manage. I've got this with Emily. We'll call you later, thank you.'

'OK, anything y'all need, just let me know. Angela and Emily will both be in my prayers today. Speak later, bye for now.'

'Thank you again, not easy news to deliver on the phone. Goodbye, Mary,' and I close the call immediately to cut off the opportunity for a return comment.

Looking at Emily, she's not expressing any emotion, which doesn't surprise me. I pull my arm in again, squeezing her to reinforce I'm here for her. Her mind will be in overdrive now, working out how to approach this situation, coming on top of the ordeal she's just been through. Does bad luck reside in Emily's shadow? It never seems that far from her.

We sit there for a few minutes, both thinking of what to say next, and it's Emily who breaks the silence.

'I have something to tell you about Angela.'

50

Martin

White Creek Ranch

I have to hand it to Job Gunnarsson, using a remote derelict ranch is a perfect place for what we do. No CCTV, no prying eyes or curious neighbours, no one to hear the screams, nothing to worry about. This is one of the advantages of having access to all this wide open, remote land for people who do what we do.

'So, you thought you could have the kill for yourself?'

She nods frantically, then realises that was the wrong response and shakes her head from side to side vigorously, the lashings keeping the rest of her body immobile. I take a grip on the gag tied tightly across her mouth and release the pressure slightly, slipping it down off her chin so that she can speak.

'How many have you dispatched like that?' I ask her calmly.

She coughs and tries to lick her lips, her mouth evidently dry as she hasn't had any water for a few hours now. I reach around and lift the bottle from the workbench, unscrew the top and place it to her lips. She tries to gulp at the water as I trickle it over her lips and mouth. 'Slowly, slowly, water is a precious resource that must not be wasted.'

She clears her throat and, in doing so, tries to spit at me, but she can't muster enough moisture to make it meaningful, reminding me of Gunnarsson's last moments.

'That's not very nice, especially from a nurse; tut, tut, and I thought you were from the caring profession.'

I watch her as she struggles against the restraints but gets nowhere. I start to pull the bottle back from her, and she cranes her neck, following it as I slowly withdraw it, tipping it upright and replacing the plastic cap. Dropping her head down again, she licks her lips, seeking every bit of the water that she can.

'So, how many have you killed then? And lying to me wouldn't be a good idea.'

'A few,' her curt reply, followed by a large sniff and grimace, as though in defiance.

'Umm, a few. More than five?' She doesn't answer straight away, probably thinking of how to reply to maximise the chance of being spared from this situation. 'Well?'

'Yes.'

'So, you are officially a serial killer. Umm, I now have an immobilised serial killer at my mercy; what do you think I should do with her?'

She coughs again. 'You should be a hero and turn me over to the police; you will be the person who captured the killer of Angela Collins.'

'And the others… how many others, Grace?'

'Why?'

'Then I'll know what to say to the police to big up my hero status.' I say this with confidence, knowing there is no way she'll be turned over to the police, but I may uncover the truth if she thinks there's an outside chance of surviving this.

'She was my seventh.'

'Seven? Wow, you have been busy. And these other six, were they all as deserving as Angela Collins?'

'In my eyes, yes, I thought so.' She pauses, thinking of what to say next. Quite calmly and almost disturbingly, she continues, 'They were all a burden in some way to our system, a burden to their families and to society.'

'Oh, is that in your opinion?'

'Yes, it's my opinion, and if any rational person were to take a step back and examine this logically, sensibly, they would come to realise this provides the best all-around solution, and they'll come to agree with me.'

'Is that so? They will allow you to enact euthanasia without the victim's consent, really? So, the family members don't get a say; they don't even get to spend the last minutes of life with their loved ones? How can that ever be right?'

'Because, if we leave it to them, they won't make the hard decision that is needed… the right decision; their emotions will get in the way of reaching that logical conclusion.'

'So, the basis of your ideology is that a sane, logical person would shoot a lame horse or a sick dog, but that same person would let their loved one suffer on.'

'Yes, that's what happens; people are too emotional for their own good. We both appreciate this, don't we?'

She is trying to reason with me and win me over to her way of thinking. Whilst I appreciate some of her logic, my reply scotches that plan. 'No, Grace, no, that isn't right. There has to be a right of choice, a decision made by a loved one or family member or the patient themselves; anything else is just murder, and anarchy would follow. Anyway, who appointed you as the righteous taker of life?'

I watch the glimmer of hope slowly disappear from her eyes. She knows now that this is not a debate she is going to win. She switches tactics.

'Where are we? What is this place?'

'We are at the end of the world. We are nowhere. There is nothing out there, and there is only us in here, just us.'

'How did you find out about me, that it was me that killed her?' she asks. 'I'm always very careful.'

'One simple mistake tripped you up. I didn't see it at first, even though it was staring me in the face. I didn't notice that one tiny detail that led to your downfall until recently.'

'I don't make mistakes,' she replies.

'Oh, but you did on this occasion. It was the camera in the room; it was the only hospital room with a camera fitted, and the output was monochrome, old-style black and white output, but with good definition and audio capability. The rest of the cameras in the hospital are all high definition, full colour, high quality outputs, but without audio. In hindsight, it was clearly a different installation, eventually dawning on me that your camera was a parasitic attachment, piggybacking off the hospital-installed system. At first, I thought it was odd for a hospital to install room cameras to monitor patient activity, but at the time, I didn't give it much thought as I rejoiced in what I'd hacked into and the benefits it could bring me for the book, including collecting information on Angela covertly. Sometime later, when I did think of it further, the difference in the output, I considered it may have been put there by a journalist or someone looking for a scoop or inside line on Angela, but it still allowed me access to her without her knowing, and I just accepted it for what it was. But then, no one released the scoop that it captured, no one sold Angela's confession to the newspapers or wider media. So, that got me thinking, who, having heard and seen Angela's confession and had a recording of it, would choose to ignore it and not take material advantage of exploiting the death out of it? And, importantly, why? Who would gain an advantage in another way, and what could that advantage be?'

'It could have been installed by anyone.'

'And yet it wasn't, it was you. It recorded the very moment you killed Angela, picking up the words between the two of you; even though faint, they can be heard. When you stood up, you turned and looked up at the hidden camera's location, smiling. You. You put it there as you wanted a video record of your kill. It reminded me of a similar event I was embroiled in some time ago…'. I pause, taking some pleasure in remembering the holiday cottage, of what happened there and what followed afterwards. 'Anyway, that's another story, a different time. All that I want to know now is how many you have killed so I can include them in the aggregate count and won't be forgotten.'

She looks at me puzzled, 'What?'

'So that their deaths now contribute to the total count.'

'What, you mean your count?'

'Umm, well, they shouldn't be lost, should they? They all have meaning. We are in a small, unique club, you and I, a club of exclusive membership. When it dawned on me what you were doing, I was surprised I hadn't spotted it earlier. Angela did, though, didn't she? She saw it in me, too, the hidden darkness within a killer.'

'Angela only saw it in me at the very end.'

'Yes, maybe that's true, or maybe she saw it earlier and thought you were to be her release, giving her the confidence that she could speak the truth about what she did and not be around long enough to be returned to prison.'

'You give her too much credit; I don't think she was that smart.'

'Oh, she was, possibly a few errors along the way, but she made her own decisions right until the end. And now look where we are.'

Not wanting to hear any more from her, I try to replace the gag back across her mouth, and she resists, violently twisting her head from left to right and shouting out. Placing my right hand around the grip, I gently withdraw Gunnarsson's stainless-steel hunting knife from its sheath fastened to my belt and slowly but carefully move it across her face, making sure she sees it, bringing it to rest, hovering with the point about half an inch above her right eye. She freezes.

As I re-affix the gag with my left hand, the fear in her eyes intensifies.

'Is this what you revel in, Grace, enthralling in the victim's fear? I must admit, it is a rush. I can see how this can be highly addictive.'

I step back, moving half a pace away from her, watching her closely as she starts to sob. Noticing the dark, wet patch slowly expanding in her light blue jeans, I decide the time has come to end this. My weapon of choice has always been a blade. I trust in the steel and my ability to use it effectively. Holding the knife vertically over her heaving chest, her head is violently shaking from side to side again. With both hands wrapped tightly around the handle, I raise my arms and hold them at full height above her. Our eyes lock, and I can see the pleading in hers, the will to live and no doubt repent. I wait, hanging in this pose for a few seconds, then slowly, I lower my arms and, with my left hand, release her gag once again.

She speaks rapidly, 'Thank you. Thank you. Thank you.'

And I reply, 'Yes, no doubt you are thankful, but what choice did you give your victims, especially the innocent ones; did you give them back their life? Goodbye, Grace.'

I pull my arms back from her and look over her, into the shadows beyond. Switching my hold on the knife, I put the blade in my palm with my thumb holding it in place, and I offer out the knife handle to be taken.

'Yes,' she says quietly, confidently, 'I want to.'

Grace's confused look initiates the knife's transfer as I gently nod. Silently, Emily's hands pierce the cone of light first, reaching over and across Grace, ready to receive the knife. She quietly steps fully into the light. Grace's eyes widen to their extreme when she sees her, and the realisation of what this is hits her.

Taking the knife from me in both her hands, I let go completely and step backward, observing her deft and confident movements with the blade. Gripping the handle with both hands, she draws up both her arms to full height, pauses for a few seconds and then swiftly plunges the knife down into Grace's torso with all her upper body weight behind it. To me, it's in slow motion, the knifepoint puncturing her blouse and skin, the blade sinking into Grace the entire length of the fuller, only stopping when the quillon hits the outside of her chest. Emily keeps her hands wrapped around the handle, and I notice her loosen the pressure of her grip slightly, allowing her to feel Grace's final movements transferring through the steel. Grace's scream is piercing, but no one can hear her here; there is no one to come to her aid.

Red oxygenated blood flows quickly from the entry wound, her panting chest moving at a speed even I hadn't expected, her fast, sharp breathing elevating the excitement beyond anything I'd felt before. Keeping her hands lightly wrapped around the handle, Emily holds her breath and waits, just as I had advised. As Grace's breathing slows and subsides, so does the minor trembling through the knife until it stops altogether.

I release the air in my lungs, take a step forward, back into the light over the table and corpse, and breathe in again deeply, taking in what life has just escaped her body, hold myself upright for a few seconds, and then exhale slowly. Emily, following my lead, also inhales deeply.

As she releases the knife and takes a step back, I admire the clean rosewood and brass handle of the antique knife standing vertically from Grace's chest. This, to me, was another worthy kill, one to avenge all those Grace had taken, replacing the one Emily or I should have done if we'd had the opportunity with Angela.

Picking up the water bottle and taking a long drink, I survey the clean-up scene needing attention. Her body will never be found out here in the desert lands. As I wrap my right hand around the handle of the knife, I wonder if anyone will actively look for her, possibly the authorities, for a few weeks until they register her as just another one of their missing statistics, filing it away to then focus on other crimes, as if there are any more serious crimes than this.

Emily's breathing is slow and deep. As I start to slowly extract the knife, she steps forward again and places both hands around mine, gripping the handle.

'Together,' she says sweetly to me, looking deeply into my eyes.

'Yes. Together.'

51

Emily

Leaving Texas

Looking across at Martin driving with the sun slowly breaking the horizon behind us, I recall how he said he could help me, show me ways to confront my anger and emotions so that I could breathe again and take control of my life. And he was true to his word; he has done.

I have a man who completely trusts me and one I can completely trust; there are no secrets between us. Isn't that what all successful relationships are founded on, mutual trust, respect, and support?

It has been a long day and an even longer night. I'm tired. Leaning my head back on the headrest and closing my eyes, I relive her confession, my so-called mother who brought all this together, helping Martin and me to become one.

Confessing that she planned Barry's murder was shocking enough and brutal to hear, but for her then to confess that she didn't want me after my birth was even more shattering. Topping these confessions, she went a step further, confessing she was actively involved in planning my abduction, this being a further cruel, insidious act, not only to me but also to her husband,

Barry. She told me everything, the whole, horrid tale as her final confession.

In the beginning, they truly loved each other. They had a happy relationship, but then his want to have a child and their inability to conceive eventually drew Barry to the private Letona Pro Clinic in London for help to receive IVF treatment using sperm donations from my biological father, Graeme.

After a few years of trying to conceive, they had tests carried out, and Barry was devastated to find out he was sterile. This was bad news for him but good news for Angela, as she had been secretly taking birth control pills since they met. She never wanted a child or children. His insistence to have tests done meant she had to stop taking the birth control pills, or they would have shown up in her medical screening tests. During the period between no pregnancy prevention, until the results were known, she feigned her interest in having sex, saying it was due to the pressures around them, but really, she was worried about the risk of becoming pregnant. Thereafter, with the news of his sterility, her pregnancy worries were removed, and they continued to be a happily married couple.

A year or two after receiving the news of Barry's sterility, he announced he had been quietly saving up what money he could with the intention of approaching a private fertility clinic. She loved him dearly and didn't want to lose him, but she still didn't want the burden of a child. He was always talking of having a family, and now he had planned a way for them to have one. Her plan, however, was to go through with it and hope that either the process failed, or the money ran out first. However, when she became pregnant following the clinic's first treatment, she even tried on a couple of occasions to lose the pregnancy, to abort the baby, me.

Then, she had a chance encounter with Julia and Duncan Leyden while attending the clinic, the people I thought were my parents, and they hatched their plan together. Ahh, now it all makes sense, that's why Duncan said what he did when I saw him in prison, when I mentioned her illness, *"Oh, I'm so sorry to hear she's unwell"*, it's because he knew her; it came from a place of their shared knowledge, and him holding some respect for her; the bastard. Angela didn't do it for money; no, she just didn't want me - she never had. But she couldn't say that to Barry for fear of losing him. So, when the police investigation started, they could find no evidence of cash transfers or deposits, and Angela had a cast iron alibi at the time of my abduction. Angela could never really have predicted what the police would then allege, infanticide and a missing body, and how grotesque public sentiment would be to her and Barry. Poor Barry.

Barry didn't know what she had done and outwardly portrayed my abduction as a momentary lapse on her part, but all the time, quietly, he was harbouring a belief that she was negligent, blaming her for my disappearance; that belief festering all those years within him. What Angela didn't expect was for him to hold onto this belief for such a long period, never really letting it go, allowing them to move on. She half expected the public outcry, even some of the extreme comments and actions of some, but she never thought Barry would become one of them, maintaining a subtle but consistent resentment of her; she naively thought they would become closer still, sharing the grief of their stolen and lost child.

Their relationship had become one of strained existence, both believing that their wedding vows were important to the extent they stayed together. Then, that day arrived when he allegedly went too far with her, causing her to snap.

However, in her own words, Barry's treatment of her was not as extreme as she made out in her statements and in court. She told me he would drop odd comments every now and then, the occasional statement or quip, insinuating it was still her fault, but secretly knowing her role in it all, she would merely shrug it off. But then on that day, the day she killed him, he told her he'd had enough, that he was leaving her. He never said why, just that his mind was set, and he was leaving, wanting a divorce. That was the catalyst to unload on him, to tell him everything that had happened, and naturally, he was stunned. She then simply walked across the kitchen, picked up the kitchen knife, and stabbed him multiple times to death. In her words, "*He made me do it. I'd suffered the enormity of holding it all in for all those years, for him, for us, and then he just said he was leaving me, giving me no reason, just that he'd had enough, and I thought, why have I wasted all these years living this existence, living this lie when he was the one that started it all off by wanting a child?*"

Knowing what I now know, I feel genuine sorrow and compassion for Barry, the man I never met, the man that the world thinks was a cruel, sadistic, vindictive person, driving her to breaking point. He only wanted what he thought they both wanted, simply because she never told him she didn't want children. He got over the fact that he was the reason they couldn't get pregnant and proactively moved on to find a clinic that could help them. Then, after my abduction, when their world was falling apart around them, he stayed with her through it all, showing true loyalty, sympathy and support for his wife and their relationship, understandably still carry his own emotions and baggage, although now it was all clearly misguided.

Using my book, his story will be told, and she will be fully exposed for what she was and what she did. The secret the Leydens hold over me about my husband's death, if ever they disclose it, will, by comparison, be dismissed as mere fiction.

Angela's interest in me, since I was identified as her child, was really only ever about how she could use my identity to help her escape prison. Initially, she displayed the lost love and affection for her stolen baby, keeping up appearances when others were around, but it was all a front; she was different with me in private. She was adept at maintaining a false front, masterly even. Perhaps I have inherited some of those traits from her.

To the world, Angela died an expected death in hospital, the result of previous self-inflicted injuries. Only Grace, Martin, and I know the whole truth, and with Grace now dead, Angela's murder and the knowledge of Angela's confessions died with her. When we release my book, with Angela's full confessions stated, the world will then appreciate why I wasn't with her in her final days, why I couldn't bear to be near her. They will never know about Gunnarsson taking me and my time at the ranch, but hopefully, they will one day find out about the other women he took, and they murdered. Someone will stumble on Job Gunnarsson's body, lying beside Kelly's body, and that of his mother, and the note that Martin left, hopefully leading the authorities to locate the bodies of the other missing women buried out in the woods, thereby allowing some closure to the poor families.

Ernesto is back with his family. Martin is confident he will keep secret his involvement in my rescue, especially following the death of Kelly and Gunnarsson's mother and the unofficial and possibly illegal rescue he planned to free me. To help retain Ernesto's silence, Martin cleverly agreed to set up a trust fund for Ernesto's children to be used when they reach college age. Ernesto, the proud and brave man that he is, would not take anything for himself, and the fund was Martin's way of showing his, our, gratitude, and, at the same time, ensuring Ernesto's trust by playing on his integrity and family devotion.

'Tired, darling?' Martin asks, breaking the gentle hum of the car on the freeway.

Without opening my eyes, I reply, 'Yes, a little; just thinking back over the events of the last few weeks.'

'A penny for your thoughts?'

'I think, for the time being, that we should remain in the U.S. We have a new future to build together, and we still need to sit down and complete my story, finish writing the final chapters of our book; there is a publishing deadline to meet, and I hate leaving things to the last few days.'

52

Martin

Home, Los Angeles

'It feels like all those events in Texas weeks ago were actually years ago now. Our relationship is the best thing that has happened to me, ever. Between interviewing Emily for the various stages and chapters of the book, the story of her life and her rebirth, we have grown very fond of each other. I'll go to the extent of confessing to you my love for her. She is the one I want to spend the rest of my life with. I truly believe I have found my soul mate.'

'Oh, are you sure, Martin? I recall you saying that about your first wife, and look how that turned out, she was having an affair with your best friend, and they planned to murder you. Besides, my experience has told me never to mix work with pleasure, and to me, this is what you are doing.'

'Nico, Nico, you always bring my dreams down to basic facts and past events, but this time, I'm not having any of it; she is the one, and I can prove it.' I know I've had a few drinks, probably a couple too many, but I can speak like this with my brother with complete confidence, knowing it will go no further.

'If you say so, little brother, if you say so.'

'Yes, I do, I mean it. Stop being a sceptic. We have a bond just as close as the bond between you and me.'

'How can that possibly be so? Blood is thicker than water; there is no greater bond than a blood bond.'

'We have a blood bond too, Emily and I. We are bound by shared blood.'

'What does that mean? Oh, I see... is she pregnant?'

'No, no, she's not. What I mean is that we have shared a kill together. She is like me, she knows me, accepts and loves me for who I am, what I am.'

'A kill together, umm; and what are you, little brother?'

This throws me, I didn't expect him to be so blunt and ask, but I have recognised and accepted who and what I am. 'I am a serial killer. But I'll stress this, big brother, I will not and do not kill innocent people, only those that deserve it, and Emily shares this principle with me.'

'Oh, I see. So, who was this shared blood, this tie creating a close bond between the two of you?'

'She was a bad person, a nurse who killed innocent people, well, mainly innocent people. She killed old folk in their hospital beds; she thought she had a divine calling or something, doing them a favour by releasing them from their torment. Anyway, while we were rescuing Emily, this nurse actually killed Emily's mother, the mother that Emily came out here to be with. Anyway, this nurse has been released from her own torment now by Emily's own hand. I set it up, and Emily killed her while I observed. She used a knife, wanting to be up close and personal. So, we are tied together now, forever.'

'Was this the first time Emily killed a person?'

'Yes, well, no… I mean, yes. It was the first time she had actually killed someone herself.'

'You don't seem so sure, Martin.'

'I am, yes, it was the first time for her; she had only facilitated a death previously; it's a long story.'

'Umm, and why did she kill this nurse? Was it because the nurse killed her mother?'

'In part. I could see it would help her with all the turmoil and anxiety she had buried deep within her, especially after her recent kidnapping that you helped me with.'

'Ah, I see, and you love this Emily then? She makes you happy?'

'Yes, very much.'

'OK, then that is all I need to know. If you are happy, then I am also happy. Does she know of me, this love of your life?'

'Yes, I have told her all about me, about you, our past with Papa, what happened to me, of my wife, all of it. In turn, she has told me of her husband's death and her part in that. See, we have a common ground between us as we have no secrets.'

'Yes, I see. Will she come back to England with you sometime soon? I would like to meet this woman who has stolen my baby brother's heart.'

'Yes, the next time we are over the pond, I'll bring her to meet you.'

'Good, I look forward to meeting her and, of course, seeing you again. Now, you'll forgive me, I have somewhere else to be to address a matter that needs my personal attention and cannot wait.'

'Yes, of course, of course. I'm sorry for rambling on like this, I've been drinking in celebration, and I know I've probably woken you up. Emily is special to me, and I wanted you to know, Nico.'

'Do not apologise. It is good to hear from you again, to hear of your new happiness. I'm glad my man helped you when it was needed, and you managed to rescue Emily. Remember, little brother, I am always here for you, to look after you, whatever and whenever you need it.'

'I know, Nico, and I for you. Good night, big brother. I love you.'

'It's good morning here; we will speak again soon, Martin. Good luck with your book, although I am certain it will be a big success. We will speak again soon. I love you also.'

Nico ends the phone call the same way every time, never saying "goodbye" or "au revoir," just finishing his sentence and then killing the call. It's good that I can talk with him openly; he's the only man who really knows me and, until recently, the only person. But now I have a partner who really knows me, and I love her dearly.

Turning off the lamp in my study and heading into my bedroom, the bedside lamp is still on, illuminating Emily as she sleeps, a deep, peaceful sleep now that she feels safe. It took some time for her to stop having nightmares and panic attacks, and my coaching has helped her quicker than any other person I have assisted. She has such a strong personality and a determination within her that I love. She also has a caring, loving side that is bigger than I have seen or experienced with others, and with our newfound binding secret, we are inseparable.

Sitting down in the chair across from the bed, I sit quietly, looking at her, her breathing soft and serene. I never thought I would find another life partner, especially after what I experienced with my first wife, Tanya, but I have in Emily. She accepts me for what I am and who I am, and I her. There are no longer any secrets between us, and there never will be again.

She stirs slightly, and I see her open an eye slightly. Noticing the lamp is still on, she reaches from under the duvet toward the lamp switch.

'Sshh, I prefer to watch you with the light on, darling.'

She partially lifts her head from her pillow to look at me. 'Why sit over there when you could be in bed here with me? Come on,' she replies, peeling back the corner of the thin duvet and slowly stroking the bedsheet.

This woman must know now that I can never say no to her.

53

Emily

Martin's Home, Manhattan Beach, Los Angeles

It's been another full day of book discussions, experience sharing, and revelations, and Martin has thoughtfully entwined the book's development with coaching techniques to help me address the issues in my life. I have come to terms with what has happened to me and around me and why, and he has provided me with the training and coaching to handle future events should they trigger emotional responses.

Sharing his past with me has also been immensely important and cathartic for Martin and, at the same time, has helped affirm our relationship together. Killing Grace, especially in the way we did, helped break down any final, unspoken barriers between us, allowing us to be truly one. Her killing gave me an outlet for all my anger and frustrations, a channel to funnel my energies into a specific intense event and then release it. That release was intense. When Martin first suggested taking Grace and then killing her, I was shocked, but when he talked it through with me and told me he knew of Angela's confession and appreciated my need for a release, I began to see the benefit, coupled with the societal benefit of taking a callous murderer out of circulation; it felt the right thing to do, and afterwards, I was sure of it.

Martin told me about the hospital camera and how he used his brother, Nico, for a contact to identify Gunnarsson and locate his ranch. It all made sense when I heard him out, and I now appreciate why, of course, we couldn't go to the police with this knowledge; if he had done so, then Gunnarsson, his mother, and his daughter may have escaped, or I may have been killed in the middle of some botched rescue attempt, and poor Martin would have been in trouble for accessing what became apparent, an illegal camera installation, and not reporting any of it immediately. Having Ernesto assist us made all the difference, and I will be eternally grateful to him for his commitment, discretion, and the devotion he has to his own family, and how his wider family accepted me that night without question.

Angela's funeral was a surreal event. I gave strict instructions that it had to be a closed family event, meaning only Martin and I attended. Martin let it be known that media attention would be inappropriate at that time and that, in due course, the book would address personal matters quite openly. Angela was cremated, and I threw her ashes in a trash can within a mile of the crematorium without a second thought. I will include this in the book, and the world will appreciate my decisions when they become aware of all the facts. Martin still has a copy of Angela's video confession in case it is ever needed for corroboration, although I'm unsure how we will justify why we had it and how it was acquired, we can cross that bridge, if necessary, in the future.

Nico sounds like a fascinating man; Martin mentioned their recent conversation, and I'm looking forward to meeting him soon. The bond between the two of them is intense and understandably so. Before this whole event in the States, I would probably have been horrified to meet such a person as Nico, especially in the knowledge of some of his business dealings that Martin has mentioned, but strangely now, I feel like he is family, that he has a love for his brother which is unbreakable, and he only has the very best intentions for Martin's protection and future. I love that about him. I wish now I had grown up with an older brother or sister to look up to and share things with, but that possibility was taken from me years ago by Angela and the Leydens. I have my half-siblings, but after all that happened, we rarely communicate. It's such a shame as we could have been close; maybe I'll try harder to reconnect with them when we're back in the UK.

Now, to this evening, what shall I wear? Martin is attending a high-power dinner meeting with a film production company, with the agenda focussed on film potential, syndication, royalty rights, and all those other matters that, quite frankly, bore me, although I do accept that they are essential as it's the way the media business operates. I have suggested to Martin that I am willing to invest a substantial sum of my inheritance from my former husband in the film production in exchange for a sensible shareholding, and he has my blessing to explore this opportunity during the discussions this evening if the opportunity arises.

The book deal is done with only two people at the publishers having knowledge of the book's most explosive content. I'm absolutely convinced it'll be a bestseller in its first week of publication, especially given the pre-release marketing and airtime that the publishers are planning.

So, rather than stay home alone tonight, I'm going out to meet up with some new friends I've made down at the local gym. A few drinks and a bite to eat, and I should hopefully be home by eleven to hear what news Martin brings. These are exciting times for us both; I never thought that one day I'd be in Los Angeles involved in the movie-making business.

Anyway, back to the present. Staring into my open wardrobe, I'm unsure whether to wear something more formal or dress casually. I should have asked Martin for his opinion before he left.

54

Martin

Manhattan Beach, Los Angeles

Sitting back in the Uber and reflecting, that meeting could not have gone any better. The last-minute, unannounced invite of mine to the dinner of Victoria, one of the book publishing directors, was a masterstroke by me; she is well known and respected in the publishing world and is one of the few who know the content of the book and bombshell revelations; she was instrumental in helping me strike a fabulous outline deal with the movie company, and I must thank her properly tomorrow. Of course, her interests are also well served. A successful book launch, followed by an award-winning, high box office movie, can only lead to more book sales, serialisation, and international recognition for her publishing company. It's a win-win outcome for all.

I don't think I could be any happier in my life than right now. I have a woman who loves me, trusts me, and I her; we are on the threshold of fabulous wealth and celebrity status, industry recognition and adoration, and both our pasts are behind us. We have a future to plan together now, and I'm itching to get inside and let Emily know the outcome of tonight's meeting. Surprisingly for me, I declined the offer of wine and champagne for most of the evening until the deal was summarised, as I wanted to keep a clear head and stay on track with the discussions; thereafter, I took a few drinks in celebration. I'm now feeling quite merry, although a little tired, the recognisable symptoms of an adrenalin drop that I've experienced before.

Entering my front door, the house alarm warning is activated, and I punch in my six-digit code to disarm it. I expected Emily to be home by now, and focussing on my wristwatch, it's just after eleven thirty. Pulling out my mobile, I navigate to my favourites and call her mobile; if she's still out, I'll go and join her to celebrate some more. The call instantly goes to her voicemail service, and I leave a short message for her to call me back.

Heading into the kitchen, I decide on a glass of water to help my hydration in anticipation of another round of celebratory drinks. Taking a bottle of spring water from the refrigerator, I unscrew the cap and take a large drink of the cold water. As I place the half-empty bottle back down on the worktop, my mobile rings in my pocket. Aha, Emily. Fishing it out, the screen shows "No Number", and decide to cancel the call; if they don't share a number, then I won't share a conversation.

Placing my phone down on the worktop, it rings again; persistent beggars they are. Ah, but it could be Emily using a borrowed phone if her battery has run out, so I pick it up again and press the answer button.

'Hello, Martin speaking, is your battery dead again?'

A female voice replies in a soft Californian accent, 'Is that Mr Martin Nicholson?'

She seems rather officious. 'Yes, who is this, please?'

'Officer Remes, LAPD, Sir. I understand you know a Miss Emily Collins, a British citizen; is that correct?'

'Er, yes, I do. Is everything OK?'

'Mr Nicholson, we obtained your name and cell number from a friend of Miss Collins. Can I ask, what is your relationship to Miss Collins?'

'We are working on a book together. She came over to the States to meet up with her dying mother, and we have become quite close friends over the last couple of months or so. What is it I can help you with? Is Emily OK?'

'Sir, I have to inform you that Miss Collins was the victim of a street robbery earlier this evening after leaving the… Conshellia Restaurant, on Broad Avenue, where she had dined with friends.'

This news startles me, 'Oh my god, yes, that's correct, that's where she was going. Where is she now? Is she OK?'

'Sir, it is with deepest regret I have to inform you that Miss Collins died as a result of injuries sustained during the robbery.'

'What?' her words are spinning around in my head. 'Died?'

'Yes, Sir, unfortunately. We will require you to attend the police station and to make a formal identification of her body as you seem to be the closest person to her here in Los Angeles.'

'Wait, what, Emily is… dead? No, that can't be. She's just out with friends, having dinner and some drinks.'

'I'm sorry, Sir. I realise this will have come as a shock to you. It seems that after leaving the restaurant and before entering a waiting taxi, she was approached by an unidentified person who proceeded to rob her at gunpoint, attempting to steal her bag and phone; she resisted, shouted out, and this person shot her twice in the chest at close range, snatched her belongings and ran off into the night. The attending paramedics attempted to save her, but she died at the scene without recovering consciousness. The perpetrator is still at large, and multiple units are working to locate them. It seems Miss Collins may have been in the wrong place at the wrong time.'

'Oh my god, no, this can't be true.'

'Sir, are you able to come down to the police station in the morning?'

I don't know what to say; is this some kind of cruel, sick joke someone is playing on me? What possible enjoyment could they get out of this?

'Sir?'

She can't be dead… We have a future together. We have plans, everything is in place. We have each other, and our future is set.

'Sir? Are you still there?'

'Er, yes. Yes, I'm still here. I'm sorry, can I take your name again?'

'Officer Remes, badge number 8763. Are you willing to come down to the station in the morning to assist us with this incident? The investigation is being handled by the Robbery Homicide team at Precinct Fourteen, located on Culver Boulevard. If you ask for a detective from Robbery Homicide at the front desk, a Detective will meet with you and bring you up to date on the latest information. They may also want to ask you a few questions for background.'

'Er, yes, er, I can. Wait while I find a pen, will you? I need to take down some details.'

'Of course, Sir, sure thing.'

I scribble down the details on a notepad in the kitchen and confirm them back to Officer Remes.

'Yes, Sir, that is correct. Thank you for your time this evening, and I am sorry for your loss.'

Sensing the call is about to end, I call out to Officer Remes in a raised voice, 'WAIT!' Then, realising I was abrupt, add, 'Sorry,' toning it down a little. 'What, er, what kind of questions will they be asking?'

'Well, Sir, I guess if Miss Collins had any enemies, received any threats recently, if there were any disagreements that could have escalated, that kind of thing.'

'Oh, right, yes, I see.'

'Once again, Sir, I am sorry for your loss,' and this time the call ends abruptly.

Standing and staring at the screen of my phone, it hits me that this must be real; Emily is dead, murdered in a street robbery. Everything starts to spin, and I feel sick. Running to the kitchen sink, I only just make it before I vomit heavily.

My eyes begin to well up, and I want to burst into tears, but the darkness within me emerges and takes over, an automatic control mechanism that detaches my emotional response and starts to bury it deep within me. But this is real; this is my Emily, my partner, my love; I mustn't bury this within me. I must act like a normal human being; I cannot let her simply become another person I knew who has died. She is my love, my soulmate. I pull my emotions back from the inner depths and scream out, loud and long, roaring out like a wounded bear in a trap. Uncontrolled tears flow down my face, and I smash my clenched fist into the door of a kitchen cupboard, splitting the timber panelling. The pain hits me, and I look down at my hand, at my reddened knuckles and grazed skin.

Enemies, she said, threats; the only thing I can think of is the Gunnarssons. Has someone linked killing Gunnarsson and his family to Emily and exacted revenge? Did the Gunnarsson's have another unknown accomplice?

I couldn't possibly tell the police what happened to Emily, what happened on that ranch, or what we did. Maybe I should warn Ernesto, though, as they could be after him or me next.

But she's dead. No, she can't leave me like this, she can't, I won't let it happen.

What can I do? Without realising, I am speed dialling Nico; I need his support, his help; I need my big brother again.

55

Nico

Arberly Manor, Northamptonshire, UK

The silent vibrations of my personal phone alert me to an incoming personal call. Looking at my phone on the desktop beside the other four mobile phones, I see it's Martin calling me via an encrypted video call app. Registering the time, it must be the small hours of the morning over there in LA. Turning from my computer screen, I stand and walk across my office to the large, armoured glass bay window overlooking the ornate gardens below, originally designed and laid out by Capability Brown, and accept the call.

Looking at the screen as the call connects, 'Hello, Martin. It must be late where you are; is everything OK?' From his breathing and his expression, he is clearly distressed.

'Nico. I…'

'Martin, what is wrong?'

'Nico… I… I don't know what to do. Emily has been shot.'

My initial thought runs to Martin having shot her, but guns are not his style; besides, only the other day, he was telling me how the two of them are made for each other, of how much he loves her; I know it wasn't him.

'What? Who has shot Emily?'

'She's… she's dead, Nico… she's gone.'

His voice is shaking, and he's in real pain; I know my little brother well. 'Oh my god, Martin, what happened?'

He starts to sob, his voice trying to articulate what happened, his face contorted, and I see the red in his eyes and the wetness on his face.

'She… she was out to dinner with friends… this evening, just… a quiet dinner, and…'

He breaks down into full crying. I catch him just as he pulls the phone away from his face, the video becoming blurred, the image moving without focussing, but the audio remains, picking up his distress. I feel his pain, his anguish. I have never seen him like this before, and I want to throw my arms around him and protect and comfort my little brother. He screams out; the sound sends a chill through me, that scream of inner pain I have heard so many times before. I continue watching the screen, waiting for him to come back to me. Waiting for more information.

'Martin,' trying to get him back on screen. 'Martin, tell me; tell me what you know? Is this someone who knows who you are, someone who knows you are my brother?'

His sobbing starts to subside. He adjusts the phone so that his face appears on the screen. 'What?'

'What happened? Do you know who did this?'

'No… no. The police said it was a street robbery gone wrong. Someone approached Emily in the street and tried robbing her, but she resisted, and they… they shot her. Why, why would she resist? Why would they shoot her? It doesn't make any sense.'

'Do the police know who the attacker is?'

'No, I don't think so, the officer never said; she said they were still trying to find the person.'

'Tell me what you know. I swear, we will find them, and we will make them pay for this.'

'I don't know much, just that when Emily left the restaurant she was walking to a taxi, they walked up to her, tried to grab her bag, she resisted, and they… they shot her. Oh, fuck, fuck... Nico, what do I do?'

It is not often that Martin asks for help, especially from me, but he did recently, and I must help him again now.

'Did they take Emily's bag? We could maybe track her mobile signal, but we must act fast.'

'I think they must have taken it; her phone is switched off; I tried calling her earlier and left a message… she must have already been…'. He starts crying again.

'Martin. Martin. I am coming to you. I'll get the next flight over; I'll get there as quick as I can. Hold on, little brother. I should be able to catch a flight in, say, four or five hours, and then I'll be with you in twelve hours after that. I will be with you today, Martin, I promise. We will sort this out together.'

'Thank you, Nico, thank you.'

'Do the police want to speak with you?'

'Yes, they want me to go the police station in the morning… why, why do you ask?'

'They must not know about me, about you, who you really are. Be careful, Martin; the police are skilled at manipulating things to their advantage. I am sorry to ask this, but do you have an alibi for the time Emily was shot?'

'What?'

'An alibi.'

His sobbing stops, and he sniffs loudly.

'Yes, yes, I suppose so; I was out to dinner with a group of business colleagues, but surely they will not think I was involved with this, will they?'

'No, I would think not, but if you have a cast iron alibi, they will focus on who actually did this rather than waste time on investigating you; many crimes are committed by someone known to the victim, and the Police always start off with those closest to the victim.'

'Me? But… it was a robbery... it went wrong.'

'I know, I know. There is a chance the L.A. police will contact the police here in the UK, and they may start to form a picture that does not exist. I am coming to you, Martin; hold tight, I will be there soon, OK, my little brother?'

'Yes, yes, thank you, Nico, I will. Thank you. Call me when you get to L.A.'

'Of course I will. I am truly sorry to hear this, Martin. I know how much you loved her and that she felt the same for you. This is a terrible tragedy, but we will get to the bottom of this, I promise. I will see you soon.'

'Thank you.'

I cancel the call and pull the phone to my chest as I look out over the gardens and sigh deeply. Poor Martin, my little brother; he really did love that woman. He is in so much pain. I wish now that I had met her.

My eyes are drawn to a movement, and I watch one of the gardeners pushing a wheelbarrow between the perfectly laid out borders, weaving around a sundial placed at the junction of crossing paths. My little brother's life seems to be full of tragedy at every turn.

Returning to my desk and computer, there are things I need to organise. Picking up one of the other phones on my desk and turning it towards me, the screen illuminates as I enter the PIN code and then tap the only contact in the phone. It rings twice before the call is answered.

'Hello, Nico.'

'Hello, Arabella, I've just received some terrible news from your neck of the woods.'

'Oh, that was quick.'

'Yes, news does travel fast these days. Any loose ends with your guy?'

'No, clean job, everything is cool.'

'Thank you for taking care of this sensitive matter for me so quickly. As we agreed, the usual delivery this month, but I will apply a twenty percent discount for your prompt action, loyalty, and, of course, your discretion.'

'Thank you, Nico, you have my absolute discretion, rest assured, but please, we remain comfortable with the price, there is no need for a discount. It is I who should be thanking you for letting me assist you with this; I was pleased and honoured to be of service to you. She was a problem to you, this woman, Emily Collins?'

'A loose end that needed tying off. Again, thank you. The matter was a personal favour you did for me, and I will not forget your loyalty.'

Closing the call and placing the phone down on my desk, I lift my personal clean phone and check my digital wallet for the open standby ticket from London Heathrow to Los Angeles LAX that I booked late yesterday and then check the times of the next available flight. Travelling first class, picking up a seat is normally not a problem, and upon checking availability, I confirm a seat reservation for a flight departing at 16:15 hours today; plenty of time to sort out what I need to do before the flight.

Placing the phone down again, I return to the window and look out over the gardens, where the gardener is now tending to some small, colourful bushes at the rear of a planted border. She had to go; there was no other way. Martin had shared too much information with her, and they had carried out a killing together. She was a liability that needed to be addressed. This Emily was not a natural-born killer like Martin or I, making her a future risk I could not accept. She knew too much, becoming a weakness that could have been exploited by the authorities or my enemies. Her sharing one killing with Martin does not ensure she is a person who lives this life path we do, and that is a risk I cannot accept, not for me or for Martin.

It's my turn now to look after Martin, to make the decisions he wouldn't make to protect himself and me, but he must never know it was I who ordered her removal.

Martin is strong, and he will get over this. At least her last days with my baby brother meant a lot to him, and he'll always have that.

56

Ernesto

Home, Louetta, Harris County

That call from Martin was unexpected, and I wish now I hadn't answered it. Thinking more about what he said, I am not convinced someone killed her because of what we did to the Gunnarssons, although I won't ignore Martin's concern and will be alert to any strangers over the next few weeks. Miss Collins dying like she did was probably nothing more than a city event, a drug-related robbery by someone out for their next fix, a senseless act. It is such a great shame; she had a wonderful future to look forward to, and she was a lovely woman.

I am saddened to hear of her death, but she shouldn't have resisted; what is the value of a purse and a cell phone when compared to a life?

Not that I believe in fate, but it seems her destiny was already written; if it wasn't Gunnarsson, it was going to be someone. This is the first time the Arabic saying that I picked up when posted in the Middle East has a ring of relevance to it, "what is written on the forehead will surely be seen by the eye", the belief that fate is predetermined and unavoidable.

I am proud of helping Martin and of what I did to help Miss Collins get away from the Gunnarssons. Her dying at their hands would have been far worse than the death she got. I am, of course, grateful for the investment in my children's future, assuming Martin will maintain his commitment now that the need for my silence is fading. Martin and I have fought side by side, creating a shared bond, and for that, he will remain my brother, always, and I expect he will stay true to his word. I owe him my life and will help him in any way I can if he needs me again.

At least now, his brother is on his way out from the UK to be with him. I didn't know he had a brother and thought he would have mentioned it in all those long hours we spent together, but still, it is a comfort to know he will not be alone.

Family… there is nothing stronger than blood for loyalty, trust, love and support. It is comforting to know he will have his family around him at this time to help him through it.

57

Nico

Martin's Home, Manhattan Beach, Los Angeles

We slowly drive through the area, and at each cross junction we approach, my driver comes to a complete stop and looks both ways before releasing the brake and moving forward; it's near impossible to get a decent speed going.

Looking out of the darkened glass, I wonder what life in the suburbs is really like. I bet a decent percentage of my income comes from homes such as these; punters looking for that weekend buzz, paying for illegal substances and warm company, watching pay-on-line entertainment, and all behind closed doors away from prying eyes, each of them looking to escape the monotony of the nine to five, the mortgage and bills, schooling the kids, cutting the grass… I could never live a life like this, and I struggle to understand the attraction this has for Martin.

Approaching his house, it is a typical property for the area, characterised by low brick wall foundations surmounted with a timber frame superstructure and painted cladding, brick chimneys, and fly screens, suburbia at its best. Most houses are one level, interspersed with a few bespoke two-story houses. The neighbourhood lawns are well maintained, with hissing garden sprinklers refracting the last of the day's sunshine. This is Martin all over: far from ostentatious living, he tries his best to blend in with everyday life, maintaining a modest existence.

My driver slows and tightly turns the Mercedes, the car dipping then bucking up quickly as it crosses the sidewalk and up onto the narrow driveway of a house, bringing my thoughts back to the here and now. As he puts the car in park, Martin appears from the front door, barefoot and dishevelled looking, stepping out before the engine has stopped.

My driver gets out and looks around before opening the rear door for me to alight. No sooner am I vertical than Martin comes around the car and wraps his arms around me in a tight embrace.

'Whoa. Hello, little brother; I said I would be here, that I would come to you. How are you doing?' and on asking, his embrace tightens even more. 'Now, Martin, shall we step inside? We should talk privately, and you can bring me up to speed with the latest information from the police investigation.'

'Sorry, yes, of course. Thank you for flying out here so quickly, Nico. Please.'

He beckons toward the open front door.

I step forward and indicate to the driver he is to wait with the car, acknowledging my instruction with a nod and 'Yes, Sir'. It's not often that I go places without my private protection team close by, but I know this place is safe for me, and no one knows I'm here with Martin.

Upon entering the hallway, the staircase to the left is adorned with artwork featuring different book covers and film posters, all in matching dark wood frames, accompanied by black and white photos of Martin with other people whom I mostly do not recognise. I follow

Martin around to the right, to an open-plan living area with its focal red brick-built fireplace and matching burgundy leather settees facing each other, separated by a large, low glass table topped with papers, magazines, and books. He turns to me again and widens his arms for another embrace; this time, just the two of us are present.

'Thank you for coming, Nico, I know how busy you are, and I appreciate the effort you will have gone to at such short notice to free up your diary.'

I haven't the heart to tell him the truth of why I'm here, and commonsense would prevent me anyway. He must remain in the belief I am here for him, which in the main I am, but I can also conduct business whenever I'm in L.A.

'There is no need to thank me. I will always be here for my little brother when he needs me. Now,' as we separate and I move towards one of the settees, 'tell me the latest from the police; do they have the person who did this terrible thing?'

Sitting opposite me, with the table between us, he looks like he's not slept since she was killed. He takes a deep breath before replying, 'No, not yet. To be honest, I don't think they have much to go on. The person hid their face and wore gloves. The gun, they believe, was a high-powered revolver, so no bullet casings were left behind.' He stops for a few seconds, composing himself, before continuing. 'The bullets passed through Emily, and the police are still trying to trace them or what is left of them.'

As he says these words, he is close to tears again, and I need to keep him focused.

'Is there any CCTV available? Have the police got any recordings?'

He sniffs loudly, desperately trying to hold it together. Rubbing his hand over his stubbly chin, 'No, that is, no, they haven't said anything about CCTV. I suppose they'll be trying to find some video of the killer outside the restaurant or on the escape route they made.'

'Yes. If you recall, my contact is the best in the business at analysing CCTV snippets; if there is some video available, we can use his skills to help track down the shooter,' and as soon as I say it, I see him look at me quizzically.

'Shooter? That's an unusual word to use for a drug addict trying to mug someone.'

'Oh, I'm sorry, it's just me and what I'm used to, you are correct, I should have maybe said… perpetrator.'

Sniffing again, his manner is becoming clearer, becoming more practical.

'Yeh, well, the perpetrator remains at large as the police have little to go on, but they have increased their resources to find him given Emily's background and her close connection with the Presidential Pardon of her mother.'

'Yes, well, I would expect no less of them. You believe this was a man?'

'I suppose, yes, don't you?'

'I'm not sure. It's just if the person cannot be identified, it could equally be a woman, no?'

'Umm, well…'

'And of course, Emily was English; such murders are not good for tourism and the image of Los Angeles; the City Mayor will want a quick result.'

'I suppose, but that is not what is important to me; she was a wonderful woman, the best thing that has ever happened to me, and I will not rest until he is found.'

Martin is crestfallen and exhausted, and I can almost sympathise with his pain; no doubt he is filled with anger and wants his revenge if he could have it. I may need to arrange for a suitable person to become the perpetrator to give him the closure he will need to move on; this is something I will discuss with Arabella later when we meet; it need not be the one that pulled the trigger, but a person of similar build with a criminal background, recently deceased will be preferable to close this out without risk of the truth becoming known to Martin. Martin will have to be content that they have been found and, alas, is already dead.

I reply, 'I understand that, Martin, but if the police get to them first, it'll be hard for us to apply our version of justice. I'll see what I can find out from my contacts over here.'

'Thank you, Nico, I knew I could rely on you.'

It is his blind faith in me that I find hard to accept, with me knowing what I have done to him, that I am the cause of his pain. He knows me, as do others; I am a person who will do what needs to be done, no matter how hard or difficult the task is. To me, family comes first, and it always will. Unfortunately, because of his lapse in keeping our background secret, this Emily had the potential to be a real risk, a liability to our family's safety and security. To the outside world, unaware of my sibling tie to Martin, my primary concern is reputation and the pursuit of profitable business interests. Removing Emily played a part in all these. I am fair but firm in business dealings and known for acting swiftly and decisively. Ordering her death removed the risk of her talking and exposing me and my family, and at the same time, reinforced I am ruthless and not afraid of removing someone who is a problem to me.

I look at him now, a shell of what he was a couple days ago when he told me of his love for this woman. He is silent again, in a world of his own thoughts, while looking down at the table between us. I follow his gaze, coming to realise the table is strewn with artwork for the new book cover and marketing releases, a string-bound manuscript with page markers, and a collection of books he has written previously; this is what they were working on; this is his chosen career, and was to be their future together.

In an attempt to distract him, I ask, 'What will happen to your book now? It is about Emily and her mother, isn't it? I presume it'll be dropped now.'

'Yes, it is, and no, I don't expect it will', he replies as he sighs deeply. 'It will still go ahead as the investors have ploughed a lot of finance into it, and they will want a return. I'm not sure I can complete the final touches, though, and will probably leave it with them to complete.'

'Is this it?' as I lift the manuscript from the tabletop.

'Yes. It's in final editing now, the last review, so not far from completion.'

'Then, you must be involved in finishing it and participate in the launch; it will keep you busy.'

'No, I can't do it; it'll be too painful. If they do go ahead with it, they'll have to launch it without me.'

'That is a shame given all the hard work you have put into this,' weighing the manuscript in one hand, 'but I understand it, you have lost your partner, and your thoughts are now elsewhere.'

'They are. I want the person that did this, and my focus is on them. I want to look them in the eye while I make them regret what they did to my Emily and to me.'

'You need to think carefully, little brother. The police are all over her murder; we do not want them looking at either of us too closely.'

'They can look at me as close as they want, I don't care anymore, so long as I get my hands on the person that did this.'

'Let me find them for you; please, leave it with me. I cannot bear the thought of you being arrested for doing something in hasty retribution and getting caught, especially if you fail to get them and kill them. If the police find them first, rest assured I will still be able to get at them wherever they are, in their cell, at a court appearance, wherever, but if I get them first, then they'll never be seen again; the last thing they see will be your face. But you must stay calm and let me do what I can.'

He turns away from me, looking at the fireplace, and I'm thankful for that; it's difficult deceiving my brother face-to-face. It is then that I see the photograph of them both in a glazed white frame on the mantlepiece, laughing in a loose embrace on a shoreline, him holding her at the very moment a wave breaks against them; they look happy. Glancing around the room, there are traces of her dotted here and there, signs of a feminine touch that Martin does not possess.

He turns back to me, 'OK… I will. Nico, promise me you will find this person before the police do.'

'I will, little brother, I will, and I will have them brought to you.'

58

Martin

Manhattan Beach, Los Angeles

I feel a little easier now Nico is here, using his contacts to help find this bastard. I would have struggled to get a lead on him, I know that, but with Nico's underworld contacts, I have more confidence in Nico locating him quickly, allowing me to bring him to account without the police ever knowing. He will come to regret what he's done and plead with me to spare his life, but there's no chance of that; this will be a life I will take satisfaction in slowly extinguishing.

Looking at Nico, he seems a little uneasy, not his usual self. He's keen to find this person without my involvement, and I understand that. I'm useless at this kind of thing, whereas this is his speciality; it's his world we're in now, one that I try to stay away from, unsuccessfully. God, I need a drink.

As I stand and turn, heading for the kitchen, I ask over my shoulder, 'Do you want a drink? I'm going to get wasted.'

'Yes, I'll have a drink with you, but then I must push on and make some calls, meet some people and get things moving before this person goes to ground and becomes impossible to find.'

'Yeh, I know.'

Picking up the bottle of bourbon and two glasses, I return to the settee, place the glasses down on the manuscript, pull the stopper from the bottle, and pour two large measures.

'Whoa, easy, I must keep a clear head, remember?'

'Yep.' Still standing, I offer him a glass, and without hesitating, I pour my drink down my neck in one large swallow and follow it with a cough. He watches me, and I'm almost sure he slightly shakes his head from side to side.

'What?'

'Nothing, little brother, nothing. If you think this will help, take more, I won't stop you.'

'It'll help me forget for a while.'

'But then you will remember, it's benefit is short-lived.'

'Like my love with Emily.'

'No, do not think of it like that; you had good times together, you found each other. Bad luck happened, and it has separated you, nothing more.'

'Bad luck... Huh, whatever.'

I pour another large measure, this time only drinking half of it as I sit back down opposite him. He takes a sip and pulls his face as he looks at the liquid swirling in the glass, 'Ah, an acquired taste, I think,' he follows with.

'Haha, yeh, not your usual single malt.'

He takes another sip, then asks, 'Does Emily have any family that needs to be informed?'

I sigh. The thought hadn't occurred to me until the police asked earlier. 'She has a half-brother and half-sister back in the UK, Oscar and Sarah. Oh, and another half-sister, Jody, but she's in prison. She's kind of estranged from all of them because of something that happened when they all got together,'

'Ah, I see. This will be in her book, I take it?'

'Yes, mostly, well, what she wanted the world to know will be, but there are some things that can't be put into printed word. She says you can pick your friends but can't pick your family… Shit, she used to say you can… Fuck, I keep talking of her as though she is still here.'

My rage flares up again, my grip on the glass tightening before I throw it into the fireplace, crystal shattering into a thousand pieces. As the pieces tinkle about the brick fireplace, I become aware that Nico doesn't so much as flinch; he simply leans forward and offers me his glass. 'Here, take this. I will leave now and let you finish your bourbon. I regret I did not get the opportunity to meet Emily; she was very beautiful and would have made a remarkable sister-in-law had we spent time together, of that, I'm sure.'

'You would have loved her, Nico, you really would. I'll never find another like her. She was the only person, besides you, who knew all about me and had no concerns or reservations.' As I speak, I start to feel tears welling in my eyes, and I try to hold it together in front of him, but I'm struggling to hold it together. I feel he senses this and stands to leave.

He places a firm hand on my shoulder and closes his grip tight, his large hand exuding strength and love. 'Please stay here, I will see myself out. I will call you a little later with hopefully news of this perpetrator.'

Reaching across my chest, I place my hand over his and lower my head, 'Thank you. Thank you, Nico.'

59

Martin

Off Hangman's Tree Road, Santiago Canyon

Very cleverly done, I have to give them that. Masquerading as two police officers, I was too eager to buy into their story and their request to join them at the station after they told me they had caught the mugger. It wasn't until I got in their car that they pulled a gun on me, zip-tying my hands and legs and putting a hood over my head. How could I have been so stupid, so gullible?

God only knows where I am now, but I know it's remote. As soon as we left the surfaced road and I could hear gravel under the tyres, I was starting to worry but then recalled how Nico had me picked up like this before back in England, lifted from the street by a couple of his men who conveyed me to his country mansion; I made a note to tell him to stop doing this when I meet him again and relaxed a little.

But then it started to change; this is different. On the drive here, after about an hour trussed up in the rear seat, I began asking questions, which no one responded to, and that's when I started to worry again. When the car eventually came to a stop, there was no nicety about it this time. Being manhandled out of the car and dragged over dirt and gravel to some kind of building was nothing like how I was treated at Nico's home. I guess we're in a remote rural area, for in those brief seconds being dragged from the car, I clocked that the air was clear, a little chilly, and the absence of traffic or town noise. Now, I'm tied to a chair, shivering in a cold room where noises echo around, waiting for what I don't know.

I can hear two voices talking quietly off to my right, and I'm sure one has a Texan accent.

Gunnarsson! No, he must have had an accomplice. Stupid! Stupid! How the hell did they find me? Did these guys kill Emily? My frustration gets the better of me, and I start banging the chair up and down. I want to break free; the urge to kill someone is screaming within me.

'Hey! Ya better knock that off!' the Texan voice bawls back at me.

'Fuck you! Fuck you!'

The hood played its part, as the blow across my head was unexpected, hard, and painful. My left ear is ringing, and within a few seconds, it feels like something warm is running down the side of my neck.

'Sit still and keep quiet, or you'll get more of that.'

My forced immobility and vulnerability are making me even more angry, and I bark back, 'What the hell is this? Vengeance for killing Gunnarsson and his sick, sadistic family?'

'Shut the hell up! Anyway, Nicholson, who the fuck is Gunnarsson?'

Whoa, that stops me. So, this is nothing to do with the Gunnarssons. Oh my god, what is this then? They mean business; they know exactly who I am, and they've brought me here for a reason.

I hear a car pull up outside as a large roller shutter door opens, accompanied by a commotion as someone else is brought into the building. Pulled chains indicate the door is closing again, as multiple feet shuffle on a hard floor heading towards me, with murmured voices and someone groaning. The sounds of another person resisting but being tied up near me. What the hell is going on?

Then, a clear voice cuts through the confusion.

'Take these bloody headphones off! Do you know who I am?'

60

Arabella

405 Freeway, Los Angeles

I never thought I would be presented with such an opportunity, gifted to me, without him considering the consequences of his actions. I still cannot believe he travelled to his brother's house without his personal protection. I'll never have another opportunity like this again, and I'll take full advantage of it. He often talked about the importance of family, leaving me to consider his family a potential weak link, as it has proven to be. Yes, family is important, and now he's going to find out just how much.

My drivers are waiting for my signal to surround his car and take him, three vehicles carrying ten of my best, handpicked men, all of them aware I want him taken alive, if possible, but if he fights back, he must not be allowed to escape, and, as a last resort, he can be taken out. Two other cars and men have been sent to his brother's house to pick him up as well; he'll be the lever I'll use to make Nico talk.

As we trail his Mercedes, some distance ahead of us in the centre lanes, we slowly start to move up in traffic on the freeway with the intention to effectively box him in. The sun has settled now, and darkness is helping us stalk him, to creep up from behind and both sides ever so slowly so as not to arouse his driver's attention.

His driver, keeping at a steady fifty-five, indicates to change lanes and moves across, showing intent to take the next exit ramp; this is our opportunity to strike. As the Mercedes leaves the main freeway, taking the exit down ramp, I give the order to strike. Two SUVs accelerate and drive down either side of the Mercedes, and before his driver has time to react, they quickly overtake the Mercedes and converge in front of it, forcing the driver to hit the brakes to avoid a collision. The third SUV runs up the rear of the Mercedes, blocking any attempt to reverse out of the roadblock created by the other SUVs. Within ten to fifteen seconds, all the vehicles have stopped, and my armed men are out and swarming the Mercedes as we roll up alongside, completely blocking the exit ramp. I can hear cars behind us screeching as they slam on their brakes to avoid colliding with us. Two of my masked men turn to face these cars, raising their assault rifles to firing positions, intent on keeping the occupants away and suppressing any heroic attempts to intervene should anyone try.

The Mercedes doors are locked, and my men are struggling to gain entry. One opens fire at the windshield, and it's clear the glass is bulletproof, as expected. Two men quickly apply shape charges around the locks of both rear doors and expertly detonate them simultaneously to gain entry to the rear seat. As they use lever bars on the buckled doors, the driver, seemingly armed, tries to engage with one of my men through a gap and is swiftly cut down in his seat in a rapid exchange of fire.

Prising one of the rear doors open, one of my men reaches in and struggles to pull Nico from the backseat, but he succeeds with the help of a colleague. As they drag

Nico out, I've never seen him so stunned, so dishevelled. They handcuff him swiftly, pull his arms upward behind him, and frog march him to one of the front SUVs, throwing him in the rear seat. A man climbs in on either side of him, and as the doors close, the SUV is pulling away at speed. The remaining men climb aboard the waiting SUVs, and we all pull away at the same time. Paying top dollar attracts the best talent; it's having this type of experienced and trained talent that helps me stay on top of my patch.

To any spectator watching this unfold, it will appear to be a well-rehearsed SWAT team or DEA operation. The way our vehicles move through the streets, deftly blocking cross traffic so we can speed through, will have everyone second-guessing for the next few hours as to which agency we belong to.

At speed, we enter an industrial area and stop the vehicles inside an abandoned warehouse. Switching vehicles, we each go in different directions on leaving the property, leaving two men behind to set the intervention vehicles alight inside the warehouse and then make their escape.

They'll all get a bonus for this evening's work, as he is still alive; the lift executed professionally to perfection.

So, now I have him; he doesn't know it's me behind his kidnapping, but he soon will. I look at my cell phone and see a message that his brother has been picked up without any issues, and soon we'll all be together.

I'm looking forward to this next meeting on my terms.

61

Nico

Off Hangman's Tree Road, Santiago Canyon

This can't be one of the cartels; surely, they wouldn't risk taking me and treating me like this. I started to think it was a DEA snatch operation, but when we switched cars and sped away again, I knew this wasn't a law agency. As no one is speaking, it's impossible to pick up anything useful. There are no radio noises or call signs being used, again reinforcing that this could be far worse for me than a DEA arrest.

As the car comes to a rapid stop, I sense the tyres skidding slightly on gravel and all the doors open. The vehicle rises as bodies get out. There are some garbled words spoken, but I can't decipher them through the hood they've pulled over my head and the headphones they then placed over my ears.

Roughly dragged along, we enter a building, and I make out what could be a shutter door rolling down behind us. It feels like I've reached my destination.

Pushed down onto a chair, my legs are zip-tied to the chair legs before they uncuff me and then tie my arms around the back of me and the chair. Again, they are talking, but I can't understand what they are saying.

I hear another voice, distant, muffled, but I can't make this out either. Then nothing. Silence. It's about time I got some answers, I deserve them.

'Take these bloody headphones off! Do you know who I am?'

A few seconds later, I hear a voice beside me, faint through the headphones but unmistakable, 'Nico, is that you? What is going on?'

My heart sinks. They have Martin, too. Whoever this is, they have us both, and I instantly know this is not good. How could this have happened? When I get out of here, I pledge to myself to kill them for this, kill them all.

'Yes, Martin, it's me. I'm sorry.'

'Sorry for what? What's going on.'

A pair of hands removes the headphones, and now I can hear clearly, although I still have a slight ringing in both ears from the earlier blasts tot eh car doors.

'I am sorry, Martin, it's me they want, not you. Just let them know whatever they want to know, and it'll all be OK; you will be fine.' I say the words in the full knowledge we won't be. I have an idea of what this is now.

'Take off their hoods,' the female voice instructs, but before my hood is removed, I already know it's Arabella, and my thoughts are confirmed; this is a takeover.

'NO!' I shout out. 'Leave the hood on him. He's not seen you. He doesn't know who you are, and no names have been said.'

'Oh, how very gallant. Remove both hoods.'

Unless I can talk my way out of this, we're both dead. As my hood is being removed, I speak to Martin. 'I'm sorry, Martin, I really am.'

The room is bright, and the sudden rush of light hurts my eyes for a few seconds. Squinting, I try to get them accustomed to light. My first thought is to Martin, and I instinctively turn to him beside me, a couple of yards away, strapped to a chair just like me.

He's struggling with the light as well, and a few seconds later, he turns to look at me. This feels like the endgame for me, I'm sure of it, but I hope to bargain or plead for Martin's life.

Redirecting towards her, I try to take control of the dialogue. 'Arabella. I never thought you had it in you. Very well done.'

'Thank you, Nico. I aim to please, as you know.'

Then it dawns on me, the realisation hitting like a truck. Following my instructions, she arranged for Emily's removal, a removal Martin does not know I instigated. She must have worked out what it was all about.

'Who are you?' Martin asks her.

'I am a colleague of your brother, Martin. Isn't that right, Nico? We have done business together now for some years, with the odd special assignment now and then, eh, Nico?'

I sense Martin turning to look at me as I continue to eyeball her and reply. 'Yes, that is right. So, what is this, then, Arabella, an attempt at a takeover? You feel you are entitled now to move up to the top table?'

'Well, yes, although it's no attempt, and this is more of a promotion, really. I know there are others you report to; I'm merely stepping into the management structure at the next level. It's my time, and I've earned it.'

'Nico, what is she talking about?' Martin asks.

Ignoring his question, I continue my response to her. 'Yes, it was inevitable, I suppose, that someone would try, but The Guild will not allow this, Arabella, unfortunately overstepping your position. And my brother here isn't from our world; he's a civilian, a writer of books. He's not a part of this and never has been.'

'Oh, I know all about Martin and his writing skills, his accolades, his colourful and unfortunate past. You may not consider him to be "one of us", but his connection to you really does tie him into our world, wouldn't you say, Nico? That's why you've kept him hidden away all these years; he's your Achilles Heel, and it seems that I'm Prince Paris, the one who fired the fateful arrow.'

'That may be so, but The Guild will not tolerate such insubordination. They will come for you unless you rethink this situation. Release us now, then you and I can sort this out amicably and come to an understanding. Let Martin go, and I will quietly step aside for you. In fact, I will openly endorse your takeover of my operation. Releasing Martin is the only condition I ask.'

'Ah, another noble act by the older brother; I respect that, but things have already moved on, making that outcome difficult.'

'What things?'

'When you requested my help in removing a problem, I asked myself, what was behind it? Why would the great Nico Costas want help from me with this? What would he achieve from this death? Why the need to carry it out so quickly?'

I must front this out now. I must remain stronger than her even though she has all the power and control, remain immovable and stalwart, even in the face of what I know must be my final hour. She is intent on letting Martin know I ordered the hit on Emily.

'It was a personal request, one that I thought you would honour, that it would remain between the two of us.'

'Yes, of course, it did, believe me. There is such a thing as honour amongst thieves, but I wanted to know, as this could provide the route to Nico Costas that I had wanted, that I needed and have been looking for, oh, such a long time.'

'Nico?' Martin tries to break into the conversation, but I must remain in control, ignoring him again and aiming my reply at her.

'So, now you have me, what are your plans?'

'Not I, Nico, no, I do not want your blood on my hands even though the Guild has already approved it and given me their blessing. Yes, they have given me their blessing. You see, you had a weakness that you kept from them, and the Guild takes a dim view on such matters. They thought that it was dangerous when they became aware of it, as it could have been the police that exploited your weakness or another group from Eastern Europe or South America. They could not accept that risk. You should have discussed it with them when they asked you all those years ago about any potential skeletons in your closet. You see, Martin,' she looks at him now, directing her words to him, 'we operate in a similar fashion to the legal enforcement agencies; we need to know about an individual's weaknesses and how they are to be controlled to prevent the risk of detrimental leverage from others. Nico broke that understanding, that trust, and I could not let it pass me by.'

I jump in quickly, 'What? For the Guild's interests or your own?'

'Both are well served in this situation, and my loyalty to the Guild will be rewarded.'

'Nico, what is she talking about?'

My mind is turning over at a speed that is making me feel dizzy. If the Guild has approved this, then this is the end; there are no options left open to me or Martin that I can exploit. Twisting to look at him as best I can, I need to come clean with Martin about why he's here.

'I know exactly what she is talking about, and of course, she is right; I was not fully open with the Guild about you. The Guild is the organisation we work for. You see, Martin, to advance in the Guild, we have to declare any potential weaknesses to them before we are selected for higher positions, and my little brother, I chose not to mention you. I wanted to protect you from this world, to make sure you had as free a life as possible, to live how you wanted, and for that, your existence had to be kept secret, or they would get you involved.'

'So, if I am a secret, how did she find out about me?'

'Well, I… it's…' This is one question I do not want to address or explain, and Arabella seizes her opportunity when I fumble my words. I remain looking at Martin as she speaks.

'Martin, your brother did his best to protect you and himself, although probably more for himself than you, in my opinion. He had to take action to keep you from exposing his deception.'

'But I wouldn't have exposed you, Nico, I never would have.' He looks at me and, with sincerity, adds, 'You know I would never put you at risk, Nico.'

'I know that little brother, I know that, but these people think differently.'

'What he's avoiding saying, Martin, is how I found out about you.'

'Well then, how did you?' Martin asks me.

'Shall I tell him, or will you, Nico?' Her pause, waiting for my reply, is short, as she clearly wants to run this narrative. 'No, let me, I'll explain. You see, a few days ago, your brother phoned me asking for some help with a delicate, personal matter, as he called it. Naturally, I was willing to assist, as that's what we do, look after each other in the Guild. So, Nico asked for someone to be removed, that is, killed, as that person was a risk to him and the Guild finding out about you, a problem given how he had not been entirely honest with them. So, I assisted and carried out your brother's request, but curiosity got the better of me, and I wanted to know who this special person was and why.'

Instantly, I am ashamed and cannot bear to look at Martin. Given what is about to come next, I turn my head and lower my eyes.

62

Martin

Off Hangman's Tree Road, Santiago Canyon

This situation is far wider and greater than I could have imagined. What the hell is this Guild they keep mentioning? Nico is looking away from me now as she takes a step closer to me.

'This special person is someone also very dear to you, I understand, Martin. Have you lost someone dear to you recently?'

What is she going on about? I look away from her towards Nico and notice his sullen posture. He senses me looking at him, and instantly, he lifts his head, twisting his neck, attempting to shuffle his chair in an attempt to face me.

'No, Arabella, I am the one to tell him.'

I register her acquiescing, taking a step backwards and bowing her head slightly. 'As you wish, Nico.'

His manner is serious, and his tone confident as he looks directly at me. 'Little brother, I have not been completely honest with you.'

'What is going on here, Nico? What are you trying to say?' I struggle with the zip ties at my wrists, wanting to free myself, but the only thing I am achieving is the thin plastic strips cutting deeper into my skin.

'It's about Emily.'

'What about her? Why is this about Emily?' Piecing together this conversation, I'm making a narrative in my head I don't want to hear. 'Nico? What have you done?'

This is the first time I have ever seen tears in his eyes, and this frightens me.

'Nico, what is she talking about?' but he doesn't reply, as though he is unable to speak.

Arabella speaks. 'Emily Collins. Umm, that's right, Martin, your brother here was the one who ordered Emily's execution; isn't that right, Nico?'

I feel the fury of a thousand volcanoes building within me. Nico ordered it? He couldn't have done this, knowing as he did how much I loved her and what she meant to me. No, he couldn't have, not to me.

'Nico, tell me she is lying. Tell me she has this wrong.' He doesn't move, doesn't react; he's simply staring at me as I see the tears escape from his eyes and run down his cheeks. 'Tell me she did this to get to you through me.'

'Yes, Martin, I was asked to kill her, to do it as fast as possible, make her death a quick one, and make it look like an unfortunate street murder. You see, Martin, when I dug into who she was, I came across you and the plans you had with Emily. Then, after informing Nico the task was done, I heard he was flying out to LA on the next available flight. Why would he do that, especially after such a high-profile murder and the police working extra hard to find the shooter?'

The shooter. She used the same term Nico did. I cannot believe this. Why would Nico do this?

Arabella continues as I stare at him, wanting a reaction from him, wanting him to voice a rebuttal to all her lies, but he remains motionless and silent.

'It was relatively easy to track Nico's car to your home in Manhattan Beach and then find out your name. It was interesting to see it was the same name I'd come across when looking into Emily Collins and her trip out here to meet her poor mother. Can you imagine the tantalising feeling of collecting snippets of intelligence when I'm looking to find something to use against my boss, something that could be useful? So, I needed to know who you are to Nico. Now, admittedly, it was difficult to find the link between the two of you, but with perseverance, I did. You see, to me, information is everything; it is power and control. So first, I followed the money, the money behind that pending movie deal, and it wasn't hard to find out that a sizeable proportion of the investment was coming from a single source; it was all clean and easy to find on a web search, and it turned out to be coming from one of Nico's many investment companies.'

She paces slowly about the room in front of us, like a schoolteacher giving a history lesson; she has all the facts, and we are here to learn them.

'However, if that was the basis of the link, it didn't seem enough to want her dead, especially as she played a major part in the success of that investment. There had to be something more, something that would prompt Nico to change his plans at short notice, fly across the Atlantic, and call at your home in LA in person, all without his usual protection team, indicating he felt safe. So, reaching out a little further, I contacted my inside person in Nico's household in the UK, one on my payroll, to keep an eye on what is happening and to keep me informed who is coming and going. I sent her your photograph, and she remembered your visit to the mansion some time ago. Then, after entertaining one of Nico's closest men, she found out about your sibling tie. Of course, it was all hush-hush, top secret, but that's the kind of information I reward well. So... Brothers. Then it hit me, Nico was always going on about blood and family ties, and it all made sense. When I mentioned this to the Guild and that Nico had ordered me to have his brother's lover killed, their deliberations didn't take long. Nico had broken their trust and their code.'

I'm speechless, shocked to my core that Nico is not challenging anything she's saying; he's just letting her talk, spouting her lies without correcting her. Is all this true? How can it be? He wouldn't do this to me. No, I need to hear it from him.

'Nico… say something. Why are you letting her say these things? You need to put this right.'

He raises his head again and looks me straight in the eyes, and without hesitation, his confession flows, 'Because it's all true, little brother, all of it.'

I have never known emotion like it since I killed Papa. The sheer rage in me conflicted with family blood and loyalty, is enormous. Papa deserved what I did to him, but not this, this can't be true, none of it.

'No! No! I don't believe you! Not you, not my Emily. Why in God's name would you do that to me?'

'Because you told her of me, that we are brothers, and you confessed to her what you had done, and… and because you turned her into a killer and were proud of it. She knew too much, and the risk of others discovering any of this was too great. She had to go, as she was a liability that you had created. She wasn't born to this. I'm sorry, Martin, but it's true, I ordered her death.'

'NO! I'm not having that; don't you go putting this on me. She was the love of my life, and I told YOU that! I confided in YOU, but YOU still went ahead with it, making it out to look like it was some random street killing. She was assassinated, executed on your instructions.' Adrenalin is coursing through me to the point I think I am about to explode, and I'm bouncing in the chair I'm strapped to. His remorse isn't enough; it'll never be enough; he is no better than Papa was. He's not repentant at all.

'ARRGHHH!! You bastard, you deserve what you're going to get here tonight!'

'Martin, please, I know I have wronged you, but you have to appreciate why I did it. It was for us, for you. You went too far, telling her of us, and I had to consider damage limitation and control the situation. For one, I never thought you would find out.'

'AND THAT MAKES ALL THE DIFFERENCE, DOES IT?' screaming at him at the top of my voice. I can feel the zip ties cutting deep into me as I try to free myself, the pain pushing me even more.

'Martin, please? I did it for us. You must see that?'

I know if I could get out of this chair, I would finish him myself with my bare hands. But it's useless; I cannot escape these fucking restraints.

63

Arabella

Off Hangman's Tree Road, Santiago Canyon

I watch this pitiful display unfolding before me, the meltdown of family ties and bonds. I half-expected trouble between them, but I didn't expect this level of reaction. Martin is furious to the extent I think he would kill his brother right now if he could, of that, I'm sure.

My plan was to have a couple of my men take them out and shoot them, bury them in a grave out there in the remoteness, but a thought now crosses my mind that Martin could be useful. Nico is living on borrowed time now; if I don't do this tonight, the Guild will want my head for not carrying out their orders. I feel excited observing the rage within Martin and surprised at the collapse of Nico, a man of power and dominance, begging his brother for forgiveness for a killing he ordered.

But bringing down Nico has always been my goal, and I praise the heavens for providing me with this opportunity. Protected by the Guild, I always needed to obtain their approval, or I would join him very quickly in an unmarked grave. Nico was born into criminality, clawing his way up the ladder, but his infamy grew overnight following that weekend when he tortured the family of a man accused of being a grass, an informant to the NCA in the UK, that I later proved he was innocent of, the real informant deflecting allegation on to him. Nico butchered them slowly with a scalpel, peeling his wife and child in front of him to the point he confessed just to free them of their pain. They all died horribly, and we were all made to watch, an example of what would happen if we betrayed him. That was nearly seven years ago now. I never believed it was the man accused, and when I eventually found the real grass, I presented the piece of shit to Nico, and Nico simply brushed it off, shot the informant in the head, and ordered it was never to be mentioned again. I still hear the screams of that little boy and his mother when I close my eyes at night, and the thought that they will stay and haunt me forever is all on Nico. Now I have Martin, I am going to use him like Nico would.

'Martin. Martin, look at me. Now you have found out the truth, I see and appreciate the anger and the rage within you; I have experienced that same anger myself over the years. You must understand that I had to follow my instructions to kill Emily. Emily's death was not personal to me, I did not know who she was or what she was guilty of, but it was a personal order from my boss, one that I could not decline; that is not how these things are done. Rest assured, I used my best man, and her death was quick. I have my instructions to terminate Nico, instructions that I must carry out. However, I can show compassion to you, Martin, if you want it.'

On these words, Nico looks up at me, 'Please, Arabella, please, spare him, you know he is not from our world. He does not deserve to be buried in the desert, whereas I do. I beg for your compassion. Please, Arabella?'

Before I can reply, Martin speaks. 'Do not beg on my behalf, my so-called big brother. No, I have no brother now to speak of anymore. I am an only child, orphaned by destiny with no family to speak of.'

Nico slumps limp in his chair, his head dropping to his chest. He knows his fate now. He has betrayed his brother's trust, like the man alleged of betrayal all those years ago, except that man wasn't of his family and was innocent as I suspected all along; he just wouldn't wait to find out, to see how it panned out, instead acted out of haste and arrogance. Nothing has changed; he's done it again, but this time with Emily Collins and his own brother. I am not Nico; my actions are all well considered. I look back at Martin, registering the man wanting to avenge the killing of his love and offer him his opportunity and lifeline.

'Martin, I will free you on one condition.'

Nico looks back up at me. Martin continues to stare at his brother as he replies, 'And that is?'

I step closer to Martin, to be near when I say the words, 'I see your passion, and I feel your rage. You want your vengeance. I will let you go free, but only on the understanding that you kill Nico for me, here, this evening.'

64

Martin

Off Hangman's Tree Road, Santiago Canyon

I loved Emily, and for sure, I would have died for her, and certainly, I would have killed for her. Will I kill for her now? I want to, I want to kill the person that was behind her murder, but this is my brother, my protector all these years; well… at least I thought he was. I am not sure who he really is anymore.

It does not bother me if we both die this night. I had already checked out on hearing of Emily's murder if I couldn't get my revenge. It is near impossible for me to accept Nico was behind her death, that he killed her, knowing how I felt about her, what she meant to me. He could have spoken to me about her before giving his orders; in fact, he should have been fully open with me about the Guild, my anonymity and why I had to stay invisible. I always thought that he was the top dog in his world, ruling his fiefdom successfully off the back of all his hard work; now I find out he is a mere employee, in the employ of this Guild, some kind of dark corporate criminal organisation I never knew existed.

'Yes, I can accept that,' Nico responds to Arabella, nodding, 'I would prefer it by his hand; retribution and atonement in one; it is only fitting. He twists in his chair to me, 'It's OK, Martin, it really is, I want it this way.'

'This is Martin's decision, not yours, Nico,' she replies to him, trying to cut him out of the decision process. Looking at me again, 'Well, Martin, will you do this for your freedom?'

Nico twists towards me again, 'Say yes, Martin, please. I am truly sorry, my little brother, I should not have done what I did. I know I am not walking out of here tonight, and I would prefer my death to be at your hand rather than hers, it will be meaningful and just.'

I look up at Arabella. She is serious, nodding gently, offering me my freedom if I kill him. Although I couldn't care less about my freedom, I do want a reckoning, retribution for what he has done.

Calmly, I ask her, 'Why me? Why ask me to kill my own brother?'

'You said it yourself; you have no family, you are an orphan. This is the man behind the murder of your love, the man that is the cause of all your pain and suffering; he is the reason you are here tonight. Clearly, he has not been honest with you, for if he had, Emilly Collins would still be alive, and you would be with her.'

As she talks, my rage continues to boil away inside, urging to be released. Nico is not resisting her words, not rejecting anything she is saying; he is guilty of what she accuses him of, and as she speaks, her words drive deeper into me, turning the heat up on my rage.

'You will find a release from this Martin, trust me,' she adds.

How many times have I uttered those very words to others? How many times have I reinforced this belief in those I have helped? Emily was the last; to her surprise, she acknowledged after killing Grace that it provided her with a release for her pent-up frustration, aggression, rage and anger. I can readily accept that this is something I need to do, as I also need that same release.

'Yes, Martin, it's OK, I want it to be you, please.' Nico adds, almost pleading.

'Well, Martin, what do you say, yes or no?'

I am not interested in being set free; it doesn't bother me one way or the other anymore, but I am interested in exacting my sentence on Nico, my retribution. But can I? He is my brother, my blood. This isn't right.

'Martin?' she prompts again.

So many times, I have found that killing has provided me relief from pain, the pain I carry within me. Papa, Tanya, Craig, the Gunnarssons… they all deserved my attention, and I the medication and satisfaction their deaths provided me. Looking at Arabella, I must decide, and my reply is calm and deliberate, 'I don't want a gun; this is personal, and I'll do it my way.'

'Good. It's not like I'd give you a gun now, is it?' One of the men near the door laughs, and she turns to him, admonishing his interruption with a mere look. Turning back to me, 'So what is it to be, Martin, a knife or a rope?'

I turn my head to look at Nico, his face showing contrition with a hint of gratitude that I will be the one that ends his life. He knows what I'll pick. He knows me.

'A knife,' I say as I look into his eyes.

A smile softly radiates from him with a gentle nod of the head, 'A knife; that is fitting, my little brother.'

Arabella turns to one of her men, asking for a knife to be brought over. They look at each other before one of them bends, lifts a faded denim leg, and extracts a knife from the inside of his cowboy boot. He steps forward, holding out the knife by the blade to Arabella. She takes it by the handle, twirling the knife slowly in her fingers, and compliments the owner, 'Nice balance. Now, keep your guns on him.' Turning back to me, 'I don't want you getting any ideas; fair enough?'

'Yes, fair enough.'

She walks to me, squatting down on her haunches, and cuts the zip ties holding my legs to the chair. She then stands, slowly walking around me, twirling the knife gently as she does, almost as a taunt to Nico. I feel her push the steel blade between skin and chair to get at the zip tie, and, with a sharp jolt, the severed tie releases my left wrist, followed quickly by my right wrist, and the relief is instant. I pull my hands around in front of me and look down at the red, raw and broken skin on both wrists. She steps back, placing the knife on the floor between us, then steps further back to stand beside her men.

'Your downfall, Nico, was your own doing, you know that. For what you did to a friend of mine and his family years ago, this is personal for me, but having your own brother kill you will bring me greater satisfaction. I will enjoy watching you pay for your sins.'

'Arabella, having Martin do this is an honour for me; there is no better person I can think of that I would embrace to do this. Enjoy your promotion, Arabella, with all its trappings and comforts, for it won't last long. There is always another wanting more, to move up and replace you.'

As he speaks, I step forward and bend, reaching for the knife. As I put my hand to the handle, I hear two clicks, pistols being cocked, and I look up and see at least two guns trained on me. The thought briefly occurs that I could fight my way out of here, but they would shoot me down, then Nico, before I got within two yards of them. Besides, it is me who must silence Nico, and in doing this, she will let me go free… then I will find the person who shot Emily and end this.

Slowly wrapping my fingers around the handle, I lift the knife from the floor and mimic Arabella in twirling the blade between my fingers. Standing upright, I slowly turn to Nico, my grip tightening now around the handle, the blade out in front of me. I decide on a quick kill, a deep stab to the heart; after all, he is my brother, and I hold those tenuous strands of family bond still, even at the point of my killing him.

Taking a step forward, we look at each other, neither of us speaking. He smiles softly, almost sweetly, to me, and I see the tears in his eyes. Does he love me, still? At the very moment I am about to end his life, does he still love me? Did he truly do this for me? I hesitate.

65

Nico

Off Hangman's Tree Road, Santiago Canyon

It was always going to happen one day; someone was going to come for me. I have been lucky, averting the two previous attempts, but this time, Arabella is right; my pride and arrogance got the better of me. Watching him pick up the knife and turn back to me, I am glad it is Martin, but sad it was for this reason. I hurt him badly, and now I must atone for my actions.

Watching him almost in slow motion, I remember the times we played together, how we wrestled, how I taught him to climb trees, pinch fruit from a neighbour's garden, grift extra sweets from the owner of the corner shop, and how we used to sing on the way home. Papa deserved what he got that night. He deserved to die. He was brutal, cold, and the cause of Mama's passing; if I had been stronger, it would have been me that killed him; it should have been me. I should have stopped him, and I'll regret that I didn't spare Martin that burden which he has carried for all these years.

As he stands in front of me, looking down at me, the thought of my actions fill me with shame and regret. I look up at him, feeling the tears welling in my eyes, overcome with how much I hurt him, that I stole from him the happiness he so deserved and found.

I'm not frightened of dying, I never have been, as the end is a fact of life. I keep my breathing calm, not wanting to show any kind of weakness in front of Arabella, not wanting to give her greater satisfaction.

I look up at him as he stands over me, poised with the knife in his closed grasp, its tip pointing at me. Nodding gently, still bound to the chair, 'It's OK, Martin, it is. I am ready. I love you, my little brother. I only wanted to protect you, and I did what I thought was necessary to keep you, us, safe. I am so sorry and ask only for your forgiveness.'

He pauses, motionless, looking into my eyes, and for the first time, I see his are cold and empty.

'Goodbye, Nico.'

His thrust is rapid, precise, and deep into my chest. The instant shock hits me, frozen in pain. His hand is still on the knife handle as I struggle to look up at him, but as I do, I see the gun levelled at his temple as he looks back at me, unaware.

'NO!' is all I can manage as the gun fires into Martin's head, spraying blood and bone and brain outward.

I can't breathe, my lungs won't work, the pain is searing through me. He falls away, crumpling to the floor to my right, his grip loosening on the knife still stuck in my chest, coming to rest in a limp, bloody pile at my feet. Arabella is standing in front of me now, holding the gun, smiling with vicious contempt as she glares down at me. My eyes close as my body begins to shut down.

I feel her lean into me, whispering close to my ear, 'This is my vengeance for Robert Lloyd, my father you murdered.'

I hear the name…

66

The Guild

Quarterly Board Meeting, Oslo, Norway

Looking down the agenda, I see there is an item for which Arabella will be discussed. She has done well; her intelligence, along with her qualifications and experience in international finance and law, makes her a most suitable candidate to step into Nico's shoes. I am incredibly proud of my protégé, and I am sure I will have reason to congratulate her later this evening.

Two knocks on the tabletop resonate off the oak-panelled walls, bringing us to order.

'Good afternoon, ladies and gentlemen. Shall we begin?'

The room falls silent, and we all look up, along the polished mahogany table, to the Chairperson.

'Thank you all for confirming and accepting in advance the Minutes of the last meeting; we will address the actions arising therefrom as we approach the respective items on the agenda.'

There is general agreement by nods.

'However, and I ask you to forgive me a slight digression, there are two items I wish to bring forward to ensure we address them today. As you are aware, Nico Costas, having recently departed, has created a vacancy, and we are required to appoint a replacement head of operations for Europe, the Middle East, and Africa. Only one candidate has been nominated and given her demonstrative and commendable loyalty over the last few days, I am confident you will all agree and support me in accepting the nomination of Miss Arabella Moffat to the position. If there are, however, any objections, please raise your hand now?'

I look across the table to the vacant seat, seemingly soon to be occupied by Arabella. There is a brief pause without any movement or comment.

'Very good, thank you. I will confirm Miss Moffat's promotion following this meeting. The second item I wish to bring forward is item nine on the agenda, as it relates to certain business dealings of the late Mr Costas, which now fall within Miss Moffat's portfolio. Mr Costas apparently invested heavily in the film adaption of a book draft written by author Martin Nicholson, who we now know to have been the brother of Mr Costas. The film company involved has requested additional investment to kickstart the next stage of production. However, I am minded not to support this request at this time. The further investment carries the risk of potential scrutiny by the authorities, thereby increasing exposure to our broader interests. We can decline, citing as reasonable grounds, the absence of the two key persons in this project; the first being the subject of the film, Emily Collins, who unfortunately was the victim of a street murder in California recently, and the second, the aforementioned Mr Nicholson, being the author of the book the film is based upon, and his subsequent disappearance following her murder, the man who it now transpires was also the, ahem, romantic partner of Miss Collins. The authorities continue to investigate both matters, and I think it prudent that we maintain a lower profile for the coming months at least. We can request Miss Moffat to report further on this matter at the next meeting. Once again, if we are all in agreement, please indicate with a show of hands.'

All twelve sitting around the table acknowledge the motion by raising their right hand and stating 'aye', and I note the Chair place a tick alongside both items on the paper in front of him. Arabella has won this quorate over, and I'm confident she will further distinguish herself in her new role.

'Thank you. Now, let us return to the other matters on the agenda in due order.'

67

Epilogue

Arabella

Signal Hill, Los Angeles

I cannot believe he thought I would let his brother live; the mighty Nico Costas thinking he could still trust me. Before this opportunity arose, I had never heard of Martin Nicholson, but I'm grateful he became known to me and our paths crossed. He unlocked the future I've been aspiring to achieve for a long time. Unfortunately, Martin had to die, as he would only have come after me. Besides, the Guild instructed that both were to be disposed of, ensuring the matter was fully closed.

No one, not even the Guild, knows I am Robert Lloyd's daughter. Mummy and I were in Switzerland when we heard of his murder, and we ran. Daddy had always planned an escape route for us just in case, and she took it without hesitation. They did come looking for us, but with different identities, passports, and moving from country to country using the money Daddy had banked in numerous accounts, we were impossible to find. When she died suddenly in a car accident in Thailand just after my fifteenth birthday, in my loneliness, I vowed to exact my vengeance on the man who killed Daddy and those who ordered it done, causing our life on the run, hiding, and, as I still maintain to this day, being the catalyst to Mummy's early death.

The man who killed Daddy is now dead. Nico was a young man then, one looking to make his mark. He accepted the tough jobs and soon began to move up the ranks. With his ability to exact punishment and mix with the higher social circles, he made valuable connections and became useful to the Guild. However, the Guild demands one hundred percent loyalty and trust, and my exposure of Nico's disloyalty earned me the right to respect and the promotion I received.

Now, I am closer than ever to finding out the identity of the person who gave the order for Daddy's assassination. My time will come, and I will honour my pledge to avenge the deaths of both my parents. One has to play to win, and I do. I will not accept defeat or second place, and my goal is not to settle until I have achieved absolute retribution, which drives me to excel. And, on my chosen path, I know what it takes to excel, and I'm prepared to do it. Did I anticipate the opportunity Nico inadvertently provided would allow me to be one step away from achieving my goal? No, but making the most out of an opportunity is what epitomises a winner.

Nico's last image was that of his brother killing him as I killed his brother, and that image will stay with him for eternity in the afterlife, whatever that looks like for people like us. Nico deserved that for his past deeds, and I am proud to have procured it by my actions. As for his brother, he is collateral damage, unfortunately, just like Emily Collins. Her life was unique, but her death was not; it'll remain another unfortunate street mugging that went wrong, another statistic, one more unsolved city crime added to the list.

The knock at the door brings me out of my thoughts. 'Enter.'

Donny enters with his usual swagger and closes the door behind him. 'Morning Boss.'

'Good morning, Donny. Is everything OK?'

'Yes, I think so, but… well…'

'Come on, out with it.'

'You see, Boss, I caught something on the news last night, and it reminded me of what that guy said, you know, Nico's brother, the one you whacked a couple of weeks ago.'

'Before you tell me, please don't use the word whacked anymore, I prefer disposed of.'

'Sorry, OK, Boss.'

'Well then?'

'Er… well... when we lifted Nico's brother, and we took him up to the shed, before you arrived, he said something about a Gunnarsson family and how they were all sick or twisted or something. I think he thought we were working for them.'

'Well, we weren't.'

'I know, Boss, we work for you, but that's the weird thing. On the news last night, three members of the Gunnarsson family have all been found dead on their ranch outside of Waco, all with gunshot wounds.'

'Yes, well, what of it? I'm busy.'

'Whoever took them out left a note saying that the Gunnarssons had abducted and killed numerous women and buried them nearby. The police started searching with special dogs and have located multiple bodies on the ranch, buried in the woods nearby, and they believe the bodies are of women and girls that were reported missing over the last few years… I can't help thinking that Nico's brother had a hand in killing the Gunnarssons, and he might be the one that left the note.'

'Just coincidence.'

'I don't know Boss, I think it was him, he said their name and…'

'Forget about it. There's nothing to be done now. Anyway, how are you getting on with that next shipment? It will all be ready for tonight's transfer, won't it? I want everything to be perfect when my replacement arrives on Friday so I can leave for Europe at the end of next week.'

'Er, yes Boss, I'll get on to warehouse now and check all is OK.'

'Good, you do that and be sure to let me know.'

'Sure thing, right away, Boss.'

He turns and leaves the room, closing the door behind him. Sitting back in my chair, I start to ponder what he just said and how there could be some sense in it. Martin was a cool customer, killing his brother with that knife without any real hesitation; preferring a knife over rope takes a special kind of someone, a person willing to look into the face of their victim as they die.

I open my laptop and search for the news Donny mentioned, and it's there, breaking in all the nationals. I then type Martin's full name into the internet search engine, and there are quite a few hits and recent uploads relating to books, therapy coaching, a possible film deal, and rumours of a relationship with Emily Collins; it's all there, but this is old news to me. On the face of it, he appears to be a regular guy, but as I delve deeper into his background, especially older articles from the UK a couple of years ago, I come across news reports relating to his wife and her lover. They were both murdered in the same bed with a sword after they had already pre-staged an attempt to murder Martin, which later failed but tragically caused the death of a close friend of his. The alleged murderer was reported to be one of Nico's men, who was later found dead in his prison cell during the murder trial, a suicide, it seems. All that while being the secret brother of Nico Costas. There seems to be more to this man than I first thought.

Coincidence? I'm not so sure now.

Who were you really, Martin Nicholson?

ALSO BY MARK HURST

The Lies

When Samantha and David decide to have a night out separately with their friends, events overtake them, and the lies lead them down a path of destruction.

To everyone else, it looked like Samantha and David had the perfect life. From meeting at university and falling in love to starting a successful business together, they made a great team. However, as everybody knows, appearances can be deceptive…

That one night out changed everything between them and things would never be the same again; not unless they could face up to their own truths and correct the wrongs.

Neither thought they could become the people they became and do the things they did. But that's just what happens when two people wronged become consumed by a need for the truth, for justice, and ultimately, for the price to be paid.

If either of them had let it go, it could have all been so different – but neither of them could.

The fast paced and gripping debut novel that will keep you turning the pages as you try to answer the question yourself – would you have let it go?

Lies Never Die

In the sequel to 'The Lies', Samantha and Blade continue playing the game of truth versus lie, reality against perception.

Dame Samantha Walsh, now a world icon, a person of respect, wealth and charity, flawless and untouchable in equal measure, continues to grow her empire on her terms. Her enormous wealth and reach bring about power and control never before contemplated, opening up new interests and outcomes for her, both inside and outside legal and moral boundaries.

Blade, recently released from prison, needing to re-integrate with society, has his path to follow to find the truth. He needs work, he needs income, and what better way to fund finding the truth than by taking paid work doing what he is good at, what he was trained to do?

The race is on to find out the truth of what happened to their loved ones. Who will find out first, who will win?

Fast paced and gripping, 'Lies Never Die' is the sequel to the bestselling debut book 'The Lies' from crime and psychological thriller author Mark Hurst.

My Partner's Friend

Should you trust the people closest to you?

A well-deserved weekend away in the English countryside, a time to catch up with friends and have fun. Martin and his wife Tanya, meet up with friends Melissa and her husband Craig, in a luxury barn conversion outside the small village of Brambleside, in the tranquil Lake District in the north of England.

Four close friends, each with very different professional careers, enjoy their collective time together, reconnecting after Martin's recovery from a recent illness. Within forty-eight hours, two are dead, one is unconscious in the hospital, and the fourth is charged with double murder and attempted murder.

With unexpected twists and revelations, who can be trusted? Is everything as it seems?

Would you trust your partner more than your friend?

To accompany the book "**Your Secret**"; these two stories then converging to bring two destinies together… in "**Her Last Days**"

YOUR SECRET

Can you trust what you've been told?

Paul marries his second wife, Kate, in front of friends and family and they set out on a new life together. Shortly after the wedding, what starts out as an innocent gift between friends becomes the catalyst to marriage difficulties, family tensions, the testing of friendships, a brutal murder, and much more.

Can Paul get the outcome he desires? Can Kate find the truth she is searching for?

Decisions made now, and in the past, unleash a series of challenges leading to deception and death.

Will the full truth be known and the secret revealed…?

Knowing what you now know, can things ever be the same again?

To accompany the book "**My Partner's Friend**"; these two stories then converging to bring two destinies together… in "**Her Last Days**"

A note from the author

Thank you for reading my book, I hope you found it entertaining. If you would like to forward a comment to me, please do so via email to mark@markhurstauthor.com *and I will reply.*

You may have already downloaded my FREE shorter story "The Last Woman", but if not, it is still available; please visit my web site at www.woodedhillbooks.com and click on the download link.

About the author

Born and raised in Bolton, UK, a true Lancastrian and a child of the sixties, Mark finally decided to pursue his passion for storytelling after a long and eventful career in a completely different industry, that sometimes involved more fiction than fact!

Mark entered construction at the age of eighteen and has been involved with hundreds of large civil engineering projects for the last 40+ years as a Civil Engineer and Surveyor, Estimator and Commercial Director, working in various far-flung locations such as Hong Kong, Scandinavia and Wigan.

Mark has a passion for reading legal, crime and psychological thrillers and enjoys firsthand accounts of military and espionage events. When he's not reading and writing, he can be found watching the History Channel.

Married with two grown children and four grandchildren, his son Daniel convinced him it was time to start committing some of his own stories to print ... and there are a few. Drawing on his own life experiences, Mark weaves them into his stories but with a twist ... it all could have happened.

Why Wooded Hill Books?

The origin of the surname Hurst – an ancient Anglo-Saxon topographic name for someone who lived near a wooded hill or thicket.

PLEASE KEEP IN TOUCH

Facebook.com/markhurstauthor

www.woodedhillbooks.com

Front cover design by 100Covers

Wooded Hill Books Limited

Printed in Dunstable, United Kingdom

65503649R00190